If anyone had taken the trouble to count the known methods of reproduction that exist on the Earth today, the figure would surely go into at least several hundreds. Survival has to be a highly adaptive process or benign old Mother Earth kills off the species.

What then of other planets, other stars? What unimaginable strains, stresses, conditions will produce how many thousand different ways of perpetuating a race?

Miriam Allen deFord here considers a few possibilities—funny, tragic, tender—in every range of human emotion and several unhuman ones, on Earth and off it. And always with the vivid sense of joy in living which she brings to all her writing.

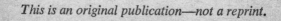

This is an original publication—not a reprint.

XENOGENESIS

Miriam Allen deFord

BALLANTINE BOOKS • NEW YORK

Contents

The Daughter of the Tree   1

The Superior Sex   13

The Ajeri Diary   24

Quick to Haste   44

The Smiling Future   56

Gathi   69

The Children   76

Throwback   105

One-Way Journey   118

The Season of the Babies   129

Featherbed on Chlyntha   143

The Transit of Venus   160

All in Good Time   171

The Absolutely Perfect Murder   181

Operation Cassandra   192

The Last Generation?   219

XENOGENESIS

The Daughter of the Tree

What worried Lee chiefly was the silence. Back home, in Boston, he had been taught his Longfellow— "the murmuring pines and the hemlocks." There were pines and hemlocks here, though the forest was mostly spruce and, above all, Douglas fir; but none of them murmured. There were no songbirds, and only once in a while did he hear the rallying call of a quail. He missed even the roar of the Snoqualmie River that had annoyed him so much the first night. Perhaps—he set the tin oven and the pans and canisters on the ground, to rest his shoulders, and took a long drink from his water flask— perhaps he had been a fool not to try to cross that half-made bridge after all.

But he could never have done it. All Watt's gibes and sneers about husky eighteen-year-old boys who couldn't keep their balance could only bring the blood to his face; they could not make him set foot on that swaying contraption with the big gaps between. He had never been able to endure heights: that time when he was a tiny tad and his father had taken him up to Vermont in the summer, he had learned that he grew sick and dizzy when there was no solid ground under him. He would be all right alone. He had a hatchet to cut away the undergrowth if the salmonberry bushes and rhododendrons grew too thick, and if he met a cougar or even a bear, the chances were that it would back away hastily at sight of him. He was not afraid. Only, it was so dreadfully quiet.

To cheer himself up, he began to whistle: "Down went McGinty to the bottom of the sea"—a tune from two years ago, 1890, in Boston, before his father had died and he had been set adrift. It had seemed like a romantic, adventurous dream then, to leave school and use up all that was left of the insurance money to go with Watt Gibson to Seattle. Washington had been a state for only a year; Watt, from his seniority of five years and an uncle who had been West for a decade and had sent for him, had been full of rosy stories of prospects in which money and excitement were inextricably mingled. But the boys had arrived on the heels of a great fire which had left the little city prostrate, with only two business buildings standing: people were living in tents, and there was little work except for skilled carpenters and builders. Then Watt's uncle had joined a party which was going to open up the country east of the Snoqualmie; and Lee, who had seldom been out of a city in his life, was overwhelmed with gratitude at the chance to go with them as cook.

Tramping miles around a gorge, all by himself, until it had narrowed to where he could cross it, and then tramping back again to join the squatters' camp, had been something he had not figured on.

Well, if the others could live that long without bacon and flapjacks, he could live till he got back to them. He stooped and shouldered the heavy kitchen-pack again. There was no least crackling of twigs or swish of air; but as he stepped around the huge trunk of a fir-tree he came face to face with a man, standing silently to await him.

Lee jumped and the tins rattled, but the man simply stood and waited. He was an Indian—one of the Flathead Indians from the big hop-ranch, probably, since in slack seasons they sometimes came into the wilderness for salmonberries and grouse and deer.

"*Klahowya sikhs,*" Lee said tentatively. All these Indian tribes of various descent and language spoke Chinook, the trade jargon; so did all the white men who had dealings with them; and Lee had amused himself for nearly two years by learning fluently the weird mixture of English, French, Spanish, and disparate Indian dialects.

"*Klahowya,*" responded the stranger briefly.

Lee was not so glib as he had imagined. The impassive dark face before him almost smiled as he explained laboriously where he was going—not why. Those fellows could cross the Grand Canyon on a plank—they were like cats in their delicate sense of balance.

He learned that it was nearly five miles to the end of the gorge. He had already come at least three, so there would be eight miles back on the other side. It was still early in the day; with luck, he could rejoin his party by dark. If they were hungry, they could make a fire and heat coffee and eat some of the cold biscuit from breakfast, but though he had the stove and all the kitchenware, he carried nothing edible except salt and baking powder and a stray small tin of flour. He was considerably relieved when the Indian remarked: "*Mesika olo?*"

Yes, he was very hungry, as only a healthy eighteen-year-old can be. The Indian had a pouch full of salmonberries and two quail. They would have a feast.

Gravely, without much conversation, they set up the stove and gathered kindling. Lee made flapjacks while the Indian gutted and spitted the quail. They set to with hearty appetites.

Suddenly, with scarcely a sound, the rhododendron bushes at the right parted, and a girl appeared. The Indian nodded curtly, and the girl smiled shyly, but said not a word. Lee sat with his mouth half-open, staring at her, a forgotten drumstick between his fingers. The girl sank in a graceful heap beside him on the ground, and still without a word prepared to share the food.

In his amazement the boy forgot to eat. He glanced inquiringly at his companion, but the Indian only shook his head very slightly and impassively went on with his meal. Not a sound came from the girl, and she did not seem to notice Lee's covert glances.

She was dressed like an Indian, but she was plainly of full white blood. Her hair, worn in two long plaits, was a soft chestnut brown, and as she stretched out her arm for a flapjack he could see the white above the sunburn. Once she looked full at him, with curiosity equal to his own, and he saw that her eyes were a dark blue.

Then, as silently as she had come, she stood up, raised her hands for a minute above her head, in salutation and apparently in thanks, and quietly slipped away. There was no sound of her going in her buckskin moccasins, and though Lee jumped to his feet and ran a few steps after her, she was nowhere to be seen.

When he came back, the Indian was cleaning up and burying the remains of their meal. He looked amused, but he waited for Lee to speak.

"Who is she?" the boy asked in Chinook.

The Indian was busy lighting his pipe. When it was drawing properly he answered at leisure, in the same language, though not to the point.

"She no can hear," he said, "but if we talk about her when she is here she know, and it make her sad."

"But who *is* she?"

"*Okustie stick*," said the Indian, and puffed away in silence.

"The daughter of the tree." Lee flushed: was the man making game of him? But the Indian gazed at him with sleepy amiability.

A little offended, the boy finished his packing, and prepared to continue his journey. He felt the man's eyes on him, but he did not look in the Indian's direction. When his task was done, he said stiffly: "Thank you for the food. Goodbye, friend," and turned to leave.

The Indian chuckled.

"Wait. I tell you," he proferred dryly.

That was just what Lee wanted. He dropped the pack immediately, and squatted beside the man, with his back against the big fir.

There was a comfortable silence. Then the Indian

said, smoking peacefully between the guttural words of the strange language:

"Long time ago I come here, I little boy. Long time ago my father come here sometimes to hunt. Sometimes he give big potlatch, he want much dinner to give his friends. We live then on seashore, we fish. Sometimes we want bear-meat, deer-meat, my father come many miles, hunt here in woods. I little boy, he bring me, teach me how to hunt. So long time before she born, I know that girl's mother."

"She's a white girl, isn't she?" burst from Lee.

The Indian frowned; the order of his narrative had been interrupted.

"Her mother white woman."

"But she looks all white. Is her father an Indian?"

"Her father not Indian, not white man. You listen, no talk. I tell."

Lee settled back. Let the men wait; they would be comfortable enough and glad of the enforced rest after days of blazing trails and chopping underbrush. The Indian, raising an admonitory hand against further inter-ference, continued:

"That girl younger than you. This I tell you happen since I grown man. But begin long time ago, when my father bring me here little boy, teach me how to hunt. When I big, I come by myself. Then white man and white woman come here from far off, live here in woods.

"Pretty soon maybe white man live all around here, chop down trees, build houses. You come today, tomor-row plenty more. Some day no more woods, all houses, all white men. But that time he first white man ever come here, and he bring woman with him.

"Why he come I not know, my father not know. Maybe he do bad things, run away. Maybe he sick, want get well in woods. You come here sick, trees cure you. But no, he strong man, do much work, he not sick. Maybe he crazy, I not know. But he come, and he bring woman.

"He camp first, then he chop trees and build house. House all gone now—trees grow over it. But he build, and he hunt to eat, and woman pick berries. She clear ground and try grow corn—no good. She not woman to do hard work. When I see her I see from her hands she not woman to do work.

"Man very busy, all day, chop trees, build fence, hunt. When day over, he very tired; eat, lie down, sleep. Morning he get up, go to work. Never talk much; very quiet always for woman."

Lee thought of the silence of the woods which had so oppressed him. He imagined a gently bred white woman condemned to this forest forever, and he shuddered.

"Every year, white man go away, back to his own country. So maybe he not do bad things, maybe he come here just because crazy. But he not too crazy, he take care of everything all right. He gone maybe two moons.

"Those days, our people keep slaves. He come to us, borrow use of slave to help him carry load. He come back, bring back slave, leave us presents. Sometimes we want things, we tell him, he buy them, bring them to us. Always come back with big load, all he need till next year. While he gone, he leave woman alone in house.

"One day he come our place like that, he talk my father. He say: 'My woman run away.'

"My father say: 'You no find?'

"He say: 'Oh, yes, I find. She run away two time, three time, I think maybe she go crazy.'

"My father say: 'What she do, you think she go crazy?'

"White man say: 'I find her, she make love to fir-tree. She put arms around fir-tree, say to it like to man, "You understand me, you love me." '

"White man laugh, but my father shake head. He know trees good medicine sick people, bad medicine crazy people. You see big tree here?"

Lee nodded. The Indian touched lightly the huge fir-tree against which they were leaning.

"Trees like people, some trees once people, long time ago. This tree, he hear everything we talk. He no can answer, but he hear."

It sounded silly, but in spite of himself a little cold

shiver trickled down Lee's spine. The Indian went on gravely:

"You treat woman bad, leave her alone, maybe whip her, maybe speak bad to her, some tree it hear. That tree, it call that woman, it take her away from man, maybe it be her husband."

That was a bit too thick. The boy laughed. The Indian frowned.

"You no laugh. White man, he laugh when my father tell him. He say: 'You crazy too, like my woman.' He go away.

"By and by, I grown man, I go alone hunt in woods. My father old man now, no go with me. We get poor people, leave our home, no more slaves, go work for white man on hop-ranch. Sometimes I remember, like now, when I boy. I come to woods again, live here two, three days. I remember good times I know, forget bad times.

"Every time I come, when I young man, I see white woman here.

"Sometimes her husband work in woods, sometimes he far away in his own country. But always the same—she walk around woods, not afraid of anything. Cougars, bears, deer, she talk to those animals, they never hurt her. Sometimes she sing. Once I see her, long time ago. Somebody kill doe, maybe her man, maybe Indian. Little fawn left, baby, maybe one moon old. She hold little fawn in arms like baby, sing to it. I see that.

"Always too she talk to trees, just like they people. That is bad, talk to trees. They listen, they no can talk, but they hear. One big fir-tree—big like this—I see her put arms around, kiss bark, talk to tree. I see, I run fast. I no want tree punish me, I see it with woman.

"You no believe me, but I tell you.

"Then come long winter, very bad. Plenty snow, very deep. I no can work, I say to boss man I come here to woods, maybe catch something to eat, maybe not. This seventeen year ago, maybe."

Seventeen years. The girl, Lee thought, judging as well as he could, must be about sixteen.

"All day I hunt, no grouse, no quail, no deer, nothing. Snow come down hard, very cold. I come near white man's house—house all gone now, trees grow over it. But house there then. Inside I hear talk. I no want go in, maybe people quarrel, not want stranger hear. I wait outside, I listen.

"White woman she very angry, she cry, she say: 'Put down that axe!' I look through window—just paper over window, and wind tear corner, so I see. White man have axe, she hold his arm, hold on tight.

"He say: 'I stop this nonsense! I put end to that!' I think maybe he going hurt her, I must stop him, but she let go arm, run to door, and he no touch her. He say: 'What you do? Where you go?'

"Then I hear her talk in other woman's voice, not her voice; if I not see, I think other woman in room. Wait. I remember what she say, the words: not Chinook, I say them in *King Chautch le lang.*"

The Indian paused a second, as if to recollect with accuracy, then slowly, in his guttural voice, he said in English:

"I'm through with you. I'm going where I'm wanted."

The sound of those slow, badly pronounced words, in the Indian's harsh monotone, sent a tremor of horror through Lee's veins. He was an imaginative boy—an unimaginative one, like Watt Gibson, would have crossed that swaying bridge without a thought—and suddenly he heard that lost, desolate creature, worn to insanity, uttering her dreary challenge. In the silence that followed, he fancied for a second he could hear the girl's light footfall. But when he turned sharply no one was visible.

"So," the Indian went on deliberately, "I know because she speak in other woman's voice, she truly crazy. I rather stay out in snow than be with crazy woman. I not listen any more, I go."

"And didn't you find out what happened?" Lee cried. "He must have been fixing to chop down that big tree she was so fond of, wasn't he, and she was trying to stop him. Did he cut it down?"

To his embarrassment, he suddenly discovered he had been speaking English, of which the Indian probably knew only a few words. But the man paid not attention to his outburst. He went on placidly.

"I go away, but I not find anything to hunt. Night come, still snow. I very cold, no can make fire in snow. Nothing else to do but pass night next crazy woman. I go back to white man's house.

"No light there. I go to door, to knock, no noise in house. At door I stumble, stoop down. I pick up branch of tree, lie across doorstep. I shake snow off branch, I feel. It is branch of fir-tree. Then I know."

"Know what?"

"I know fir-tree has come for woman. I know it hear her, come for her. I know another thing. I open door. White man is lying on floor. I light lamp, but I know before I look. He is dead."

"Dead?"

"He has been dead four, five hour. I look to see sign how he die, but I know before I look. The back of his head is broken."

"By the axe?"

"Axe is in corner, it is clean. The tree has heard; it has come to get its woman, it has killed him."

"But, good Lord!" Lee burst out. He recollected himself and went on haltingly in Chinook: "Tree no can come in house, kill man."

"Spirit of tree come anywhere, kill anybody. You listen.

"I go back to ranch, but I come here again. I see white woman maybe two, three time before summer. I no tell anybody, not my father, not anybody. I no want tree come, punish me. First time I come back here, next moon, house all clean, dead body buried. Woman, she can do that, work slow in frozen ground. Very cold all time, he keep till she ready. One time I come again, just before summer. I see her, she say: 'You come here again when first snow fall.' I say: 'I come.'

"First snow fall, I tell boss man I no can work, I come here, go to white woman's house. Her house now, man dead. But most time, she live out in woods, with tree. I go in house, she very sick. I see she going die. She have little baby. That girl you see.

"She say: 'I going die, you take baby, take to your wife.' I say: 'I stay. I wait.' I stay maybe two, three day, give her food. Then she die. I dig grave, I bury her. Then I take baby to my wife.

"She daughter of the tree. Tree hear too much, so she no can hear, no can speak. But very good baby, very quiet. She live with us, like our daughter. Very pretty, very good, but no can talk. When she grown girl, she run away. I know where she go. I come here, I get her, I bring her back. By and by she run away again.

"Now all winter, she stay our camp. She help my wife, she work hop-ranch, she very good girl. But come spring, she run away, stay till first snow. I no follow her now, I know where she go. I come here, sometimes I see her, sometimes no. She live here, live on berries, wash in river, sleep on ground. She stay with her father."

Instinctively Lee edged away from the giant fir-tree against which he had been leaning. The Indian almost smiled.

"Not this tree. I no lean on that tree. That tree far off in woods. White man ever cut that tree, maybe he be sorry. Maybe tree kill him when it fall."

"The whole thing's impossible!" exclaimed Lee, a little too loudly. Then he switched again to Chinook: "She grown girl. She safe in woods?"

"She safe," said the Indian grimly. "My wife see she safe in camp, her father see she safe in woods. I think maybe she never love man. She only half like you and me."

Lee glanced at him dubiously. The girl was very pretty.

The Indian stood up. Doubtless he was due at the hop-ranch at Snoqualmie by morning.

"You get back your friends, maybe tonight. Full moon tonight, very easy." He raised a hand in farewell. *"Kla-howya sikhs."*

"Klahowya," responded Lee. Then, already a few

steps off, already wondering with a quickened pulse if the girl might not emerge from the bushes again when the man was out of sight, he called back:

"I no believe. White woman kill man. Girl his baby."

Or yours, he thought to himself.

The Indian turned too, and smiled condescendingly. He had lived with white men: he knew how their minds worked.

"Girl not his baby," he said dispassionately. "Girl not my baby, too. I no touch woman belong to tree. You young man, you no child, you not talk like child. That girl not baby any man.

"She born ten full moons after man die, when snow begin to fall. She daughter of the tree."

Lee smiled too, and shook his head stubbornly. The Indian shrugged his shoulders and turned to go. The boy watched him disappear among the trees; then he adjusted his heavy pack and started to trudge on down the trail. It was true, as Watt had told him; these Indians had the minds of children, once you got them off the beaten track of everyday practicalities. Of all the fantastic yarns!

There was a slight rustle to his left, in the underbrush. Looking up sharply, Lee caught a glimpse of long chestnut hair.

Aha, he thought, so she did notice me! He had plenty of time; the day was young yet. Deliberately he laid down the pack, tied his handkerchief to a branch to mark the spot, and plunged off the trail.

She was fleeter-footed than he, and the woods were her familiar territory. But she kept sufficiently in sight and sound to lure him on. Suddenly she paused, not fifty feet away; and there was invitation in her eyes.

"Wait!" he called, forgetting that she could not hear him. There was no other sound; the trees stood about him like solemn guardians. He began to run.

He found himself sprawled ridiculously on the hard ground, his knees scraped, his left hand bleeding.

Stiffly he got to his feet again. There lay the fallen branch that had tripped him.

He stooped and picked it up. For a long minute he stared at it. The trees around him, he saw at a glance, were spruce, with a few pines.

The branch he held in his hand was fir.

The girl had disappeared. Around him was only silence.

Shivering in the warm sunshine, Lee limped back to the trail. As quickly as he could, he shouldered his pack and faced toward the camp. All he wanted in the world was to be with Watt and the others just as soon as his hurrying legs could make it.

The Superior Sex

She stood proud and tall like a Viking woman. She would have made a wonderful model for an ancient sailing ship's figurehead, fair hair blowing in the wind and blue eyes fixed on far horizons.

She glared at him and said: "How dare you come into my presence unsummoned? Go back at once to the seed-bearers' quarters where you belong!"

His bravely planned speech forsaking him, he slunk back and scuttled off, knowing all too well what would happen to him if he disobeyed, remembering only too well what Harry's corpse had looked like. He was still, a week later, more or less in a state of shock. It was hardly sensible to have made this foray, evading the guards, into Her Highness's private suite. He was not prepared to defy her.

In the harem they laughed when he reappeared. They all spoke English, though with a strange accent, and interspersed with words which were either neologisms or from some unknown tongue.

If he could only make out *where* he was, and why, and just what had happened!

"Here comes the brave rebel," jeered Thom. And Bawb added, "I thought the handy-robots would be called for a burial detail."

Danl, the Chief Husband, hushed them with a frown.

"It's not funny," he snapped. "What kind of crazy upbringing did you have, Willem?" His name was William, but that was how they pronounced it. "It's a disgrace to our men's quarters to have such an unmasculine creature in it!"

It was all like a reversed caricature of the relation of the sexes a hundred years ago, William reflected. Only it was worse, for apparently wherever he had landed there was a large superfluity of males over females. The result was polyandry, as in the opposite case it would have been polygyny. And these kept males were as smug and complacent, as self-degrading and superficial, as kept females had ever been. They might have greater physical strength than the females, but they would never have dreamed of using it.

One of them echoed his thought. "It isn't *nice* for a may to try to set himself up as a woman's equal, which nature never intended him to be," he pronounced. "No lady can be expected to be chivalrous to an unmanly man."

Chivalrous—a polite word for the jocular condescension with which Her Highness had first accosted them, before poor Harry had brought her wrath down upon them by his open truculence.

They had been delivered into her presence bound and gagged, after their rough capture, and as soon as his gag was off, Harry had defied her. The only reason William had not joined him and met the same fate was that he was still too dazed and bewildered. His mind was whirling with unanswered questions: Where and when had the crash landed them? On another planet? In an alternate universe? In the future?

He couldn't take any more from his harem mates. He stalked into his sleeping alcove—it had no door but it was at least curtained—and sat down, brooding. It was growing dark; soon, after dinner, the command might come for one of them. Not for him—not at all so far, and certainly not after today. He had come to the conclusion that she was keeping him merely as a status symbol—a curiosity. Nobody else had a husband like him!

"Which of you fathers her children?" he had dared to ask in the innocent early days. Danl was shocked. "If Her Highness should wish to mother a child, she has all the sperm banks in the world to select from," he said stiffly. "We are the relaxation from her duties and cares."

There was a slight sound at the curtain. William looked up, and saw the ingenuous face of Chass, the youngest of the husbands.

"May I come in, Willem?" he murmured. Without waiting for a reply he edged past the curtain and settled on a floor-cushion at William's feet. For a moment William felt his blood rising and his fist knotting, but it was nothing like that. Chass wanted to be where a whisper would be audible.

"They're all dressing for dinner," he breathed. "Making up and titivating, each of them hoping he'll be favored tonight." He giggled. "I don't bother—it'll probably be me again, if it's anyone, and she doesn't care how I look. I'm new and she's not tired of me yet. I thought you'd take over when you came, and give me a rest, but I understand now why not."

"That's more than I do," William growled.

Ignoring the interruption, Chass went on.

"I've been waiting for a chance to speak to you privately. I can't tell you how thrilled I've been by what you've said that shocks the old boy so. All the things I've hardly dared to think—I was afraid I was the only man who did!"

"Such as what?"

"Oh, I know it hasn't all been explicit, but I can read between the lines. Willem, I want to be your disciple! I feel just as you do—we men *aren't* just seed-bearers and playthings. We have brains too, and if they'd educate us and give us a chance, we could do everything that they can.

"In fact, I think we're *superior* to them—not just more sensitive and high-minded and pure, the way all men claim, but potentially above them mentally, too."

"I never said that. That isn't what I mean at all. Where I come from—well, anyway, what I mean is that *some* of us are better and more able than some of them, and vice versa. In other words, we're all human beings together, with immense variability, and sex isn't the limiting factor."

"I don't dig that," said Chass sulkily. "The way I look at it, people are either slaves or masters. We're slaves, and they're masters—or mistresses. I'm not interested in equality with them; I'm bottom dog and I want to be top dog."

"But—"

"Sh! There's the dinner bell. Can we talk some more some time soon? If we could start a *movement*—if we could find others who think as we do—"

"Beat it, Chass," said William wearily. "I've had enough war in my life. I don't want to get into another one. All I want is out of here."

"Well, if you're going to be like *that*, when I've offered my help," Chass said with spite, "I wash my hands of you!"

"O.K., just as you like. I don't want any dinner, tell Dan!"

He watched Chass retreat, anger implicit in his very walk. He needed friends badly, and now he had made another enemy.

At least he was sure that now he would be safe from further instrusion behind his curtain. The men would be on the *qui vive* all evening, though her Highness seldom sent for any of them, despite Chass's adolescent boasting. There was great agitation and tittering and bitchy comment when she did. Apparently, procreation—and she must have provided herself with at least one daughter as heiress—was done by test-tube impregnation; and she seemed to have only a moderate interest in or desire for sex.

Obviously she was somebody very important in wherever-he-was—a queen, or a great feudal lady at the very least. Since he had never been allowed to leave the—castle? fortress?—after he and Harry were brought there, blindfolded and fettered, from the wreck, he had no idea of the social set-up among the lower orders. Undoubtedly the excess of males must have made polyandry the rule, but he doubted if ordinary women had anything like Her Highness's harem—probably 2 or 3 husbands at the most.

Deliberately William let his mind wander, on the principle that if you have forgotten something, you will never remember it by straining for it, but if you let it alone, the subconscious may eventually deliver the memory to you.

The crash, though it had not injured him physically, and the rough treatment they had received after their capture, must have induced some sort of selective amnesia in both Harry and himself. Certainly Harry had seemed as bewildered and ignorant as he was. In the brief time before Harry had defied Her Highness and she had ordered him disintegrated, they had been kept apart as much as possible, but there had been occasional moments when they managed to ask each other questions neither of them could answer.

If only he could remember what had happened *before* the ship fell! Harry, he was sure, had been the pilot. He was also sure that they were not old friends, that they had met seldom before they were briefed for this expedition. Briefed by whom? Where? With what objective? All that was completely lost. He knew his name was William, that he spoke English as his native tongue, that he was somewhere in his early thirties. The rest was sunk in the mists of forgetfulness.

No, one other memory clung to him vaguely. In his former life, wasn't he married? And wasn't there something unusual about his wife? He couldn't come any nearer to it than that, but somewhere in his mind something important lurked which, if he could clear it, would help to explain his present predicament.

He had volunteered for something, he thought: but what? And though he was sure he hadn't known Harry well before (before what?), the idea clung to him that he *had* known a lot about him. Somewhere in relation to him was a woman named Janet.

One thing was certain: it was Harry who had played the hero, not he. In consequence, Harry was horribly dead and he was alive—a virtual slave, but a live slave. It was guilt and revulsion that had impelled his rash act today. What he had intended to do when he entered her presence puzzled him now; what he *had* done was shrink back from her anger, yet he did not believe he was a coward.

Could it be, he wondered, that some substance in their food or drink made of them all the foolish mental and moral weaklings they were? Or was it simply the inevitable effect of slavery on the slave?

His musing was interrupted abruptly. The curtain was jerked aside.

"Her Highness wishes me to conduct you to her—at once," Danl announced. His face showed a mixture of curiosity, resentment, and envy.

"But I don't particularly want to see Her Highness," William responded lightly. "She ordered me away when I called on her this afternoon."

Danl's expression turned to horror.

"But you must—when she—no one ever—" he sputtered.

"Oh well, anything to oblige a lady." He got up lazily and stretched. Underneath his nerves were tense.

She looked more than ever like the figurehead of a Viking ship. She dismissed Danl with a smile and a pat on the shoulder that left him quivering with happiness, and then she sat down. There was only one chair.

"I have been thinking over your—shall we say your visit to me," she said coolly. "I could have had you executed for invading my privacy, you know. But I realize that you are a stranger unfamiliar with our laws, and besides I can make allowances for the weaker reasoning powers of the male. Your companion showed himself obviously untamable, so I had him destroyed. You seem to me a more teachable type, so up to now I have spared you, and even made you a part of my household. But my mercy is not irrevocable."

"Your Highness," William said politely, "you have me at a disadvantage. You, if you will forgive me for saying so, are as ignorant of the customs of my world as I am of yours. Moreover, I am still not entirely recovered from the shock of a crash landing, followed by my rough capture and then by the horrible death of my pilot, right before my eyes."

"Go on," she said icily. Her finger hovered over a button on the arm of her chair. William fought down a rising panic.

"To be frank, I don't know where I am, or when this is, or what has happened to me. Worse, I have amnesia as to the trip itself; I don't remember where I was going, how I came to be in that space ship at all, or even just who my pilot was—all I know about him is that his name was Harry. I am sure that a great lady like yourself, apparently a queen or near to it, will have consideration for my plight, and help me to orient myself so that we can talk to each other on a plane of approximate equality."

She almost smiled. She looked at him with candid curiosity.

"'Equality,'" she said, "is a word that can hardly apply except between equals. But I do realize that you are a superior specimen of your sex—or I should not be having this interview with you at all—and if you want to ask me questions, I shall reply to any that I think reasonable."

"What year is this?"

"It is 943 of the 2017th Cycle."

"That doesn't help me, except to show that you keep a different time from mine. What is the name of your sun?"

"The sun, of course."

"Then what planet is this?"

"Argyth, the great moon of Oxod."

He sighed.

"I am afraid I am as confused as ever. Tell me, was ours the first space ship that has come to your world?"

"That is no concern of yours."

"All right—security; I understand that. Well, then, how does it happen that you all speak English—a rather strange and mutilated dialect, but still English?"

"English? What is that? We speak our own tongue."

"But not mine? Then how is it that we can speak and understand each other?"

"Oh, that," she answered carelessly. "Of course we're not speaking—what did you call it, English, or whatever your own language is. You are speaking and understanding ours. While you were unconscious our surgeons planted a translator in your brain. What you call a mutilated dialect is your own uneven auditory response to our speech."

He was silent for a while, digesting this. Then he took a deep breath.

"Would you be willing, Your Highness, to answer any questions about your social structure here?"

"Possibly. It would depend on what they were."

"As I understand it," he said hesitantly, "in this world it is taken for granted that men are mentally inferior to women?"

She looked surprised. "But they *are*," she said.

"Not in my world. There, in the past, just the reverse was thought to be true."

He remembered suddenly a passage from an ancient poet he had read in college: "Woman is the lesser man, and all thy passions, match'd with mine,/Are as moonlight unto sunlight, and as water unto wine." He decided it would hardly be diplomatic to quote it.

"Nowadays," he went on, "we are, to some extent at least, on a basis of equality, though there are still some hangovers from the former time. We think of ourselves primarily as human beings, born of the same parents and with the same inherent natures."

"That, of course, is pure nonsense," she replied crisply. "The mere fact that there are so many more males than females is proof that the male is in essence only a seed-bearer. It is to flatter your masculine vanity that we call you husbands and pretend that you are completely human beings in the same sense we are."

Just like the bees and ants and termites, he thought.

"In my world," he retorted, "the numbers of each sex are about even; there are disparities one way or the other in some regions, but this is true on the whole. At one time, up to a few centuries ago, the official system—often breached, but still the norm—was monogamous marriage, one wife to one husband. And even today very many people prefer it."

"It sounds horrid," she said. "I have important affairs to attend to, heavy responsibilities. My husbands are for recreation. As one of our poets has put it. 'Men die for love, which to women/Is but rest at the end of the day.'"

Another ancient couplet floated through William's mind: "Man's love is of man's life a thing apart;/'Tis woman's whole existence." He suppressed Byron as he had suppressed Tennyson.

She frowned. "Well, all this is irrelevant. Have you asked all your questions? Do you understand better now what your situation and your duties are?"

He braced himself.

"I understand," he said deliberately, "but I don't accept it."

Her blue eyes flashed dangerously.

"I don't tolerate rebellious husbands," she said menacingly. "If you are going to turn out as insolent as your fellow was, you will meet the same fate."

Suddenly William lost control.

"Then do it!" he shouted. "I'd rather be dead than live like this!"

Her Highness touched the button. The door opened and two burly robot soldiers entered. Before he could move they had him by both arms. Behind them, a human officer aimed her weapon at his head. That was what he had seen happen to Harry, before the pilot swelled up, turned black, and then exploded in a dreadful mess of blood and tissue.

He shut his eyes. At least he would die like a man—a man as men were understood to be in his own time and place.

"That's enough. We've proved our point," Her Highness said from far off.

But it wasn't Her Highness's voice. It was Janet's.

"He's coming out of it," she said. "Help me with him, Harry."

His eyes opened and he stared groggily at the two bent over him. He was lying on an operating table, and above him loomed the anxious faces of his wife and of Professor Ranleigh, whose associate she was in the university's psychology department. Janet's dark eyes were full of concern.

"Lie still, darling," she said, "until we get all the electrodes out."

"How are you feeling, Barton?" asked the professor, whom William had never called Harry; they had met seldom and only formally.

"O.K., I guess. How long was I out?"

"About 15 minutes."

"Gosh, I lived through a week. Was it a success?"

"We can't tell till we've gone over the recording. But it looks like a breakthrough at last. As I explained when you were good enough to volunteer—against your wife's wishes, I can tell you now."

"I was so afraid it might do you some harm," said Janet.

"He knew that, didn't he?" Ranleigh snapped.

"Don't fight over me, you two," William said, amused. He was still somnolent, and still full of relief at his escape from Her Highness. "After all, I may be only a lowly astrophysicist, but I do understand the scientific method!"

"Of course you do," the professor said heartily. "And if this has worked with you, now that we're sure no harm's been done, we'll have no trouble getting a few more volunteers and perfecting the technique. Janet was reluctant to ask you, but as I told her then, we had no choice; the thing has to be kept top secret, and I couldn't think of anyone else we could trust to have even an inkling of it. I'm not married, and neither of us could be the subject, because it needs the two of us to administer it."

"Of course. I understand. Don't fuss, Janet; I'm all right." He grinned. "Don't fuss as a scientist," he added wickedly, "but maybe you'd better worry as my wife! While you two were digging data out of my brain with your electrode tips, I was being the husband of a beautiful blonde!"

Suddenly his amusement faded.

He began remembering other things. *Why* did Janet keep her professional associations so separated from her personal life? *Why* was her co-worker Professor Ranleigh to him and Harry to her? Why *had* she consented, even under protest, to his volunteering for this dangerous experiment? And for what subconscious reason had he himself been so willing to volunteer?

Almost without volition he heard himself saying smoothly:

"And as for you, Harry, if I may be so chummy, I saw you exploded into a viscous, bloody pulp by a disintegrator, at the express command of my beautiful blonde wife—and I didn't turn a hair to protect or defend you.

"What has your investigation of hidden psychological impuses to say to that?"

The Ajeri Diary

May 29, 2297.

As I have done in all my previous expeditions, I am starting a private diary before I leave for Algol IV. I find it supplements my official report and is of great value when I begin to tape a new book on my latest findings.

Ever since the Patterson Differential made it possible to transmit ourselves and our paraphernalia practically anywhere in the Galaxy in the same time it would once have taken to visit Mars, there are few new fields for discovery left for the exobiologist, but some still remain for the exosociologist, so I am lucky in my special area of research. To be sure, Algol IV has been visited many times by now, but only briefly and mostly by explorers and trade scouts; for my purpose it will be almost virgin territory, and I am very grateful for the Federation grant which has opened this new enterprise to me.

I am even more fortunate in that the necessary spadework has already been done: i.e., we know that the planet is livable for Terrestrials without space suits (and can one imagine field work conducted through a space helmet?), that the inhabitants of the dominant race are not so much humanoid as practically human, at least in outward appearance, and that thanks to the initiation of trade-centers, an appreciable number of the urban residents now speak some Neogalactic. I have of course also begun to study their own language (or anyway that of their principal city, which will be my headquarters), and I already know that they call their planet Ajeri, that the city is called Bafik, that "eskon" means "man" and "org" means "woman"; and while I am in deep freeze on the two-month journey, I am confident that I can acquire through sensor-instruction enough of the tongue to be able to find my way about and settle in. As a crowning benefit, I am assured that they are a friendly and outgoing people who will not resent my investigations—though I can hardly expect that my name or my series, "With Our Galactic Neighbors," will be familiar to them, as it is throughout our own solar system.

The one wrench in this trip is that it means absence from Mara for almost a year and a half. I suppose we are what our ancestors used to call "in love" with each other, and though under the circumstances of both her work and mine we can hardly arrange to be constantly together or to remain what used to be termed "faithful" to each other so far as our physical needs are concerned, yet for both of us this is the most satisfactory partnership we have ever experienced. I shall be sorry to leave her and delighted to rejoin her on my return, and I know she feels the same way.

This, then, is my preliminary taping; and I shall take up the diary again as soon as I reach Bafik and am actually on the job.

September 8.

Everything goes swimmingly so far. Naturally, the persons concerned on Ajeri knew I was coming and were acquainted with the objects of my research. I speak of them as "the persons concerned" because (probably because of my being still unfamiliar with the finer nuances of their language) I am still rather vague as to their governmental set-up and the proper titles of its leaders. However, when after the always rather disagreeable process of being "unfrozen" the ship dropped me at Bafik's spaceport and proceeded on its way, I was pleased to find that someone apparently in authority had come to meet me. This was a man named Olven, as near as I can make it out; I was happy to discover that he did indeed look very much like any middle-aged, intelligent man on Earth, despite the rather scanty garments he wore, for Bafik is near the Ajeran equator. He spoke a fair Neogalactic, and I made what polite rejoinder I could in my elementary Ajeran. He had already made arrangements for my lodging in two very pleasant rooms in what I suppose might be called a hotel, and after my first meal I found the unfamiliar food quite digestible, though not too appetizing. (That is just as well, since I have a tendency to overweight.)

Olven has remained my chief point of contact; the day after my arrival he took me on a tour of the city and that evening had a little gathering of his friends in his own apartment for me. They were the first nucleus of my acquaintance, which has now grown rather wide in just a few days. I plan also, of course, to roam the streets at random with my recording apparatus and to get into conversation with any strangers willing to become my informants. With this in mind, I am studying the language intensively, and I believe in a week or two more I shall be able to get the whole project definitely under way.

One thing struck me very sharply in that first evening, and that was that the company was entirely masculine—or perhaps I should say it was made up entirely of "eskons." When I realized this, two possible explanations crossed my mind: was it possible that Olven and his friends were members of some monastic religious order—or had I been unlucky enough to have my first contacts among homosexuals? (I have no idea as yet of their religious beliefs; their sexual life, of course, is of primary interest to me.) But nothing in either demeanor or speech confirmed either conjecture.

I am still considerably in the dark about this. Even in these few days I have observed that one *never* sees a man and a woman (an eskon and an org) together, indoors or out. All the staff at the hotel are men. I have frequently seen women on the street or going in and out of buildings that are apparently stores, but always in the company of other women or with little girls. As for the small boys I have noticed, if they are with adults, it is always with men. This is naturally going to be one of the chief puzzles for me to solve, but I don't feel that it would be tactful, so early in the game, to ask direct questions about what is seemingly a deep-seated social custom.

Incidentally, none of the men I have met thus far seems to be married, or whatever the equivalent is on Ajeri; in answering, fully and frankly, all my questions about their society, no one has ever made any allusion to a wife—or, for that matter, to a sister or even a mother. Yet of course they all have or had mothers—they are obviously mammals like ourselves—many of them must have sisters, and some certainly must have "wives," whatever their form of sexual partnership may be. But I have not yet met one woman socially, or spoken to one. When I tried to accost one group emerging from a store, they fled abruptly as if terrified.

No one but myself, probably, will ever read this personal diary, but in the remote case that anyone ever does, perhaps I should repeat that all my sociological findings are given in detail in my reports to the Federation, and will undoubtedly appear in more popular form in my next book. What I tape here are my own experiences and reactions, with only enough generalization to remind myself in later years of things I might otherwise not remember clearly.

As to the political, economic, and social system in Ajeri, therefore, I shall only note briefly that it is utterly unlike any known to us in the past or present on Earth. I could call it anarchistic or socialistic, but actually it is neither. They simply do not seem to have the concept of government as we understand it. Apparently the dozen large cities of the planet, which has no separate states or nations, are surrounded by enormous tracts of agricultural land which is worked by machine under the supervision of resident engineers and economists. They have reached an industrial age but not a technological (robotic) one like our own. The first time Olven took me to visit a large factory, I asked to speak to the manager. He said to the first man he encountered, "Who is manager here this month?" The man answered, "Maluk, I think," and Maluk it was. Then I found that every month all the employees choose one of their number as manager, and he appoints his assistants; *everybody* employed in a factory or on a farm is fully qualified to fill *any* position. The same applies to schools, hospitals, courts, etc., and when I tried to explain our executive class, they were bewildered.

In the same way, they have semiannual elections, at which men are chosen for every political office for the next six months. Always men: the women I saw going in and out of the buildings were collecting good, clothing, and so forth from what they call the storage houses, but they take no part otherwise in Ajeri's political or industrial life. Moreover, no wages or salaries are paid to anyone; everything produced is stored in these warehouses, and every citizen takes from them whatever he or she wants. There is no luxury of any kind—I have not seen a single piece of jewelry on anyone—but everybody appears well fed and comfortably housed and clad. Intellectually they seem to lead a pretty full life; though their art and music make no appeal to me, and I am still unable to read their literature, they have innumerable equivalents of our theaters, concert halls, museums, and libraries, and education is free and compulsory until boys come of age at 20.

Boys: girls have no education at all, and the audiences are completely male. I still have to figure out just what the women do or how they live. I know they live apart from the men in their own section of the city, and never leave it except to "shop." Presumably they keep their own homes in order and take care of the girl children. All I can guess is that the men visit them at night; otherwise there would *be* no children!

But enough of this. I am sufficiently far ahead now in my inquiries to begin going deeper, and then some of these puzzles will be solved. So far as I myself am concerned, I am physically well taken care of, but by this time I do crave some feminine companionship, and as soon as I can do so without violating any of their taboos, I intend to direct my investigations to an area where I, too, can find an opportunity to lead a normal life!

One thing I had not expected is the natural beauty of this planet. The plants and trees are not our own, but they are luxuriant, even in the city gardens, and lovely. The animals—none I have seen higher than an invertebrate, but there must be domestic beasts on the farms, for I am served meat daily—are as colorful as butterflies. Bafik is not far from the seashore, and almost every afternoon now I drive the little ground-car I have been given the use of to the beach and enjoy a swim.

That is the one place where I *have* seen women and girls—and very attractive girls at that. They stick together at a distance from me or other men, and neither group ever approaches the other. But I think that this may provide my opening wedge into this strange separation of the sexes, and as soon as I happen to be alone at the beach (I mean without any of my male companions who are on holiday), if I see any girls, I intend to go up to them and try to establish some sort of contact with them. I know enough of their language now, and it seems better than to try any more to ask questions on the subject of my masculine acquaintances—who always evade them and obviously are politely overlooking an enormous *faux pas* on my part.

October 12.

Well, I tried it yesterday and it was a complete flop.

I went to the beach with two other men, and when they proposed leaving, I said I'd stay a while longer and go in once more. (This ocean water is beautifully warm and very buoyant and a delight to swim in.) I'd noticed, far down the beach, a little knot of girls, as I can't help calling the orgs, and one among them particularly stood out—tall and lithe and fairer than most of them; the Ajerans are a bit on the swarthy side for the most part. I'd observed before that late afternoon seemed to be the favorite org bathing hour.

I had my plans all made. I was going to stroll lazily down toward them, and when I got within hailing distance, wave amiably and make some casual, friendly remark that might start an acquaintance. (Aside from my professional interest, I don't want to spend a whole year here is if I were a novice in a monastery!) Probably they are just shy because the eskons are so domineering and snooty, but they must surely, little as they participate in society, realize that an alien from another planet is among them. If they have any curiosity at all, I should think they'd welcome a chance to meet him.

... Only, as soon as they saw me approaching, the whole lot of them hastily packed their belongings and ran like mad to the ground-car they'd come in. Poor things, in this aggressively male set-up, they must be simply terrorized by anything masculine!

However, I'll swear that tall, fair girl looked back at me and hesitated; only, one of her pals grabbed her by the arm and hurried her off. I'm going to try again tomorrow, going there by myself, and see if I have any better luck.

October 13.

I did. It's quite a story.

I arranged to go alone to the same part of the beach where I *almost* had made my first approach to any of the ladies. Sure enough, there they were, half a dozen of them, at their own private bathing spot within sighting distance—and the tall, fair girl easily observable among them. While I meditated my tactics, I had a leisurely swim, and then lay down on a blanket I'd brought with me, to dry off and perfect my plan. I hadn't had much sleep last night, for a number of reasons, and the warm sunshine got the better of me. (Incidentally, actinic rays

from Algol burn just as badly as those from Sol! I have a
fine sunburn today.) I fell sound asleep.

I started awake with the sound of a giggle in my ears.
I opened my eyes, and saw that the sun had set and it
was full dusk. Over me stood three young orgs, my fair
lady the nearest to me.

As I sat up, the other two ran like deer, but the tall
girl lingered. They called to her, but she stood still. I
smiled placatingly. In my halting Ajeran I said, "Don't
be afraid."

Her eyebrows went up. "Afraid?" she asked. She
laughed, and I discovered the charming giggle that had
awakened me had come from her.

"I came here from another world than Ajeri," I went
on disarmingly, quite well aware that I was probably
murdering the syntax of her native tongue. "I am here to
learn and to tell my own people about yours. But until
now I have been able to talk to only half of you—the
men. May I not ask you too questions about the women
of your world?"

Her companions had halted at a safe distance. One of
them held her hands to her mouth and called: "Lemblad!"

So that was her name.

"I am coming," she called back. "One minute." She
turned to me.

"What is it you want to know?" she asked crisply.
Seen so close, she was more than pretty; she was a
genuine beauty. I couldn't guess her age (that is true of
the men also; their life-span seems to be much the same
as ours, 100 years or so, but it is hard to tell how old
they are once they are fully grown, until they reach
extreme old age), but she was not a child, and I should
think she was somewhere between 18 and 25.

"Everything," I answered. I had risen by now, and she
stiffened and stood back a little, so I was careful not to
frighten her by coming within reaching distance. "How
you live, what you do all day, what your lives are like."

She thought a minute, then nodded decisively.

"Since you are from another world," she said, "I think

it might be done. I shall speak to my friends—there are a few, I think, who would be willing to talk with you."

"But first," I said, greatly daring, "couldn't we meet alone? Then I could give you a better idea of what things I want to know, and you could tell from that whom else to ask."

"Not now," she said nervously. "What is your name?" I told her. And I told her the name of my hotel, but she shook her head.

"We do not go into the eskons' section except to collect from the storage houses."

"Lemblad!" her friend called again. She sounded desperate. Lemblad turned to go.

"Come here tomorrow," she said hastily. "But come late, after the moons are up."

It is never really dark here at night; one or both of the two moons, as large as ours, are always visible overhead.

She ran back, her white robe dancing in the breeze. Both men and women wear the same kind of garment— a sort of cross between a toga and a sari. As a matter of fact, I have adopted it myself; it is cool and comfortable. I have put away all my ordinary clothes and wear nothing but what they call a "budong." Perhaps I should add that they do not swim nude; they wear a sort of abbreviated budong, so I do too.

Well, things are prospering. Tonight I am to meet her at the beach—and perhaps that will mean the end of these hard months of celibacy. She surely wouldn't have given me an assignation like that, at night, if she didn't understand very well what our interview might lead to.

It is almost night now, and in a few minutes I shall drive out to meet her. I find my heart is beating pretty fast. Lemblad is a very attractive girl.

October 14.

Well, I've never been so puzzled in all my life.

Was it a put-on? Is there something wrong with me? Or is there something very wrong with Lemblad? She is *not* stupid. In fact, her being willing to meet me again is proof that she has more curiosity than any other of the orgs seems to have. I'll swear she is not only smart, but a natural born rebel. And there is nothing in my past—I can be frank in my own personal diary, can't I?—to make me think I am repulsive or undesirable to women. (Unless, as an alien, I am repulsive to Ajeran women?)

She was there waiting for me when I arrived. I couldn't see much point in sitting on the beach or in walking around, so I suggested that we adjourn to my ground-car. No, she said, let's go to hers, which was near by. All the better.

We drove—she drove—away from the shore and parked again in a driveway in front of one of the huge apartment houses in which all the Bafik inhabitants seem to live.

"This is my home," Lemblad said. "We can talk here and then I'll take you back to your car and come back home by myself."

I didn't expect to be invited in. I understood that there was no privacy—nobody I've met seems to understand what the word means; they live huddled together like bees in a hive. I'd much rather, of course, have been farther away from prying eyes, but we were out of hearing distance and the driveway was lined with trees and bushes that concealed us from sight; so it could have been worse.

"Now," said Lemblad with the air of a VIP being interviewed by a reporter, "what are the questions you want to ask?"

That wasn't exactly the approach I had in mind, but I remembered that the orgs are intimidated by the eskons; so I said, "You mustn't be afraid of me, Lemblad."

She opened her eyes very wide.

"That is what you said yesterday," she said in a surprised tone. "What do you mean? Why should I be afraid?"

"Well, I realize that all you orgs are shy and timid. In my world the men and women associate freely, but here I suppose the eskons forbid you to appear in public with them."

She laughed aloud. Then she drew herself up haughtily.

"The eskons," she said icily, "work for us and provide us with what we need and want. An org who would have any personal association with an eskon would have to be mentally ill."

I did a double take. So my theory was all wrong. The orgs weren't a subjugated sex; they were aristocrats who considered the eskons their inferiors! Except, of course, for the fact that without the eskons there wouldn't be any more Ajerans! Perhaps they deal with them like an empress with her favorites—or like an empress and her slaves whom she condescends to bed with and then dismisses!

A lot of things passed rapidly through my mind. So orgs weren't included in the governmental system because that was of concern only to workers, and orgs didn't work. Orgs took, they didn't give. And they weren't educated because education was merely a technical convenience to keep industry and business going, and they had no need of the arts because they made a satisfactory art out of their own way of life. They weren't curious about anything outside their own social group. What I had taken for fear was disdain.

Professionally, the revelation excited me tremendously. Personally, it was rather disconcerting, and all the more so because Lemblad asked bluntly:

"Are you an org or an eskon in your world? It is hard for us to tell."

"I'm an eskon," I said humbly. "But in my world we live and work and play together. And make love together," I added daringly.

I had had to say the word in Neogalactic. I suddenly realized that I had heard no Ajeran synonym.

"Love?" Lemblad repeated. "What is that?"

"Like," I responded awkwardly, "the way an eskon and an org feel toward each other when they want to do things like this." And I pulled her to me and kissed her soundly.

She didn't respond, but she didn't, rather to my surprise, repulse me, either. She drew away a little and said in a rather fluttery voice, "I never did that before. It feels nice. Do it again."

I did.

"Oh," she sighed, "that *was* nice. I must tell my friends about it. We must do it together."

"It is much nicer," I breathed, my arms around her again, "when you do it with an eskon."

"Oh, no!" She shuddered in disgust. (Doubtless to her I, as an alien, rated rather higher than a mere Ajeran male.)

"And there are other things—even better—" My breath was coming fast. I reached for the fastening of her robe.

With a violent strength I hadn't dreamed she possessed, she pushed me away.

"What are you doing?" she cried. "Are you crazy?"

I tried to pull myself together. I didn't want her screaming the house down on me.

"All right, all right," I managed to mutter. "I wasn't trying to rape you. I thought you liked me. I thought you'd want it too."

"Want what, you crazy eskon?" She stared at me blankly.

I got angry then. Young as she might be, she surely wasn't as innocent and ignorant as all that.

"Don't be a fool," I said harshly. "Don't pretend you don't even know where babies come from!"

"Babies? What do you mean? I have already had two babies."

"Well, then—you can't have babies without an eskon, can you?"

For the first time she seemed frightened instead of indignant.

"Now I know you must be really crazy—maybe everybody in your world is crazy. What have eskons to do with babies?"

My head was in a whirl. What do they do in this

place? Do the eskons creep in at night, anesthetize them, and fertilize them while they're unconscious, or what? She wasn't putting me on; she was obviously sincere. There was the ring of honesty in her voice, I could tell that. Here, instead of being a young, virginal girl, she was a grown woman who had already been a mother twice over—and she wanted to know what a man had to do with that! I wondered again if under the surface intelligence Lemblad was really an imbecile.

Suddenly I felt very tired.

"I give up," I said hoarsely. "I can't make you understand. Drive me back to my car, Lemblad, and we'll call it a day."

She hesitated. I achieved a smile.

"Don't worry," I said. "You don't need to call for help. You'll be perfectly safe."

She looked at me as if from the summit of a high mountain. Without a word she took the wheel. We drove back in silence, and parted the same way.

I am writing this before I go to bed. I am going to make an appointment with Olven, and somehow get this whole insane thing cleared up. What kind of exosociologist am I, anyway, to have become involved in so giant a piece of confusion? If I can't get things straightened out, the Federation has wasted a lot of credits on me.

October 20

Well.

I couldn't get hold of Olven till today. Olven's some kind of governmental executive this month, and very busy.

We met this afternoon and went to a sort of restaurant and got a booth in back where we could talk in private. I certainly wasn't going to mention anything that happened that night, but I said bluntly that the time had come when I needed explicit answers to some questions. I wanted a clear explanation of their methods of sex and reproduction.

Olven didn't seem upset or offended, just surprised

that I needed any explanation of something that seemed, to an Ajeran, self-evident.

He said—I don't know what pronoun to use; I'll just keep on as I've been doing.

The eskons aren't men. The orgs are female, but there are no males. The orgs reproduce parthenogenetically.

If the child is an org, they keep and raise it. If it is an eskon—a neuter worker—as soon as it is old enough, it is handed over to the eskons to rear.

It isn't even like the bees or the ants; there the queen is fertilized by a drone and the neuters are produced by a difference in feeding. Orgs and eskons are born that way and never change. The eskons revere the orgs because the orgs keep the race alive; they accept without question the fact that they themselves have no sex life whatever, that they exist only to work and serve society. I had the greatest difficulty in trying to get Olven to understand what I was talking about. And when he (it?) finally did get a glimmering of our strange system on Earth, he responded just as Lemblad had done—with revulsion. He was polite about it, but I could see that he regarded me as some kind of monster.

Well, my job is going to be a lot harder from now on, I can see that. The word will spread, and I'll be a freak, instead of an equal to themselves though an alien. They'll be doing research on *me* more than I'll be able to do research on *them*. And if Lemblad gossips, I'll be a figure of fun.

It can't be helped, and I'll have to make the best of it—but eleven more months!

I must watch out to keep my official report purely technical, with no hint of my mortifying experience. Might as well end this diary, too—there'd be nothing in it but griping. And there won't be any book from this expedition—my books depend for their popularity on their personal revelations! Ajeri won't appear among our "Galactic Neighbors."

A whole year or more, living like some ancient monk or hermit! I haven't had that happen since I was sixteen.

I hope there'll be a real human woman, an unfrozen crew member, before they put me in deep freeze on the ship that takes me back next August.

And I hope to Space, Mara will meet me when we land!

January 15, 2298.

I am reopening this diary after all, though it is less than three months since I closed it. It is the only place I have in which to confide my private worries.

I'm becoming really uneasy.

Could the strange method of reproduction here be due, in some way I don't understand, to climatic or other planetary influences? Could there be some electromagnetic effect that alters not only the Ajeran genes but even and also the cells of a mature alien body?

All this speculation is because I have just begun to realize that I haven't given a thought to sex—I mean to myself and sex—for weeks. Only this morning I happened across the little triphoto of Mara that she gave me when I left, and it came to me with a shock that she hadn't been in my mind for I don't know how long.

Oh, this is nonsense! I'm working very hard and taking a lot of exercise. This is just my sensible subconscious mind telling me that what can't be cured must be ignored.

Still—

March 2.

It *isn't* nonsense. Yesterday I was at the beach as usual—a new beach, though, so I shan't run across Lemblad—and as usual a bunch of orgs were cavorting within my view. I watched them for a while as I lay half-asleep sunning myself. And then all at once I woke up with a start, as it struck me that my watching had been purely aesthetic, as if they were graceful athletes of my own sex.

Is it possible that prolonged celibacy could make one impotent?

May 18.

I might as well face it. I'm beginning to feel about things the way the eskons do. The other day I was talking to Olven and he (I keep thinking of the eskons as "he"; you can't call another human "it") said something casually about a shortage in one of the Bafik storge houses because blue budongs had suddenly become a craze among the orgs, and they would have to borrow a supply from another city until more could be made.

He spoke rather complainingly (he has some kind of storage supervisory job this month), and quite without thinking I found myself saying reproachfully, "Well, Olven, it isn't for us to question what the orgs want."

I stopped short in utter amazement at myself—and in the same moment it came to me that my feeling toward the orgs has become exactly the same as the eskons'—one of reverence and awe. As for Olven, he looked at me, not quizzically, but rather ashamed of himself and also relieved that at last I was taking a "normal" attitude.

So that's that. Psychologically I seem to be turning into an eskon! I've got to the point where my work and my social associations with my eskon friends completely satisfy me. I'd be quite content to spend the rest of my life on Ajeri.

August 1.

The ship will be along for me very soon now. What shall I do? I *must* go home. I accepted that grant, and I must report my findings. I have a reputation to sustain on Earth.

And I'm *not* an eskon. I'm a human male—or at least I was once. Anatomically, I'm just as I always was.

When I get back home, one of two things must happen. Either I'll stay permanently the way I am now, or whatever this inexplicable contagion is that seems to have turned me mentally and emotionally into an Ajeran will gradually disappear in time.

That's the rub—*in time*. How am I going to face my

public for an indefinite period—or for the rest of my life? And my friends? And Mara? It took months for me to change here, and it's not likely the process could be reversed more quickly, if it ever is. Everybody who knows me will consider I'm out of my mind. Mara will think I'm rejecting her without cause. Other women will decide I've gone queer.

And I can't bear to humiliate Mara that way. I don't desire her or any other woman any more, but I do love and respect her.

And how shall I explain that there won't be a new "With Our Galactic Neighbors" about Ajeri?

It's out of the question for me to stay here. Aside from everything else, though Ajeri welcomes visitors, it has no provision for permanent immigrants.

It's no use trying to start out immediately on another expedition after I return to Earth—I'd never get a new grant right away, and I'd have no reasonable explanation. Besides, I am sure Ajeri is unique among planets, and so I'd be no better off wherever I went.

There is nobody whose advice I can ask; even Olven, who has become my greatest friend, would be entirely unable to comprehend my dilemma.

I'm afraid there is only one way out. I never expected to end up as a martyr to science, which I suppose is what I am.

I must get my report in final shape and arrange for it to be delivered to the Federation. I accepted that grant and I must carry out my obligations.

Then there is only one thing left for somebody who is unfit to live with his own kind and unable to live where he does fit in.

Before the ship is due, I must go out for my daily swim.

And not come out of the water.

August 2.

No: that is defeatist nonsense. I'm not going to die for dear old Ajeri—or for my own reputation or my own sexual problems, either. I've got to go back and face it and do the best I can and see what happens.

The ship should be here for me by the end of this month. (I have kept my own private calendar all along, of course, according to Earth time.)

Since no one will ever see this diary but myself, I might as well acknowledge that I'm scared.

August 15.

My work is finished and my notes and material are all in order. I can get ready to leave on a few hours' notice.

A funny thing happened yesterday, and I can't quite understand what it meant.

I was sunning myself (Algoling myself?) after my swim—and that's something I'm certainly going to miss when I get back to our over-urbanized planet. As usual, there was a group of orgs doing the same at the other end of the beach, and, also as usual nowadays, I noticed them only to make sure I was deferentially sparing them any undue curiosity. Suddenly one of them detached herself from the group and walked down the sand toward me.

It was Lemblad.

At first I thought of scrambling to my feet and getting out of her way. Then I decided just to lie there and pretend to be asleep so as not to embarrass her. I heard her approach me and felt she was standing beside me looking down.

"Are you awake, Stranger?" she said. "I wish to speak to you."

So naturally I had to open my eyes and stand up. If either of us was embarrassed, it wasn't Lemblad.

"I am told that you are soon to return to your own planet," she remarked.

I nodded. "In about two weeks, I think." Then I realized I had said "weeks" in my own language and that it meant nothing on Ajeri; so I added, "Soon."

"Then I think it is right that I tell you I am no longer angry. I understand now that you did not mean to offend me."

I felt myself flushing. "Indeed I did not, Lemblad," I said. "I too understand now, and I have felt deeply sorry. Please believe me, my whole feeling about the way things are on Ajeri is very different from what it was then."

She laughed that unforgettable laugh of hers.

"I should expect so!" She glanced at me quizzically and smiled.

"After that night," she went on, "I told my friends what had happened. It was as outrageous to them as it was to me, and they were very angry. Some of them wanted to tell the eskons to keep you in custody until you could be removed from Ajeri. But even then I had the impression that you meant no insult, that you were merely ignorant."

"Thank you," I answered, and I meant it. "That was indeed true."

It was on the tip of my tongue to add that I had paid dearly for my ignorance, but I knew that would only confuse her farther. So I kept silent.

"So I persuaded them," she continued, "not to take such harsh measures against you, but only, for our own protection—for we did not know what you might do next—to safeguard ourselves while you were still here. I shall know when you leave."

For some reason she laughed again. Then she waved, turned, and walked rapidly back to her companions. I left then and returned home, considerably bemused. I still am. I didn't realize I was being deliberately avoided by the orgs, whom now I revere so highly.

December 29.

I am completely out of deep freeze now, and the ship is preparing to land. It will be an hour or so yet, and I have time to make a last entry in this diary.

"Safeguard." I thought she meant they had taken care to keep out of my way. But how do I know what advanced psychological techniques the Ajerans command?

All I know is that the ship arrived and I said goodbye

to Olven and my other friends and got ready to join it. And in the midst of my last-minute packing, I thought of Mara and suddenly I realized that I was my old self again, just as I have always been. There was a pretty under-officer on board—

Oh, Mara, be there to meet me!

Quick to Haste

It was unbelievable. It was like a dream. No Earth-scene had ever been fairer. Under a bright blue sky, a lake reflected in its clear water the thickly clustered flowering trees. Rolling green meadows dotted with multicolored blossoms ran to the soft hills on the horizon.

And across the meadows, hurrying but obviously more curious than frightened, trooped a score of people—they could not be thought of as anything but human—men, women, and children, dressed in light robes floating behind them in the breeze as they ran toward the spot where the ship had landed.

The four of them from Terra were almost beyond speech. Year after weary year of wandering, once in a great while the find of a habitable planet, once in a vastly greater while a planet inhabited by beings with whom communication could be established. But never—never before—anything like this.

"I feel like apologizing for the scorched area," Hakim muttered.

Grosschmidt grinned. "I know what you mean," he said.

Valeri and young Don Williamson just stood and stared.

Because not only was this a beautiful, unspoiled landscape, not only was the air breathable and fresh and warm like a terrestrial Spring, not only did a sturdy yellow sun that might have been their comfortable old Sol cast light and shadow on trees and flowers that doubtless were of hitherto unknown species but looked confusingly like those on Earth—but these people crowding around them now and smiling up at them without fear or hostility were like a Greek vase come to life. The men were tall and lithe, the children graceful as butterflies, and the women——

Williamson spoke for all four of them when suddenly he gave forth with a long, low, reverent whistle.

"Exquisite!" murmured Grosschmidt. "Each one a Botticelli!" Valeri breathed. Hakim just shut his eyes in ecstasy.

They were calling excitedly now from where they stood on the edges of the unburnt field, in twittering words that were obviously human speech. Hakim, who after all was the pilot and their chief, bestirred himself from his reverie.

"Set up the translator," he ordered Valeri.

For centuries, at the beginning of the Age of Space, men had debated and deliberated about the inevitable communication barriers if somewhere, sometime, Terrestrials and Extraterrestrials should meet face to face. If spaceships from Otherwhere had come to Earth, it could be taken for granted that the travelers would be highly sophisticated in mathematics and physics, and that arithmetical and geometrical series and figures would be the best first means of communication. But so far none had ever come. On the other hand, for a long time now Terrestrials had been cruising through our end of the Galaxy. If intelligent beings were found (as now they had been, several times over), it was vitally important that somehow they should learn at once that the visitors came in peace; but it was quite conceivable that a highly intelligent and highly civilized race might exist which had no mathematical or physical knowledge whatever. How then, immediately, either to learn their speech or teach them ours?

There had been some close calls and one or two catastrophes before an obscure Icelander named Aakinbur had solved the problem—and propelled himself into world-wide fame—by his invention of the Aakinbur Instant Translator. Its heart was an analyzer which took the component rhythms and stresses of any speech system and broke them down into their equivalents in any other. Now every scout ship as a matter of course carried a portable model.

So in five minutes the scouts were conversing easily with the beautiful aliens—Isti, they called themselves, and their planet Istam—each, subjectively, in his own tongue. Here, the crew discovered, was the very situation for which the translator had been planned—the Isti were entirely non-mechanical, living in a purely agricultural world, a world where philosophers, artists, poets flourished, but material science, except for farming know-how, was unknown. It was, in other words, a world very like that of ancient Greece of its great era. Apparently, however, it differed from ancient Greece in one fundamental aspect: war, revolution, politics seemed to be outside its frame of reference, private strife and killing seemed incomprehensible to its inhabitants, and it had not even occurred to the group attracted by the spaceship's landing that the newcomers, however strange and startling, could have come in anything but friendship.

They did have some rough knowledge of astronomy, as farmers always have had, and so they comprehended easily that the stars they saw were really suns like their own, that around these suns orbited planets like theirs, and that these visitors, who possessed an unheard-of ability to construct means of locomotion between the stars, came from a solar system on the outermost edge of the Milky Way (which they called Mirat, and had thought of—incorrectly, they quickly realized now—as a bridge between two constellations which from their viewpoint seemed to hang at either end of it).

The scout ship, which indeed *was* friendly, was neither a precursor of invasion or colonization, nor a missionary enterprise. Long ago Earth had learned to control its dangerous overpopulation, and Man needed no home outside his own system, where gradually the other planets and their larger moons were being converted one by one into suitable dwelling places for any overflow from Terra. Through disaster and restoration, Man had learned also to live at peace with his own kind and hence with other kinds. Space travel now was only the Great Adventure, the dream of the extroverted young, as art and theoretical science were the dreams of youthful introverts. To find new treasures in the Galaxy, to bring home news and establish steady communication for the future, was the straight road to glory. And now that most disease too had been conquered, and Man's life span and his youth span had been doubled, there was almost no limit to extraterrestrial journeying. Man still had not wandered beyond his own Galaxy, but that too would come. Meanwhile, the great ambition of multitudes of boys and girls was to win a place in the training schools for scouts, and to spend all their earlier years in searching for still new discoveries in the Universe beyond their native planet.

But young space scouts were also young humans, with all that that implies. Often the scout ship crews were bisexual, made up perhaps of two couples. Seldom were they all female, but less seldom (because more boys than girls dreamed that dream) they were all male, as was this one. And the youngest of the four, Don Williamson, was the good natured butt of the others for his roving eye and susceptible heart.

"Here's your chance, Don," Hakim whispered with a wink at the other two. "We'll be here for a month, and knowing you, I expect at least four or five of these lovelies to be crying their pretty eyes out when we leave."

Rather to his astonishment, Don neither laughed nor counterattacked. He didn't respond at all. He was standing transfixed, his eyes on a girl in the forefront of the group.

They were all beautiful, so there had to be a new word to describe the girl in the yellow tunic. She was an angel, a bird of Paradise, an epitome of every man's imaginings. Not a goddess, for goddesses are august and remote, and if ever invitation shone in a woman's eye it shone in the dark eyes equally transfixed on Don Williamson.

"Now unless they turn out to be prim and puritanical—" Grosschmidt murmured wickedly in Don's unlistening ear.

He needn't have felt concern. As soon as the translator had done its work, and each side was speaking in its own tongue but hearing the speech of the other side transformed into their own language, quite shamelessly and yet with a kind of naive purity the girl in yellow spread her arms and cried, "You—the tall young man with the strange golden hair—climb down from your house that flies and let us walk in the woods together!"

Curiously Hakim searched the crowd for frowns of disapproval. Instead, there was a ripple of indulgent laughter, and as if the words had set off a trigger reaction, others of the girls pushed forward and called invitations to all four of them.

Surely these entrancing girls had lovers or husbands among the group, but not a man showed anger or jealousy, or even disappointment that none of the new-comers was of the other sex. Grosschmidt, who had read much in ancient history, was reminded of the first westerners who had discovered the islands of the Pacific Ocean.

"How about it, Hakim?" he asked. "Do we go down and mingle?"

"Why not?" the pilot said tolerantly. "I'll hold the fort here. But look, I'm not going to be a wallflower forever. Grosschmidt, I give you an hour. Then you come back and stand sentry duty while I take my turn. Valeri, in another hour you relieve him; and we'll give young Williamson here, since he seems to be the special favor-

ite, all of three hours. After this we'll set a daily schedule for visiting. Does that sound fair?"

"Fair enough," said Valeri. "But how about the translator? Once any of us leaves the immediate neighborhood,
we're not going to understand anybody, nor they us."

Hakim laughed. "I didn't gather that conversation was
what you had in mind," he remarked. "One thing: each
of you is to be sure to keep his fartalker attached at all
times, and his laser gun in his belt. I'm as sure as I can
be that we're prefectly safe, but if there's the slightest
sign of a trap you all know what to do."

Grosschmidt nodded. Valeri exclaimed recklessly, "It
would be worth dying for! Excuse me, Hakim, I was
only kidding; I'll obey orders, of course." Williamson said
nothing, but his face was radiant, and he was first at the
lock.

The pilot watched them make their way, each to a
waiting girl, with the men and the older women and the
children opening ranks to let them in. Two of the lovelies, he noted with a grin, had seized on Valeri; he
walked away toward the woods with one on either arm.
Grosschmidt, no beauty, nevertheless soon found a
willing partner. As for Don Williamson, he and the girl
in yellow flew into each other's arms as if they were
meeting again after a long parting. After they had all
disappeared, Hakim turned to the translator and invited
any of the group who would like to see the ship to board
it. To avoid personal complications, he suggested that it
would be most interesting to the older people.

A half-dozen of them came, and he learned a lot, and
so, he was sure, did they. But he was a young man too,
and when Grosschmidt appeared promptly at the end of
his hour, the pilot was glad to leave him in charge and
go to try his own luck.

But he *was* the pilot, and they were there for more
than dalliance. He was careful to make sure that they
were all four, safe inside the ship, with the visitors gone
and the lock closed, before dark. Williamson was the last
one back, after two commands from Hakim over the

fartalker. "Her name is Ro. She's wonderful!" he said, a dazed look on his face.

Thereafter things got down to schedule. Work—interviews, physical invesitgation and research, note-taking—through most of the day; two hours for each of them, in staggered rotation, for the quasi-Polynesian joys of Istam; nights spent strictly on base. So far as the girls were concerned, the crew members were all playing the field except Don, who kept rigidly faithful to his Ro. She made no progress in his language, but he was learning hers fast without need of the translator. There seemed to be many more females than males, which doubtless accounted for the lack of exclusiveness and jealousy among the male Isti.

It was a week later that Don confided a little in Valeri, his closest friend among the four of them.

"I'm crazy about Ro," he began. "She's the loveliest——"

"Out of this world, in fact," Valeri commented sardonically.

"Don't be funny, Val. The thing is, I'm confused."

"Confused how?"

"By things she says. Like, I spend two hours with her every day, but she seems to think it's much longer, that I'm actually living with her—she has one of those grass shacks, like all of them—and that I just go on trips away from her and come home again. The second day we were together, she made some reference to 'when you were here before,' as if it had been a long time, when it was only a day earlier."

"Time's relative. Probably they have a different way of figuring it."

"I suppose. But there's another thing. She's sixteen—she told me so that first day, and I hadn't any reason to doubt it. But today it suddenly came to me that she seemed older—if I'd just met her, I'd have thought she was about my own age."

"Girls become more mature when they're not virgins any longer," Valeri announced pontifically.

"Yeah, I guess that's it."

But two days later Williamson was so upset on his

return to the ship that they all noticed it, and Hakim asked him outright if anything was wrong.

"I don't know whether you'd call it wrong," Don said gloomily. "Hakim, how much longer are we going to stay here?"

"About two and a half weeks more. Why?"

"Could you manage the rest of the trip without me? Let me stay here for keeps?"

"Certainly not. Are you nuts? If you've got any crazy idea like that, I'll have to keep you tied up in here till we blast off. What's eating you?"

"It's just—Ro told me today we're going to have a baby."

There was a stunned silence. Grosschmidt broke it. "Good Lord!" he exclaimed. "That means they're just as human as we are—we can interbreed. Hey, I just thought—maybe we'll all be leaving little souvenirs behind us!"

"I love Ro," Don said stiffly, "and she loves me. She told me she knew we couldn't stay here forever, that we were only visiting Istam. But for heaven's sake, Hakim, I can't just desert her. I asked her how long gestation takes with them, and she said nine months—just like on Earth. I—I want at least to see my child. Couldn't you just leave me here till then and then come back for me? Poor girl, she said so pathetically to me, 'I know you must go some day, but at least I'll have you till I'm an old woman and our baby's grown up.' She seems to think we plan to stay here for years."

"Not a chance, Don," Hakim said kindly but decisively. "We'll be leaving this sector altogether. It's too bad, but that's the way it's got to be. I blame myself for this. We should all have taken precautions. It never occurred to me that it would be possible for us to impregnate these alien women."

Don looked close to tears.

"It's a mess," he said. "But of course I'll obey orders. Tomorrow I'll have to tell Ro the bad news."

"I'll give you three hours a day with her from now on instead of two, Don," the pilot promised. "That will give

you both more time to comfort each other and prepare
yourselves for the separation."

But the next day Williamson came back on board,
white and wild-eyed, long before he was due.

"Good God!" he burst out as he joined them. "Ro's—
Ro's—" He stopped, out of breath.

"Is she dead?" Hakim asked sharply, fear and worry
suddenly making him look twice his age.

Don fought himself into self-control.

"No," he said at last in a flat, tense voice. "She's not
dead. She's fine. She's had the baby."

"*Had* the baby? What do you mean? Has she had a
miscarriage?"

"No miscarriage. The baby's fully developed, a nine-
pound boy. And she couldn't understand why I was so
shocked and flabbergasted. She seemed to think everything was natural, and I'd be delighted."

"Instant pregnancy," Varleri murmured.

"You've been had, boy," Grosschmidt advised him sadly. "The girl was pregnant the day you met her, and had
been for nearly nine months. Maybe they don't show it
the way our women do."

"It's my baby," Don rejoined dully. "My son. They're
all dark-haired and dark-eyed, and you know it. The
baby has light hair and blue eyes, like mine."

"All newborn babies have blue eyes," said Hakim succinctly. "And dark hair often begins as light, even among
dark-haired people like my own. Grosschmidt's right,
Don; she'd made a sucker of you."

"Don't say that!" Don cried angrily. "I know what I
know. You can't say things like that about my girl."

"Pipe down, Don," said the pilot pacifically. "There
must be some reasonable explanation, and we'll find it.
Do you want to go back there now, for the rest of your
time today?"

"I can't. I've got to think. I told her you'd ordered me
back here for duty, so I could get hold of myself and try
to figure this out."

"Good idea," Hakim said. "O.K., I've got plenty of

work for you to do. Let me know when you want to go to see her again. I've got some thinking to do myself."

For five days Don Williamson, like Achilles, sulked in his tent. Tacitly they all avoided the subject. The other three took their turns away as usual. But somehow the zest had gone out of it; this weird phenomenon had upset and baffled them all.

Hakim was beginning to get an idea, but one so outré and unthinkable that he could not bring himself to dwell on it. The only allusion he made to it was to ask Valeri and Grosschmidt, while Don was absent—returned to Ro at last—if they had had any similar experience.

"I wouldn't know," Valeri said with a shamefaced smile. "I don't know one girl from another—I don't even know their names."

"Grosschmidt?"

"I'm afraid I'm in just about the same situation, Hakim. I'll tell you one funny thing, though."

"What's that?"

"I'm not quite as unselective as that promiscuous Latin over there." Valeri made a face at him. "I haven't kept to one girl, like Don, but I do know one girl from another and I do remember our little affairs. Well, yesterday, when I reached the settlement, a woman came up to me on the road. She looked vaguely familiar, but I couldn't place her. They can't say my name—they call me 'Mit.' 'Why, Mit,' she said, 'have you forgotten Asha?'

"Hakim, Asha was the first girl I made love to on Istam. That was less than three weeks ago. But this girl couldn't have been Asha. I'd hardly call her a girl—she was a mature woman in her thirties."

"Something very similar happened to me too," said Hakim. So his preposterous guess was confirmed. That evening he would have to call them into conference.

Don Williamson came back at the end of his three hours, looking pale and strained. The pilot glanced at him inquiringly, but he shook his head. "Later, Hakim," he said. "Right now I'm all at sea."

An air of doubt and trouble hung over them all as they gathered after dinner for the meeting Hakim had called. The pilot's concerned expression did not reassure them.

"Fellows, I've got something to tell you that you won't like," he began abruptly. "But it's got to be done. We're not waiting for the end of the month. We're blasting off tomorrow."

"You'd better tell us why," Grosschmidt said.

"Of course. We're a pretty good unit here—we stick together. It wouldn't make much difference to you, or to Valeri, or to me, if we waited till the expected date. But what I'm going to tell you is going to be an awful shock for Don, and it would be cruel to put him through more time on Istam after he learned what I've got to tell you now.

"Because I've figured out what all this means. That's your baby all right, Don."

"I know that already," Don said tonelessly. "But how?"

"I want to ask you just one thing, in front of us all. I know it will hurt to talk about it, but that'll be better than leaving you thinking either you're crazy or that the whole of reality has gone haywire, won't it?"

"I guess so. What do you want to know?"

"You went back there today after five days' absence. What happened?"

"What happened!" Williamson cried, his voice shaking. "What happened was that when I got to the shack, Ro ran out to meet me, just like always—overjoyed to see me after so long. And it wasn't my Ro."

"How do you mean?"

"Ro was sixteen, three weeks ago. This could have been her older sister. I could see it, as I couldn't when I saw her every day.

"That wasn't the worst. There was a little boy playing around outside—a little boy with light hair. And she called to him and said, 'Come and say hello to your father, Brog.'

"He wasn't a baby—he was a child old enough for kindergarten if he'd been on Earth."

Valeri drew his breath in sharply. Grosschmidt

glanced at Hakim in sudden appalled understanding. The pilot nodded.

"I guess you're all beginning to comprehend. I couldn't believe it at first myself. But it's the only answer.

"Their metabolism must be fantastically faster than ours. What we call time is only a convenient measurement. I've doped it out, roughly but fairly accurately.

"A day to us is about a year to them. Nine months is about eighteen hours of our time. If we waited our full thirty days, Don's Ro would be a woman of forty-six."

"She's remarked often lately that I keep looking so young," Don said brokenly. "I thought it was a joke— was I expected to age in a few days? And that's what she meant by our staying till she was an old woman."

"Exactly. Don, your girl was born just two weeks and two days before we landed here. By the time we took off, by our former plan, your son would have been in his teens.

"You won't ever know about it—but Don, you'll probably be a grandfather before you reach your twenty-fourth birthday."

The Smiling Future

A great many things had happened to Stort in the course of one lifetime, but this was by all odds the weirdest of them all.

If anyone had told him a month before that as Director General of the United Regions he would travel to the coast of California for a private interview with a—something: you couldn't call it a human being but you certainly couldn't call it an animal—he would have laughed in the prophet's face.

Yet here he was.

When the first group (embassy? army?) had appeared suddenly on the shore, each ensconsed in its private tank of coral or thin rock with things like surf-boards to bear it out of and back to the water, and when the leader had raised its head and addressed the frightened chlorella-gatherers in harsh and jerky but perfectly clear English, they had been too petrified by fear even to answer. Chlorella-gatherers were stupid by definition; they were about the only manual workers left in a computerized world. If every scrap of edible substance had not been vital to the pullulating billions of mankind, they would not have been set to collecting the scraps and crumbs that evaded the automatic machines in mid-ocean and drifted in to shore.

But naturally the governmental electro-spy planted near by had caught the speech and transmitted it to the nearest police station, and a copter with three fuzzes and a lieutenant had been dispatched at once.

At their approach the leader had raised its head again from the water in its tank and repeated: "I wish to speak to your highest authority. It is urgent and for your own sakes. Tell your ruler it must meet me on this spot seven suns from today, at this hour. It is life or death for you. We cannot go to it, so it must come to us."

The policemen were almost as frightened as the chlorella-gatherers, but the lieutenant pulled himself together and in a rather quavering voice blustered: "You're crazy, whatever you are! Get back where you came from at once, or we'll shoot." They all had their ray-guns out.

The leader didn't say another word. It just looked. And the three fuzzes and the lieutenant and the dozen chlorella-gatherers all suddenly found themselves flat on the sand, utterly unable to move a toe or a finger.

"You can talk," said the leader kindly. "I've left your speaking apparatus free. You do have somebody who can speak with authority for you land-people, don't you?"

The lieutenant couldn't nod; he managed to clear his throat and say yes, hoarsely.

" 'Him,' not 'it'. But—"

"Then tell him. You see what I did to you. I and every one of us here and every one of us anywhere can do the same thing to any number of you, at any time or place. We do not want to do it; we prefer to reason with you like sensible beings. But since you were so foolish as to threaten us, I had no choice.

"Unfortunately we have no fingers or thumbs like yours, so that our power to manipulate objects is limited. Therefore we have had to develop our minds, and you must believe me that this is the very mildest of the things we can do with them. Tell your ruler that. And tell him we are giving him and all of you land-people this one chance. If you do not take advantage of it, there will never be another. Tell him that.

"Seven suns from today, here and at this hour. I shall release you when we are safely away from the reach of your weapons."

They were a thin line back in the Pacific when the shaken auditors were able to lift their bruised bodies from the beach.

The lieutenant was a very intelligent man. Anybody who could be spared from the incessant labor of food-production for an overcrowded world had to be intelligent to rise above the common herd. He knew at once he had two imperative duties: first, to save face by arresting the chlorella-gatherers to keep them from talking; second, to convince his superiors of the truth of this incredible happening and to force the persuasion up through the ranks of officialdom until it reached somebody whose responsibility was secure.

Half a dozen times in the next fevered days it was pure chance that the whole unbelievable situation did not bog down. But somehow the message penetrated the ranks of command until on this afternoon Director General Stort stood face to face with a row of water-filled tanks and found himself in colloquy with something that to his amazed but scientific eye (he had once been professor of genetics in the Pan-Scandinavian University) could be nothing but a super-dolphin.

The sleek gray head with its big smiling mouth and its calm, direct, opaque eyes gazed back at him with equal interest. Obviously his thoughts had been read.

"You are quite right," said the leader politely. "In fact, I might say that you can thank yourselves for our existence. For 550 years now you have been dumping atomic waste into the oceans—in lead containers, to be sure; but in time they leak.

"You have known that, and you have known that in consequence all salt-water fish have been irradiated until they are no longer fit for you to eat. Therefore you have planted the oceans ten feet deep with chlorella, which can be decontaminated, and left the deeper waters alone.

"What you have not known is that this same irradiation has caused specific genetic changes in us also—the dolphins, the whales, all of us whose home is the sea but who also breathe air. Only, in our case, the mutation has been beneficient, not maleficent. Not only are we the descendants of those who could survive deeper pressures, but our mental powers have increased tenfold.

"With all modesty, I may say that my own kind had the best brains to start with, and we still have. The whales and their kind are very useful to us; but we are the rulers."

Stort was so bemused he forgot for a moment the reason for his visit.

"How have you learned to speak English?" he asked.

Dolphins always smile; but the smile widened.

"We could always speak, even in the old days. You must know that: you took some of our ancestors captive and taught them your language. We speak all the tongues of men who dwell along the coasts of the world. We learned them very simply—by spies who frolicked in the shallow waters and listened and reported.

"It just happens that, as your main seat of world government is in this part of the land area, ours is in this section of the seas, so naturally when someone was appointed to deal with you, they chose one who could speak the language of the nearest land-region.

"But let us talk of more important things. I am here to give you an ultimatum."

Stort stiffened.

"Excuse me," said the leader suavely. "I did not mean to use an offensive word. Perhaps I do not know your tongue as well as I think I do. Let me say rather that I am here to give you a warning?"

"What kind of warning? And by what authority?" Stort's tone still bristled.

The harsh voice dropped to a sibilant whisper.

"You know a little of our powers. I should be most reluctant to have to demonstrate how far we are in control. I am here at all only because of our sense of justice and our generosity. Do not push us too far. I implore you, as one living being to another, to take us with the utmost seriousness. Believe me, the fate of your whole kind is in your hands today."

Stort felt a chill creep over him—whether born of premonition or induced by the stranger he did not want to know.

"I am only a representative," he said, in a more conciliatory manner. "I can carry messages. I cannot make final decisions by myself—and certainly not instant ones."

The leader seemed taken aback.

"You mean you are not yourself the chief authority?" it asked. "That is not the way in which *our* society is constituted. Is there no one, then, to whom we may speak once for all? Time is running out fast."

Stort made up his mind. He was aghast at the prospect but he dared not take the risk of refusing, after what he had already seen and heard.

"Only the assembled United Regions can consider any information you have to offer," he said coolly. "If you mean it in good faith, you must arrange to cross the continent and speak to them where they meet."

For the first time the super-dolphin seemed nonplussed.

"I am sorry," it said, "but that is totally impossible. We are not equipped for land travel—it is all we could do, with the aid of trained crabs and octupuses, to devise these containers you see, and to come in this far on the waves.

"We shall help all we can, with our mental influence, to make your mission successful; but your assembly, or enough of them to make and implement decisions, must meet us here."

The leader paused.

"I cannot impress it upon you too strongly that there is no time to lose. We cannot delay much longer. You have the means of flying back and forth across the continent.

I can give you no more than another seven days. Even then it may be too late."

Stort never knew how much was his own position and influence, how much the hypnotic ability of the super-dolphins, which seemed unchanged by distance. It was touch and go. Perhaps curiosity and incredulity had as much to do with it as anything—and the fact that the United Regions would foot the bill. But a week from that day three hyperjet planes, each holding a hundred passengers landed in utmost secrecy at the nearest airport, and soon after, 260 delegates to the UR (a clear majority) and 40 technicians with all their equipment, gathered on the wide beach, cleared for the day of chlorella-gatherers.

They waited an hour, and some were already restless and complaining, when at last the thin line appeared to the west, and in a few minutes scores of the water-filled tanks that kept the super-dolphins comfortable were ranged opposite them at the edge of the sea.

This time, however, the spokesman was apparently someone of far higher rank than the envoy with whom Stort had spoken. Apparently, because to human eyes the smiling invaders all looked alike. But the first words set them straight.

"I am glad," the dolphin said, "that you have heeded the injunction of the messenger we sent to you. Believe me, it is purely for your own sakes that we have put you to this trouble. I am authorized both to explain the situation to you, to make our final offer, and to receive your prompt acceptance—for I cannot imagine that you will not accept this one chance for your racial survival.

"But first, to make things plain, I must ask your speaker a few questions. You will understand that our knowledge of you land-people is necessarily limited to what our spies have been able to see and hear along all the coasts of all the oceans. Unfortunately our cousins in fresh waters have not mutated as we have, and so we have not been able to secure much information from them.

"Am I correct in assuming that there is a certain amount of over-population among you land-dwellers?"

There was some sardonic laughter from the men and women gathered on the shore, and a confused babble of voices. The super-dolphin's expression could not change, but it gazed pointedly at Stort as the appointed spokesman.

The Director General drew a deep breath.

"Unhappily," he said, "you are only too right. For 500 years now mankind has been over-producing itself, and despite immense efforts we have been unable to cut our population down to the optimum size. Contraception, sterilization, abortion have all failed to compete adequately with the conquest of disease and the consequent increase in life expectancy. The one thing we have not been able to eradicate from human nature is the selfish desire of most individuals to perpetuate themselves, or their prejudices which prevent the establishment of proper eugenic standards."

"Strange!" exclaimed the official. "We had always understood that, next to ourselves as we have evolved, human land-dwellers were the most intelligent beings on earth. When *we* found ourselves faced with this problem, we found a solution though we had not your means of solving it; but you—

"But more of that later. Isn't the result the overcrowding of your living areas?"

"So much so," Stort replied, "that merely to feed this immense population takes practically every inch of earth that will grow vegetables or animals for men to eat. There has been one good result—wars have become obsolete and all mankind is united in a single effort to raise food. Our planet has become one huge food-factory, and the vast majority of the inhabitants are engaged in this one industry."

"By the whole planet, I take it you mean that smaller part which is dry land. But where then do you live?"

"That is our greatest problem. We had hoped to colonize the other planets of this solar system, or even to go beyond them to other systems. But every effort to do so has failed; the vast amounts of money needed to make it possible cannot be spared from the amount necessary merely to raise enough food to keep mankind alive.

"Where do we live? We live, crowded together, with the individuality and leisure our ancestors knew a luxury none of us can afford, on mountain tops, in the few deserts we cannot irrigate, in barracks in the factory-farms themselves, but mostly in a vast network of underground tunnels. A few, who are very rich, live in satellite tracts above the stratosphere."

"That is even worse than we had anticipated," said the stranger slowly. "If we had known, perhaps we would have been able to postpone our solution of our own difficulties until you had found a better one for yours. But it is too late now.

"We did, though, from the beginning try to consider your welfare in making our plans. I shall not conceal from you the fact that there are two major schools of thought among us concerning you land-people. One very large group feels that you have not fulfilled your promise as a species, and that the time has come for your extinction. The other, which I myself represent, is still slightly in the majority. It feels that it owes you a certain gratitude, because—quite without any intention on your part, I grant—you made us what we are.

"I am sure that we, or any others of us who dwell in the ocean, never entered your minds when you dumped your atomic waste in our living-space. Nevertheless, it is solely because of this inadvertent action on your part, that we dolphins, and to a certain extent the whales, have mutated into the highly evolved beings we are now. We are by nature altruistic. We feel that even accidental benefactors should be protected if it is at all possible. That is why we are making this attempt to save at least some of you."

"To save us from what?" Stort inquired bluntly.

There was no change in the super-dolphin's face, but Stort could have sworn that the small black eyes gazed on him with compassion.

"From certain and universal death," it said.

Thre was a murmur from the throng listening through their earphones. The speaker raised a flipper for silence.

"We too," it went on, "have our serious population problem. We too are finding our living-space insufficient for civilized existence. *We* can't make room for ourselves by destroying all other life except the edible—which in our case means the fish, poisonous now to you but not to us."

The fish. And it was true that no animal lived on earth any longer which could not be used as human food.

"Therefore we find it necessary to make the whole planet our dwelling-place."

"How?" asked Stort hoarsely.

"You know there are many rifts and faults in the earth's crust—more of them under the sea than in the land. There is a very deep one in the mid-Pacific; there are others, almost equally deep, in the southern portion of that ocean you call the Atlantic. When there is a break in any of them it can alter the whole relation of sea and land.

"We have no machinery, but we have unlimited animal strength at our service. With the help of our trained whales, we have found that these rifts can be widened and opened. We have known that for a long time, and have abstained from action because we wished to protect you—which I feel in all honesty is more than you would have done for us in like circumstances.

"We can no longer do so. Our population has increased too greatly, and unlike you we have no technical means of regulating it. You have such means, but you have refused to enforce them. There is only one way by which we can find enough room for us to live and build our society for any conceivable time to come.

"We are going to open all the rifts and flood the earth."

Stort darted a glance at those nearest to him. He saw faces as white as his own must be.

"You can't do that!" he gasped. "It would be inhuman!"

Again the fixed smile seemed to widen.

"That," the dolphin official said succinctly, "would hardly be a consideration with us."

Pandemonium broke out. The throng of delegates went berserk. In a hundred different languages they screamed, howled, bellowed. The super-dolphins stood unmoved.

It was not any from the "underdeveloped" Asian or African Region, but two from Europe and one from North America who broke out from the crowd and dashed toward the row of tanks, forbidden ray-guns in their hands. They took only a few steps before they fell on the sand, paralyzed as had been the policemen and the chlorella-gatherers at the first encounter.

"Don't be foolish," said the super-dolphin mildly. "You can't hurt us. And if you could, you would be only hurting yourselves, since I come bearing a suggestion by which some of you at least might be saved."

Scared and sobered, the delegates fell silent.

"Tell us your offer," Stort said.

The spokesman waited until the limp bodies had been carried to one side. All this time the other dolphins had neither spoken nor stirred. Now, at a nod from their leader, two of them detached themselves and surf-boarded their tanks down to watch over the stricken three. Then, with a glance of approval at Stort, the leader spoke again.

"You cannot live at all in our element," it began. "And we cannot live wholly in yours. We breathe air, as you know, just as you do, but we must live for the most part under water. You can swim in water, but you must spend most of your time in the air.

"We cannot adapt to land-living; we should be dehydrated in no time. That is why, for these meetings with you, we must stay in these containers, under water except when we come up to breathe or speak.

"We can do nothing for you yourselves. But if your

progeny means so much to you, we can see to it that your race shall not die altogether."

"How?" Stort's voice was thick with strain.

Instead of answering, the leader turned to its companions. There was a whistling hubbub in their own speech muffled to human ears because the voices came not from mouths but from blow-holes. Then the leader turned to Stort again.

"Do you realize," it said, "that when we flood the land it will mean *all* the land? Your highest mountains will be drowned, your underground tunnels will be flooded. Even those you say live on satellites will slowly starve to death, since I assume their food is imported from earth."

The delegates' loud-speakers burst forth in a hullabaloo of protest, threat, and pleading. The dolphin leader stood unmoving and unmoved.

"We'll kill you all first!" yelled an Italian delegate. "Murderers!" screamed a delegate from Outer Mongolia. "Have mercy on us," pleaded a delegate from Syria. "Give us time at least to find a way to save ourselves!" pleaded a Venezuelan.

Stort stopped them with a gesture. His face was ashen under his fair hair.

"Sir," he said to the stranger, "I do not know your name—"

"We have no names."

"Then, sir, let me ask you: is this decision irrevocable?"

"Unfortunately for you, yes. We have tried every other way possible to us, and failed."

"How much time have we?"

"I told you I represented a majority. But it is a small majority. Our opponents were unwilling to give us even time to warn you."

"Then," said Stort, "you might as well have saved us and yourselves the effort, unless you really have some way out for us.

"You must know that our whole economy is based on automatic machinery, and that even if any of us could survive they couldn't survive long as a society. They couldn't even live on sea-food, for that is poison to us now, thanks to our own stupidity. Oh, yes, I'm not exonerating us; perhaps we deserve to die. But if we can even leave descendants, that would be better than nothing.

"So, do you really have anything feasible to suggest to us? If not, it would have been kinder to let disaster come upon us without foreknowledge."

"Stort," said the dolphin, "you are a brave and wise man. You are the first land-animal I have heard of whom I should think almost worthy to be one of us.

"I wish it had been possible to spare you and any others of your breed who are like you. It is not. But there is one chance, if you hurry, to prevent your utter extinction."

"What is it?" asked Stort eagerly. "Whatever it is—"

There was an affirmative murmur from the throng behind him.

"In the natural order of things, our two species could never interbreed. But we have found that among our own people we can, by our mental powers, alter the chromosomal pattern. We have been able to produce experimental crosses with other species of mammals— none, yet, as far removed from us as you; but there seems to be no insuperable obstacle.

"We are a proud people, and we do not like to mix our blood with that of inferiors. But we are also a just and generous people. We owe you what reparation we can make for what, to preserve ourselves, we are obliged to inflict upon you. It is a great, great sacrifice, but we have volunteered for it. At least we can console ourselves that your presence here must mean that you are among the most worthy of your kind.

"The party among us which is impatient for action may not wait for our return. But if any or all of you wish to take advantage of our offer, here and now, we are willing."

There was a profound silence. Then Stort said stiffly:

"You mean—there are females among you here?"

"I supposed you would know that we are *all* females," said the leader. "Female dolphins have always been more intelligent than the males. Few males among us could become important members of our government, such as we are."

The silence continued. Some delegates prayed. Several fainted.

"There is no time to lose," the harsh voice said. "We have wasted too much already. If you wish to preserve your human genes—"

Suddenly all the super-dolphins raised their heads abruptly from their tanks. They conversed agitatedly among themselves.

Something's happened, they've sensed something, Stort thought. We need a miracle. Perhaps it's come.

He turned to the ranks of delegates. In the faces before him he saw fear, disgust, anger, hesitation, stoical resolution in a few.

"I think," he said quietly, "our visitors have something new to tell us." He turned expectantly.

"I am truly very sorry," the leader said. "We have waited too long. Time has run out. We have just received a mental message from our headquarters. In our absence, our opponents have overcome us. Our offer must be withdrawn.

"We could still do one thing for you—we could put you all to sleep."

"No!" cried mankind's last defiance of fate.

The super-dolphins turned without another word and glided back into the breakers.

And while the delegates stood in dread, eyes fixed on the ocean, something else arose on the horizon.

A wall of water so high it blotted out the sinking sun.

So that now we who inherited all the planet Earth will never know whether we could have mingled with the only other terrestrial race that came near to our own mentality.

Centuries later, we still keep finding the buried skeletons of what was once the Race of Man.

Gathi

I don't want to seem mean or cranky, but your father and I are getting old, and he's never really recovered from that leaf-curl, and it's too much for us to have to be baby-shading for your seedlings *all* the time. If you won't take care of them yourself once in a while, I'm going to have to complain to the grove-masters.

I don't know what's got into the younger generation. It's against dendroid behavior, the way you act. I know you and your trunkmate have other interests, and all we old trees are good for any more, in your opinion, is to provide shade for the young.

And don't tell me I don't love my own little descendants.

Of course I love them—is there a sweeter feeling than that of a tender green tendril wrapping itself around one's gnarled old bark? But they slither and rustle and leaf-talk all the time, and we're tired and need our rest. It's just as I claimed from the beginning: young couples when they're ready to root together ought to stake out a place of their own, and not crowd in on the spot they were seeded in. It isn't as if you were really my daughter, seeded directly from me; your father and I are both pushing 2000, and sky knows how many generations away from me you two really are, my dear. Calling all one's living ancestors father and mother, and all one's descendants, no matter how many generations off, son and daughter, is merely a convenience, not an obligation. My own immediate children, I seem to remember, were much more considerate—and still are, the ones still young enough to seed.

The thing is, we were brought up very differently when I was young. I can recall my mother—my own, immediate mother—giving me the rules when I was barely more than a seedling myself. "Always be thoughtful of grown trees—don't disturb them. Don't be always overroot with them. Play around all you like with your young friends—that's the way you'll be able to choose wisely when you're old enough to root and mate. Get your fair share of sun and water, so you'll grow up into a beautiful straight tree that we'll be proud to be the parents of. And never, never do anything to make us call in the grove-masters to punish you."

We were respectful of the grove-masters in those days; we were even afraid of them, though in a way they are our servants. Nowadays the young folk affect to despise them. What advantage have they over us, you youngsters say, except being mobile all their lives?—and that, you add, is only an instance of permanent immaturity we've evolved beyond; no grove-master has the intellect of a tree.

Which may all be very true—I don't pretend to understand this new psychology—but the fact remains that the grove-masters still have the power of life and death over us. If they neglect us or expose us to blight, we may live on, but we can never be parents. And then if we have the misfortune to outlive our contemporaries, we may be left solitary in the forest, with no one to communicate with for hundreds of lonely years. It's dangerous to offend the grove-masters.

Like Gathi. You came from another grove to root with our remote son; perhaps you've never heard about her.

Gathi and I were seeded almost at the same time, and we were saplings together. She budded out before I did, when she was barely 100, and right away she became interested in boys. "I'm young," she used to say to me rebelliously. "I'll be rooted soon enough, and I want to have fun while I'm free. If a boy wants to rustle leaves with me, why shouldn't I let him?"

"Gathi," I used to tell her, "it will be another hundred years before we're rooted, and you'll have plenty of time for fun and games when your buds and leaflets are a bit less green and tender. Why rush things? I know what the old trees say sounds stuffy, but it's true: a girl who doesn't know how to take care of herself can get into a lot of trouble. What tree will ever want to be your trunkmate if you let your bark be lost before you're ready for rooting?"

"Oh, you *seedling!*" Gathi would cry contemptuously, and off she'd be, rubbing twigs with some other precocious young sprout.

"He has the dreamiest green leaves!" she'd rave. "He's so tall and slender, and his trunk is brown when he's only a hundred and twenty-five!" Then soon she'd be crazy about another.

The grove-masters warned her over and over, but she paid no more attention to them than she did to me.

So what happened? When her time came for rooting, there wasn't a boy she knew who would look at her. They'd all fooled around with her for a century; she was nothing they wanted to settle down for life with. I had found my own trunkmate by then, and our roots had begun to grow around each other lovingly. Gathi was still root-loose and beginning to get worried. Is there anything more dreadful than to be an untrunkmated tree?

It cost Gathi a lot of pride to have to go to the grove-masters at last for advice and help, and she didn't like what she got.

"You belong in our grove," they told her, "and we're reponsible for you. How many times have we told you that no good ever comes of the kind of life you've been leading? We can't have wild trees growing unattached in the grove, playing rootsie with other women's mates.

Our business is to build the grove into a healthy unit, and trees that can't fit in will have to be blighted."

That, of course, scared her silly—a girl who had never suffered even so much as a branch-scrape.

"Please, please," she begged them, all her pride gone. "Anything but that—I'll do anything."

"Very well," said the head grove-master—the one with the blue wings. "There is an old tree here—you know him: Borthi. He's nine hundred, but he's still young enough to seed, and to provide shade and nourishment for his seedlings till they grow up. His mate was struck by lightning last year, and fell. He is looking for another."

Gathi turned pale chartreuse, and shook so that all her twigs rattled. But she had reached the time of rooting; she dared not stand still a minute lest her roots settle in the earth.

Oh, she fought against her fate. I don't think Borthi had much joy of his second marriage. Gathi became the scandal of the grove. She had an incurable case of wandering roots. Every married woman within reaching distance of her had grounds for complaint, and carried her grievance to the grove-masters. The boys Gathi used to play around with were all grown and trunkmated now, and their wives hadn't forgotten Gathi's reputation. I must say in fairness that she was blamed for plenty she never did; but perhaps I'm prejudiced in her favor because my trunkmate—your father—was the only one she never flirted with: she and I had been friends from the seed, and besides, my husband never so much as touched leaves with another girl after we'd found each other.

And you can't altogether blame poor Gathi. Borthi had no bad habits, and he was a good provider; their saplings, as they came along, were healthy and handsome. But he wasn't much company for a girl like her.

Things couldn't go on like that forever. The grove-masters came to her, since she could no longer visit them, and laid down an ultimatum.

"If it weren't for our respect for Borthi," they told her

right in his hearing, "we'd have skipped service to you two long ago. You'd have become a sterile couple forever. We know we made this marriage, and we've done our best to preserve it. What about you, Borthi? Do you want her blasted?"

That's probably what saved her life, for Borthi answered grumpily that he couldn't care less—he'd rather spend the rest of his 3000 years alone than with a wife like that. That offended the grove-masters with him too. One of them said to him sarcastically, "Well, Borthi, it takes two to make a happy trunkmating. There's more to life than air and water. Perhaps if once in a while you rustled leaves or rubbed branches with her, Gathi might learn to keep her wandering roots at home."

Borthi just grunted, and Gathi snickered. I heard the whole thing; they lived right next to us. I was frightened; I was sure that the grove-masters would simply end the whole controversy by condemning them both. But I suppose they felt a bit guilty themselves—after all, the marriage was their doing. So they gave Gathi another warning, and went away.

After that, Gathi seemed to settle down. Our part of the grove grew a lot quieter; there was no more of the constant leaf-shaking and branch-rattling which had been going on as indignant wives told each other their troubles, or went after Gathi. I began to hope that she had learned her lesson, and I was terribly sorry for her—she had been such a gay, vivacious girl, and now through her own foolishness she was tied to a husband more than four times her age.

It was autumn, and soon we'd all be overcome by the winter sleep, when even the grove-masters rest and the whole world lies still under the peaceful snow. I did, I remember, notice and wonder about a good-looking young sapling, a boy of the generation after ours, who seemed to be spending an awful lot of his time circling around our corner of the grove. Once in moonlight I saw him and Gathi with their branches intertwined. Borthi must have been dozing, the way we do as we grow older. It worried me, but I didn't say anything. I told myself that what she felt for him must surely be maternal love—though he was mighty near rooting-time for that.

Then winter came, and everything quieted down as always, until the grove-masters should waken us in the spring.

As long as I live—which is at least 1000 years more—I shall never forget the sight that lay before me when I stretched my branches and scratched my first leaf-buds of the season, that morning of early spring.

Near us, where Borthi and Gathi had stood in their uneasy trunkmating, he lay prone on the still frozen ground. His bark was gray and dry, and what few leaves still clung to his branches were sere and brittle skeletons.

And the Mark was on him. He hadn't died of freezing, as sometimes happens to old trees; he was far from old enough for that. Low down on his trunk was a white ring. He had been—excuse me for saying the word: only strong language can express what I felt—he had been Girdled!

And above his corpse, veiled in light green already and shimmering happily, stood Gathi.

But not alone. Next to her, rooted, was the young sapling in whose branches I had seen her embraced, that night in autumn.

There was only one way it could have been done. I had heard of such things—they were legends our parents used to scare us with when we were young—but never before had I discovered that they were true.

When we settle down for the winter with the snow coverlet over our roots, and our sap quiets for the long sleep, and thr grove-masters themselves cease their care of us—some say they go to some other forest far away, where it is summer in our winter, but that I think is a myth—then the Evil Ones roam the groves. They are mobile like the grove-masters, but they are not our caretakers and keepers as the grove-masters are: far from it—they wish us ill. They cannot harm us, the old trees told us, unless we are wicked too; but if we are, they can sense us calling them.

Gathi and her young lover had called them.

They must have been mad, both of them. Did they think they could escape?

The grove-masters let him be blighted; he died slowly.

But to Gathi they did worse. They let her live.

That's Gathi, over there—that faded, shriveled, twisted tree. A few warped leaves break out each year on her withered branches. Her saplings have long ago deserted her; when their time came to root they settled as far from her as they could go. No one speaks to her. I tried for a long time, but she never answered, so for many years now I have let her alone.

Beside her, until her isolation ends in death, lies the body of the husband whose murder she incited. There are still a few black stalks tangled in her lower boughs— all that is left of her last lover.

No, child, the grove-masters may be long-suffering, but they are not to be despised. Perhaps they haven't our intellect, perhaps their permanent mobility means that they are not evolved as far as we are: but without them, we can't live normal lives. If we offend them beyond forgiveness, as poor Gathi did, they will punish us as she was punished.

... No, of course, I'm not implying that your thought-lessness can be compared to her sin. I'm only saying that the old ways, when we were considerate of our elders, and when we went in wholesome fear of offending the grove-masters, had their points.

I don't want to have to complain to them about you, and, as I said, I don't want to seem mean or cranky. But your father and I *are* getting old, and I wish to sky you'd let us have some rest and take a little care of your own seedlings, some of the time at least.

Or let them go play around Gathi. There's still a little shade in her branches, and it would be a kindly deed.

The Children

I

"I think," said Dr. Schultz brusquely, "that this is a preposterous and essentially unscientific project. There is nothing new about the experiment itself; it was first announced nearly 30 years ago, in 1952, before the British Association. We have been using it ever since, and we know the effect remains good for periods up to five years. Longer—even immensely long—periods are merely supererogatory.

"As for the other aspect of McElroy's proposal, involving the possible future discovery of means of time-travel, that seems to me the wildest of unscientific speculations. I don't know how the rest of you feel, but so far as I am concerned, I do not favor lending the resources of the International Association for the Advancement of Science to this harebrained proposition."

Kemet Ali cleared his throat. As chairman of the IAAS, his chief asset was his unfailing tact. But before he could begin, James McElroy, his earnest eyes peering through his spectacles, spoke up.

"May I say just a word?" he asked. He was too thin, and gray hairs showed already among the brown. His voice still had the deadened quality it had displayed ever since his personal catastrophe six months before. But there could be no doubt of the continuing keenness of mind of this brilliant young geneticist who had actually become one of the most valued workers on the IAAS staff soon after he had achieved his Ph.D. and Sc.D. simultaneously at the incredibly early age of twenty-two.

"I am quite aware," he said, "that there is every chance the experiment I propose will be an utter failure. Careful as we should be, in the light of previous experience, never to prophesy what scientific discoveries may or may not be made in the future, I agree that practicable time-travel may well be a chimera mankind will never bring into actuality.

"But I can't see that it will do any harm to take so simple a chance—and if it *should* succeed, we shall have proved at least one point of immense value, which is that for all time to come humanity as a species can insure its practical immortality, at least as long as the earth itself is livable.

"I want very little of you—only permission to place my tape-recording in our innermost vaults, and the use of a very small space in our concession in Antarctica. I shall be interfering with nothing and nobody, in the little room I shall take up. And if—I say *if*—a month from now even one of the persons at whom my message is aimed should be able to visit this place and time, the result would in some ways be the most astounding revelation of all scientific history."

"Would you expect these—these visitors to give us detailed information about their own eras?" asked Dr. Duseldina Moro.

"That I doubt very much; I think in the first place they would be unable to do so, lest the actual course of history be interfered with; and in the second place I doubt if we should be equipped to understand if they did try to tell us.

"But if I, standing here a month from today, can secure actual living evidence that those phials buried in Antarctica can still be used a hundred, a thousand, who knows how many thousands of years in the future—that, while civilization continues, depleted human stock can always be renewed and regenerated—"

"Exactly," interrupted Schultz rudely. "And what makes you think, Dr. McElroy, that *you* should be chosen as the perfect human specimen? Why not conduct first a scrupulous inquiry and select the young man, anywhere on earth, whom we all judge to be, mentally and physically, the fittest subject—or several such men, for that matter?"

He stopped short, sensing the embarrassed hush around the conference table. McElroy stammered: "I wanted to spare expense and labor, Dr. Schultz. And I don't consider myself 'the perfect human specimen' or anything near it. I only felt that for this first experiment it would be better to use someone in our own organization. As a geneticist I know I carry no serious recessive defects. And—and I felt—"

Kemet Ali scribbled a hasty note and passed it down to Schultz. The biochemist read it and reddened uncomfortably. It said, in the chairman's easy American idiom, "Give the poor guy a break."

"Very well," Schultz conceded abruptly. "I withdraw my opposition. Perhaps you are right. We can use other subjects later, if this first experiment succeeds. As I don't expect it tol" he bristled.

His colleagues averted their faces. They had all been remembering, as Kemet Ali had reminded Schultz, how near they had come to losing McElroy altogether. For a while the psychologists had feared he would never recover fully from the shock of that dreadful day when his adored young wife and their infant son had burned to death before his eyes.

Dr. Norah Wong came to the rescue of the difficult moment.

"I notice," she said in her singsong voice, "that there is a slight error in your prospectus, Dr. McElroy. You name the 25th of next month for the possible visit of the—er—the time-travelers—if any. It is the next day we meet, the 26th."

Young James McElroy flushed.

"I know," he mumbled. "I just wanted—if you don't mind—I shall of course make a full recording by tridimens-telescreen. It will be the same as if you were all here. I shall present it the next day at the April meeting."

"You mean," Nigel Wycliffe put in helpfully in his precise accent, "since you yourself are the—the subject, you would prefer that this first—hypothetical meeting be made in private?"

"Exactly," McElroy said gratefully. "After all, if any of—of the results do arrive, and if they should be odd, or—or unsatisfactory—"

"Of course," Dr. Moro seconded him. "Of course Dr. McElroy does not want twenty onlookers at this meeting. We all understand."

"You have the recording ready?" asked the chairman.

"All ready, just as I read it to you yesterday. And I have the vials ready too, in glycerol deep freeze. As soon as I have your permission, I can fly to Antarctica, bury them, and mark the spot as I have indicated in my instructions."

"How many?"

"I thought three."

"I should make it five," said Kemet Ali. "After all, there is always the possibility of one of them being lost or spoiled. And you don't know how many times one may be used and the results merely added to the record, before the point may be reached when time-travel is in effect."

"If it ever is!" Schultz exploded.

"If it ever is," the chairman responded blandly. "I take it, ladies and gentlemen, there is no further objection to giving Dr. McElroy unanimous consent? Thank you. On April 26th, then, we shall hear his report."

"We shall hear that nothing happened!" grumbled the irrepressible Schultz.

II

In 2150, it was decided that the IAAS headquarters had become obsolete and inadequate. The buildings were all torn down and the site cleared for an entirely new construction. In the course of demolition, the innermost vaults were uncovered. A committee of the Association opened the vaults and went over the contents. One thing they found was a twentieth century tape-recording apparatus, marked: "To be opened by any competent scientist." They opened and reproduced it, with mingled feelings of interest and amusement.

"This James McElroy—I've seen his name in footnotes now and again—certainly believed in long-range projects," one of them remarked. "I wonder if anything happened on April 25, 1980? I don't suppose they put it in the records, for fear of influencing future developments."

"What shall we do with this thing?" inquired one of his colleagues. "Just put it back in the new vaults, to wait for our forthcoming buildings to fall to ruins in the course of time?"

"No, I think first we ought to follow instructions, as a duty to the progress of science."

"But *we* haven't achieved time-travel, or any prospect of it."

"True, but we can do as McElroy said—locate one of his phials buried in the Antarctic—at 72° 20′ S., 155° 15′ E., near the South Magnetic Pole, and see if the contents are still viable. Leave the rest of them *in situ*. If the thing works, then we add the information, at the proper time, to McElroy's recording, with data of name, place, and so on for possible future discoverers, and redeposit the recorder in our new vaults. We shall have to get official authority, of course."

"Suppose nothing happens?"

"Then even so, I think we should say so—though I agree that in that case there would be little likelihood of any success later on. Too bad we'll never know the end of the story."

The experiment succeeded, and the record was duly made.

In 2900, during the Second Dark Age following the Last Plague and the Terminal Atomic War, the IAAS buildings erected in 2150 lay a mass of ruins on the shores of the Pacific Ocean. The blasted earth around them had long lost its radioactivity, but the huge tumbled confusion of steel and stone was a forbidding and a forbidden place to the roving bands of illiterate and superstitious hunters who were the only human beings left alive in what had been a metropolitan area. When the leader of one of these groups sighted, in his tribe's wanderings, what had become known as the Devil's Castle, he hastily ordered his followers to turn in another direction. There was nothing to hunt, anyway, for miles around the desolate place, unless one wanted to eat lizards and scorpions.

But rumors and hearsay and legends grew up and seeped into the ears of children listening to stories by the campfire. Because the Devil's Castle was terrible, soon it began to take on a fearful fascination as well. Curiosity and venturesomeness do not die out of the human race because knowledge is under a cloud. Boys and girls dreamed and egged one another on to boasts and dares; young people, restless and bored, planned half-meant expeditions and forays. Perhaps, they told one another, somewhere in that ruined landmark lay hoards of jewels and strange metals, such as had been uncovered sometimes in the forsaken cities, to reward a bold invader. But time would go on, and the hunting would be bad and need all their energy, and the young people would grow up and seek mates, and the children would come, and then there was no leisure or taste at all for adventures into the unknown.

A young man named Bom was the one who did finally dare to search the ruins—all alone, in a world where the only safety and comfort came from close huddling in one's own native group. He was a strange young man, unpopular with other youths or with the girls, given to daydreaming by himself when he should be out hunting for the tribe, inarticulate and dissatisfied—a young man who, a thousand years before or a thousand years after, would have been a pioneer, a searcher, a discoverer. When from afar, on one of his clan's endless journeyings for food, he glimpsed the Devil's Castle for the first time since early childhood, the urge was too strong for him to resist. He was terribly frightened, not least from the difficulties of escaping from the band. At night, when all the others slept, and by the perilous possibility that after his adventure he might never be able to find them again: that was a much more real and dreadful danger than the stories he nevertheless half-believed, of malevolent demons guarding the hidden treasures.

He escaped unseen and unheard, and dawn found him before the tangled pile of broken ruins. No demons worse than cold and fog and wind assailed him. If the clan had missed him by now, they would never follow him here or guess that he had come here; doubtless they thought he had strayed too far from the sheltering fire and a cougar or bear had caught him—these predators were becoming bolder and venturing nearer to human camps as the hunters killed off more and more of their prey.

Valiantly Bom set to work to explore the Devil's Castle. His plan had been to leave when the sun was halfway across the sky toward the west, so as to catch up with his tribe before night if possible. He burrowed through tunnels and under heavy stones that balanced menacingly above his head; he scrabbled in the earth and searched roofless rooms crowded with strange broken objects whose use he could not even imagine. But nowhere were there jewels or any other treasure he could use—only twisted pieces of metal not fit to be fashioned into weapons, or shards of glass and hunks of plastic material unusable as ornaments or tools. In his explorations he came upon a huge underground wall of stone and cement, in the middle of which was a series of heavy metal dials. Bom guessed that this was a sort of door, such as he had seen in houses in the deserted cities. The cement had cracked, and it was possible to tear out pieces of it large enough to allow him to enter what had been the inner vaults of the IAAS.

It was a complete disappointment. There was nothing inside but shelves upon shelves of what he did not know was microfilm, and a little metal box with characters etched on it he could not read, and containing only some unguessable object. He dropped it back where he had found it.

He had delayed too long in leaving. The sun was setting when he found his way to the open air again, his hands empty after all his search. The hungry coyotes had begun to gather. He fought hard, but they were too many, and there were no tribesmen near to hear his screams and hurry to his rescue.

III

In the summer of 4016 an archaeological expedition under the sponsorship of the University of Teheran began excavation in the buried ruins of the IAAS buildings. Very quickly they became aware that their speculations, based on philological study of the few remaining ancient microfilm records, were justified, and that this was the remains of some sort of center of twentieth century science. The whole civilized world followed their progress by telaudioview. News commentators in the international tongue assured fascinated watchers and listeners in Greenland and China, in Argentina and Africa—for these local names were still used to indicate natural divisions of the World Territory—that this was the greatest archaeological discovery of the age. When at last the innermost vault was uncovered and opened, with its priceless store of microfilm—and an unexplained human skeleton lying well preserved not far away—the commentators chattered like magpies.

But suddenly their descriptions stopped abruptly, and they turned to other aspects of the expedition.

When Harduk Bal, the director-in-chief, came upon the tape-recording in its rustless alloy case, he sent for the head philologist to decipher the inscription. Then the recording was fitted to its primitive transmitter—it was totally unadaptable to a modern reproducer—and Harduk Bal had it translated by an expert in twentieth century English.

As soon as he had heard the translation, he got in teletouch with the Executive Council of World Government. The newly elected World President himself called Harduk Bal back after the Council's consultation.

"All right, go ahead," he told the archaeoleogist. "It's worth trying, long as it has been even since that additional record in 2151. But we'd better not make it public till we see if it works. We don't want to have your expedition made a laughing-stock if the experiment should be a failure, as it probably will be. Tell your publicity director to cut off further news till we've tried the thing out."

"But the time-travel part, sir," Hardul Bal objected. "I know the mathematicians keep reporting they have made progress—they've been saying that for fifty years at least—but actually we have no more time-travel now than they had in 2150—or in 1980."

"Listen, Harduk Bal." The president touched the button which made the conversation secret. "This is for your ears alone; we heard it only last week and the Council is not ready yet to make it public. I think I can say confidently that by the time it would be needed—about twenty-six years from now—time-travel will be a demonstrated thing."

"Wonderful! Really, at last!"

"We hope so. We're almost sure. But even if we're wrong, and this new method is another failure, we could still do the rest of the experiment, and add our statement to the one made in 2150. There ought to be four vials left, and surely before the last one is used up, time-travel will be a commonplace mode of transportation, and future generations, if not we ourselves, can take advantage of it—that is, if the stuff is still any good."

"Right, sir. I'll see that the whole thing is kept quiet until the Council's ready to release it. And you, I take it, will send somebody to that location in the Antarctic."

"Immediately. Do you know, Harduk Bal, I envy the young man or woman, twenty-six years from now, who is going to make that journey back to 1980!"

"I do too. But I'm afraid nobody alive today is qualified!" chuckled the archaeologist. "By the way," he added, "what do I do now with the original tape-recording?"

"You'd better send it to me. I'll have it redeposited in the vaults of World Government headquarters in London. It doesn't matter where it is, so long as it's left in a place that, some far-off day, will constitute an archaeological investigation site. And I imagine there won't be much left for future excavators, a thousand or so years from now, of the site you're excavating, by the time you get through with it.

"It's a sobering thought, isn't it? Our most elaborate constructions some day will be ruins, just as that scientific center of yours is now."

"But according to this thing," answered Harduk Bal cheerfully, "our past will still be our future, even then, and good old mankind will still keep moving onward and upward! And perhaps they already knew that for sure, away back in 1980!"

In 5891, or 91 GM, Kel 87459X2ZA of the third generation after the Great Migration was a candidate for his doctorate in Terrarchaeology at Skyros Institute of Science. As a subject for his thesis, he proposed—as did almost every other budding Terrarchaeologist—a specimen excavation on the Parent Planet.

"I don't know, Kel," his department head frowned. "It's too bad that a student as promising as you are didn't get interested in a field with more possibilities— one that hasn't been worked over until nearly all the

good sites have been excavated long ago, in the nostal-
gic rush back to Earth after we'd left it permanently.
There's still an immense amount of work to be done on
the ancient Martian remains, or on those puzzling buried
structures on Planet 3 in Alpha Centauri. But there's not
much worth while left in the old home except in the
dried-up ocean beds, and they're more rewarding to a
palaeontologist than to an archaeologist."

"There's one site," said Kel daringly. "The last World
Government Center."

The professor shook his hairless head.

"Now, my boy, you know that's totally impossible.
Didn't you learn in elementary school that it was a strict
injunction of the Migration Charter that the London
Center should be left inviolate, as a symbol of the planetary origin of man?"

"Of course I learned it—and I'm not the only one who
thinks it's an idiotic superstition unworthy of civilized
beings. It's worse—there may be important historical
material there that we need and ought to have.

"What do you suppose has become of those buildings
after nearly a hundred years of neglect? They're probably a heap of weathered rubble by now. A fine symbol!"

"They're not overgrown with vegetation, anyhow,"
said the professor grimly, "considering that the reason
we had to abandon Earth in the first place was the
drying up of the surface water and the consequent
death of all vegetation, after the collapse of the moon.
No, perhaps a thousand years from now, when nobody is
alive with even a tradition of Earth as our former home,
Terrarchaeology will revive, and then no place on Earth
may be considered too sacred to be delved into. But not
today. The Interplanetary Congress would never give
you a permit."

"Look, I'm not going to injure their beautiful ruins.
I've got a specific thing I want to look for. We took away
loads and loads of records from the World Government
Center when we left. But I'm certain there is more
there, of infinitely greater importance.

"See here—listen to this: it's a standard text you use in your own classes, the Compendium of World Surveys by Cort 27463Q5HW. 'The original plans of the Center included underground, impregnable vaults, in which World Government's most vital records could be stored in permanent safety. However, when the Great Migration occurred, searchers found no trace of these vaults under any Government building. This does not mean necessarily that they did not then or do not now exist; the required speed and enormous magnitude of the Migration operations made it impossible to make a complete and thorough investigation. Unfortunately, the setting aside of the Center as a Sacred Symbolical Area has prevented any further research.'

"The minute I read those words for the first time, professor, I decided to make Terrarchaeology my field, and to be the one to hunt for and discover the lost vaults of the World Government Center and recover whatever they contain. With the new Supra finders, which did not exist a hundred years ago, they can be located without harming or moving a stone of the upper buildings.

"I know you can't authorize me to go ahead. But will you give me a strong recommendation of my ability, that I can take to the Interplanetary Congress? That's all I want. The rest is up to me."

The professor gave up.

"That much I can do for you, Kel, and will, very gladly. But I'll have to add that I advised you against attempting the project."

"Don't worry about that professor." Kel smiled impishly. "I don't suppose it has occurred to you that this year's chairman of the Congress happens to be Mora 84912M6RG, and that Mora 84912M6RG happens to be my Chief Guardian? I'll get a hearing, anyway, and if I have your backing I'm confident of making them see the light. It would be a pretty fine medal on her chest to be able to say that the year she was chairman, the hidden records of World Government were recovered, and that the person who made them available was her own ward!"

Six months later Kel landed his equipment near the gaunt, deserted Center. It was another month before the Supra finders located the vaults. There was richness there indeed to be stored in his Contragrav ship. And buried among the records, he found a queer, inexpressibly ancient-looking metal box, marked in difficult twentieth century English, "To be opened by any competent scientist."

Kel, under the circumstances—fortunately, he even knew the language—deemed himself sufficiently competent not to wait till he got the box home to Skyros. What he heard as he listened to the recording sent him headlong to the ship, to telebeam first the professor and then the Congress. Before he returned home with his priceless plunder, he made a quick trip to the Antarctic, where the ice, though much thinner than in earlier days, still provided the only unevaporated water on the surface of the ravaged planet. Continuing deep freeze was easy in the Contragrav.

By Kel's time, travel to the past was as commonplace as space-travel. He was strongly tempted to go back to April 25, 1980, himself, to take a look at the remarkable James McElroy—say an hour or so before McElroy's appointed meeting with somebody yet unborn when Kel would have made his journey. But young and romantic as he was, Kel 87459X2ZA was also a responsible scientific worker. And so he handed over the tape-recording and the vial to the proper authorities, to let them conduct the experiment, while he buried himself in the other material he had found in the Center's vaults, to prepare what eventually became the most famous thesis ever presented by a candidate for the degree of Ter.D.

The gray parched earth grew more desolate as the centuries rolled over it. The Antarctic ice dissolved inch by inch, then evaporated in the unoxygenated air. The two vials left lay finally on bare rock.

Soon, under the sun's radiation, their contents died at last.

IV

Gord 20977F8EN stood for a moment at the entrance to the grounds of the IAAS Center. This was the right place and of course there could be no question as to the exact time. It was five minutes to three o'clock on the afternoon of Saturday, April 25, 1980. Unaccustomed emotions swept him—puzzlement, curiosity, frustration, and a sense of anticlimax. In a way his entire twenty-five years of life had led up to this moment; when it was over and he was back again in his own time and place, he would have to begin some entirely new career, with his reason for living, hitherto, no longer in existence.

He was carefully dressed in the proper clothing for a young man of the twentieth century, and in the jacket he found a pocket into which he could insert the tiny apparatus that would insure his safe return home. He had been just as carefully schooled in the English of the period, in its American version. Except for the wig, to simulate twentieth century hair, he looked like any tall, handsome youth of 1980.

What interested him more than this James McElroy to whom he had been dispatched, more even than the solution of all the vague hints and allusions he had heard since childhood, was the landscape around him. At home there were no great bodies of untamed water like this. There were hills, far higher than this one on whose summit he stood now, but they were not planted with grass and trees; indeed, he suspected, from the proximity of the site to the ocean below him, that all this verdure had been cultivated by man, and that the natural aspect of the hill would be that of a sand dune. He knew, of course, the geography of his location. He was on a flat-topped hill overlooking the Pacific Ocean, in a portion of Earth once known interchangeably, it seemed, as the United States of America and California.

As he tore his gaze reluctantly away from the view—who knew how much time he would have for sightseeing when he left, and it might well be dark then as well—and prepared to turn in at the gate in the massive brick wall, he saw a girl walking slowly up the path, trundling some kind of machine. As he watched, she paused at a thick clump of bushes and pushed the machine inside, arranging twigs and branches elaborately so as to conceal it from any passer-by. Gord's eyes lighted up with interest; in the second before she hid the thing, he had recognized it as a primitive time-travel equipment, such as he had seen in museums at home. Deliberately he waited until the girl caught up with him.

"Excuse me," she said in twentieth century English that had exactly the same slight stiffness as his own, "but is this the headquarters of the International Association for the Advancement of Science?"

Gord smiled.

"What is your century?" he asked.

She jumped, and stared at him with long, heavily fringed dark eyes.

"The—the forty-first," she stammered. "How did you know? Are you—"

"I am from long after you—almost as long as you are after the time we find ourselves in now. I take it that you too have been sent to see a man named James McElroy?"

"Why, yes. All my life—"

"All mine too. Let's go in together."

"What's it all about, do you know?"

"No more than you. Perhaps we shall find out now. What is your own language?"

"Interlingua. And yours?"

"A modified Interlingua too, but I doubt if you'd understand mine or I yours. Let's stick to this one, since we've both learned it well."

"My name is Wia Rustum." She held out her hand, but Gord did not take it; people of his time seldom touched one another casually. He noticed, however, that the little finger was complete—doubtless her little toes too—not rudimentary as his were. That, he had been taught, was the only physical change in mankind in the past four thousand years, unless one counted the loss of head-hair before adolescence, or the increasing number of babies born without a vermiform appendix.

"Call me Gord," he said. "The rest of it is just for official identification."

He noticed with approval that her perceptions were sensitive; she had withdrawn her hand swiftly the instant she received no answering gesture from him. She did not seem pretty to Gord, despite her chiseled features and her smooth light-bronze skin through which the warm blood showed; her lustrous black hair, arranged in some strange fashion which he presumed must be that of women of the time they were visiting, repelled him. Obviously she was of pure Earth descent; there was no trace in her of any off-planetary mixture.

They had reached the group of white stone buildings. "This one in the middle is probably the main structure," Gord remarked. "We can go in there and ask for this James McElroy."

A small door in an L-shaped wing opened abruptly, and a young man of about their own age stood framed in the doorway. He peered out at them anxiously.

"We are looking for a man named James McElroy," Wia Rustum told him.

"I am McElroy." The man's voice shook with excitement. "Are you—?"

"Yes," said Gord gravely. "It seems that we have both been sent to visit you."

"Come in! Come in!"

He beckoned them into a room that reminded Wia of reconstructions of primitive architecture she had seen—a sort of ancient office, with a desk and filing cabinets and chairs, to which McElroy waved them fussily. They sat down gingerly, but the chairs were more comfortable, in spite of their odd shape, than either of them had expected.

"You won't mind, will you," said McElroy, "if I make a record of our conversation?"

"Of course not," Wia answered politely. Gord only

nodded, perplexed; in his experience, records were always kept of *all* conversations, however trivial, though he wondered how the primitive machine standing against an inner wall was expected to work.

Their host sat down at his desk. He seemed hardly to know how to begin.

"Are you all that are coming?" he blurted.

"All?" Gord echoed. "I know only that I myself was sent to you. I met this young woman just outside here, and it appears that she too has been sent."

"Then you're not both from the same approximate time?"

Gord laughed.

"Hardly. I am as far from her in time as she is from you. You should see the obsolete object she traveled here on, and has hidden in your grounds. It's a wonder to me that she could travel ten years back in that thing."

Wia Rustum flushed.

"It's a very fine traveler," she said defensively. "Why, it's an enormous improvement on the first ones, only twenty-odd years ago."

Gord felt the pocket-sized traveler in his jacket and concealed his smile.

McElroy was watching them intently. His hands were shaking, in some almost unbearable agitation, but he was getting better control of his voice.

"You must both be utterly bewildered," he said. "Unless you have been told all about this?"

They both shook their heads.

"All I know," said Wia, "is that ever since I can remember I have been told that on my twenty-fifth birthday I was to make a journey back to 1980 to see a man named James McElroy, at the International Association for the Advancement of Science."

"I also—at these headquarters, on Earth," Gord agreed. "The guardians said that was why I had to learn to speak twentieth century American English, and study your history and geography and customs, though I was not in training to be a Terrarchaeologist. I had lessons with Kel 87459X2ZA himself," he added proudly.

"I don't know about any guardians," said Wia Rustum, "but I had a special World Government Council scholarship right through school, and the famous Harduk Bal, who excavated this very site in 4016, gave me my final instructions only a week ago."

"In 4016!" McElroy exclaimed. "And what year is it now, in your time?"

"Why, 4042, of course."

"And in yours?" he asked, turning to Gord.

"This is Year 117 GM—of the Great Migration—or, according to your calendar, I suppose it would be 6917."

V

McElroy gaped at them. He seemed overwhelmed. In a dazed tone he said to Wia: "And you say time-travel was discovered only in your own lifetime?"

"The first short trips were made in 4020."

"I see. So any earlier—tell me, has either of you any message for me, from a time earlier than your own? Probably you, young lady—good heavens, I haven't asked either of you your name!"

"I am Wia Rustum. You may call me Wia, James. Yes, I was told to say—but maybe Gord has a message too."

"Gord 20977F8EN," the young man introduced himself belatedly. "Call me just Gord. Yes, I was given a message also, but I was told it would be unnecessary if any traveler from an earlier era should be at the meeting. Was yours about somebody named Mark Iverson?" he asked Wia.

"Yes, it must be the same."

"You give it, then."

With the air of one repeating a lesson learned by rote, the girl recited:

"In 2150, a committee of the IAAS, in charge of tearing down the old buildings and erecting new ones, discovered the tape-recording and followed instructions. Mark Iverson was born the following February. Means of travel into the past had not yet been discovered, and so it was merely added to the record that this child was born but that he died at the age of five when a Moonplane on which he was a passenger was destroyed in a collision with a meteor."

James McElroy closed his eyes for moment. His face was white.

"Another!" he muttered. "Little Jim—and Adela—and now this child."

He took a deep breath.

"Tell me," he asked Wia, "did your message say if the child's mother was with him—and who she was?"

"How would anyone know that?" Gord interrupted. "Oh, yes, of course—in that age—"

"No," said Wia, "that is all I was taught to say, and I haven't the slightest idea what it means. Did you have more than that in your message, Gord?"

"It was just the same. But I do remember once asking Kel what tape-recording they were referring to, and he said it was one he found in the old World Government Center in London, here on Earth, and that it was now safe in the archives of the Interplanetary Congress on Skyros."

"At this moment, it is in the vaults under the IAAS buildings, right here," said McElroy. The color was coming back to his face. "I wonder how much it has wandered, up to your time, Gord—and where it will wander afterwards!

"So now three vials are accounted for, and the other two must have been lost or useless, or else I would either have more visitors today than you two, or your message would be longer.

"I know I'm trying your patience. None of this can make sense to you. Please bear with me just a little longer, and then I'll explain as well as I can. I don't suppose," he added wistfully, "that either of you could tell me anything in detail about life as you know it in your respective times? No, don't bother to answer. I told my colleagues only last month why that would logically be quite impossible.

"But perhaps you *can* satisfy me on one point. I noticed, Wia, when you gave your message, that you spoke of 'travel into the past.' Does that mean that time-travel is all one-directional? Can't you go forward into the future?"

Wia looked at Gord. "*We* can't," she said. "Can you?"

"No, and I doubt if men ever will. I could tell you why—it's elementary mathematics. But unless you're familiar with the Moitier Concept discovered in your Year 3845—"

"And the Gregi Correlary of 3907," Wia added.

McElroy smiled.

"I'm not a mathematician," he said, "and even if I were—" He shrugged. "Well, that question was for the benefit of my colleagues, particularly of my friend Wycliffe. I imagine I'd get the same kind of answer if I queried you about Moro's specialty, or Schultz's, or Wong's, or Kemet Ali's, or any of the others. We can't change history by altering the past, though I do wonder why there was so long a gap between Mark Iverson's birth and yours, Wia."

"Well, of course the Second Dark Age came in between—"

"Better not, Wia," Gord warned her. "I know what the Interplanetary Congress would do to me if I tried to scramble up history by leaking it into the past."

Wia looked frightened.

"Don't worry, Wia," McElroy said reassuringly. "You haven't said anything that could do any harm. We in 1980 have been prepared for a quarter of a century for the onset of some such interregnum. In fact, we've expected it much sooner than, apparently, it will arrive. And plenty of us also have the faith that civilization will revive and go on to greater heights. You and Gord are both evidence of that—in more ways than you know.

"Now if I may ask you both just a few more questions, I'll solve the whole riddle for you. You, Gord. Can you tell me about your mother?"

"My mother?" Gord knit his brows. "How would I know about that? I'm just like everybody else. I was produced in my local Genitorium and reared in my local Pedenid. How would I know which particular ovum gestated me, any more than I would know which particular sperm-cell activated it? All I know is that I must have a bit of native Martian heredity, since I have superexpansible lungs, and the Martian stigmata on my spine."

"I see," said James McElroy slowly, gazing at the young man with a sort of baffled wonder. "So in your time all children are laboratory products, are they? No haphazard breeding—the geneticist's dream come true! Don't you have any sex life at all?"

Gord reddened angrily.

"Naturally I have," he said in an offended tone. "I'm twenty-five years old today. I'm a perfectly normal human being. I've belonged to a sex group since I was eighteen, like any other man. But you can't mix up sex and reproduction. It isn't civilized!"

"*We* do," McElroy answered dryly. "And you, Wia. Did you come out of a test-tube too?"

"As a matter of fact, I did," said Wia, looking surprised. "How did you know? I mean, my mother was one of those selected for controlled eugenic maternity by the Biogenetics Laboratory. But naturally I know who she is—in fact she reared me until I formed my first love-union, and I never was sent to a nursery. I live near her now, and I see her often; I said goodbye to her just before I left on this time-journey.

"But I do agree with Gord on one thing. I don't want to be rude, but it does seem terribly dangerous and rather disgusting to let just any woman have a child by any man. We don't do that even in direct parentage. How do you know they have the right kind of heredity?"

"We don't," said McElroy mildly. "I'm a geneticist myself, Wia, of an antique variety. I'm not denying that our science and our culture are far behind yours. As far, perhaps"—a bit of malice spiced his tone—"as yours may be behind Gord's here. But let's not wrangle over our comparative social mores. Tell me about your mother.

What is her descent? For instance, of what nationality is she?"

It was Wia's turn to flush in anger. Her dark eyes flashed.

"If you're implying," she retorted, "that I'm a monogene, it's an outrageous lie. If you're any kind of geneticist, James McElroy, you know perfectly well that one can't parcel out the chromosomes like so many building-blocks. I may display more of the characteristics of one of the ancient races—the one they called white, I suppose, to which you seem to belong—than of the others; but I can assure you that, whoever my father may have been—and that, of course, I can't know—my mother has her Class A certificate attesting that her ancestry includes every one of the civilized types of mankind!"

"Didn't they teach you about this age we're in now, Wia?" Gord intervened sarcastically. "In this era they *favored* monogenes. You were penalized if you had even a trace of interracial heredity. I can't imagine what they would have done about my touch of Martian—except that they hadn't even reached Mars yet!"

"No, the Moon's as far as we've attained to," said McElroy placatingly. "And please believe me, Wia, I didn't mean my question in a derogatory way. I'm—I'd like to know a lot about your mother—I'd like to know about Gord's, if he could tell me, because—

"Oh, Lord, let me try to tell this in the simplest way I can.

"In August, 1952, at a meeting of the British Association for the Advancement of Science—there were still separate national associations then, instead of one International, as now—a Dr. Parkes reported on a new method of freezing germ-cells, by the use of glycerol. The cells were quick-frozen to minus 79° Centigrade, and though crystals formed, the glycerol crystals did not crush the cells, as those of other freezing media had done. In consequence, less than ten per cent of the cells died, and the rest retained vitality and fertility for an indefinite time, so long as they were kept at the same temperature. Do you follow me?"

"Of course," answered Wia. "We employ a more refined technique of the same sort. It is used to preserve the sperm of superior and distinguished men, to be used as sires for eugenic maternity. In fact," she added with an embarrassed laugh, "I have always dreamed that I myself—"

McElroy looked embarrassed too.

"And you, Gord?" he asked.

"We have a much better method, but naturally I understand what you mean."

"Well, we too began to employ this method experimentally soon after it was announced, and it worked. But we had used it only for short-time experiements, and mostly with animals."

VI

Gord glanced inquiringly at Wia. "Don't you remember?" she whispered. "In this time, they still had all kinds of living animals besides man—natural ones, not synthetics." "Oh, yes. I'd forgotten," he said. McElroy went on.

"Where I differed from the others was in the fact that I believed firmly in the ultimate discovery of time-travel. Without that, naturally there was not much point in conducting experiments which would extend beyond the probable span of lives of the experimenters. I don't know exactly what your life-expectancy is—"

"About a hundred years," said Wia.

"Somewhere around 150," said Gord.

"Ours today is in the late seventies.

"But, I reasoned, if the cells could be kept frozen for hundreds or even thousands of years, and if meanwhile time-travel into the past could be discovered, then it would be possible to prove the practical immortality of the human race. There were other important scientific correlaries too, but this alone justified trying it."

"But how could you keep up a temperature of minus 79° Centigrade—we don't use that scale but I gather that it is very cold—long after the people who first prepared the cells were dead and gone?" Gord asked.

"In the Antarctic Continent. The IAAS had a concession there, where vials of sperm could be deeply buried and the site marked. It will be countless centuries before that ice will begin to melt. I made a tape-recording, with full instructions, and placed it in our vaults here. If it were found before time-travel, then the results of the experiment were simply to be added to the recording. My idea was that eventually, as the ages passed, these buildings would fall into ruins, and some day the vaults would be found and opened.

"I find from your message, Wia, that actually the first time the recording was reproduced was less than two hundred years from now—I hadn't thought of our headquarters' becoming obsolete and being rebuilt. But obviously, after that, somebody did find the recording in the ruins of these buildings; and you, Gord, said that in your day it was found in London and is now on some planet outside the Solar System.

"Are you beginning to understand?"

Wia found her voice first.

"You mean we—"

"You two—and Mark Iverson."

There was a stunned pause. Then Gord said tautly:

"Will you be so good, James McElroy, as to describe to us the men whose sperm-cells were in those vials?"

"There was only one man," answered McElroy almost inaudibly.

"But then," Wia exclaimed, "that must mean—Gord, you and I must be half-brother and sister! And that little boy back in the twenty-second century—he was our half-brother too!"

"Yes—you see, I—" McElroy began. Gord interrupted him, his face white with rage.

"How *could* you?" he cried hoarsely. "How *could* you upset our entire genetic pattern, on which our civilization and even our continuing existence are based? *We* don't indulge in slapdash parenthood the way you people did back in your barbaric age. Our births are all carefully calculated to produce just the right number of each type of body-mind needed to maintain a balanced economy. With all the completely unknowable characteristics of a haphazard man of your era, how can the resulting child be sure of its abilities and potentialities?"

His voice shook, and his face was a mask of fury and despair.

"You did that to *me!* And my own people let it happen to me! My own guardians knew—they've always known—that I was a freak. For the sake of some frivolous bit of scientific knowledge, they let me be created a different being from anybody else in the world. They trained me for this idiotic journey back in time, so that I might hear from your own lips just what you had done to me!

"And now I am to go back home, my purpose fulfilled. And what is my life to be from now on? How is anyone ever to know what I am best fitted for, what my place is in society?

"I don't know what *your* future will be like, Wia Rustum." He turned savagely on the girl who stared at him wide-eyed, her dark face bloodless. "*We* aren't concerned with brothers or sisters. For all I know, any girl in my sex group might be my sister, though it's not likely—and what would it matter? None of us is ever born except from a regulated union of ovum and sperm, and only the best of us are ever selected to contribute our own cells for reproduction.

"None of us but me!" he concluded bitterly. He jumped to his feet and glared at McElroy.

"But I—" McElroy began weakly. Gord snarled at him.

"I congratulate you on the success of your experiment! I can't wait any longer to find out what plans my Chief Guardian has for me next!"

He put his hand in his pocket and pressed a trigger.

The next instant McElroy and Wia Rustum were alone in the room.

McElroy buried his face in his hands. A soft hand

touched his shoulder. He looked up at Wia's compassionate face.

"Don't feel bad," she murmured. "I know you didn't mean any harm. They'll calm him down. Surely, if their culture is so advanced, they wouldn't have let him be produced only as a—"

"An experimental animal?" His tone was as bitter as Gord's had been.

"I suppose so. They'll fit him into the normal life of their time, I'm certain of it."

McElroy shook his head.

"And what about you, Wia?"

"Don't worry about me. They've always told me that after what they spoke of as my 'twenty-fifth birthday project' I could go on quietly with my own life and my own work. I have a very good job with the Council of World Government," she said proudly.

"And aren't you, too, horrified at the thought that your father is one of us twentieth century barbarians?"

"It *is* an upsetting thought," she replied frankly. "But you've told us you are a geneticist, and primitive as genetics must be in your time, I'm confident you wouldn't have used cells in your experiment that came from a defective man."

Her voice grew coaxing.

"I don't suppose you could tell me, could you? Really, we're not nearly so fussy as Gord's people seem to be. Naturally, we don't let just anybody who wants to, have children. But lots of women have them by men they actually know—if they can get certificates on both sides, they often have them by their own love-partners." Her face fell. "In fact, Tir and I were planning—well, now, of course, we'll have to give that up; I see I could never be certified."

"So I've ruined your life too by my rash experimentation, have I?"

"Nonsense," said Wia stoutly. "I don't live in a one-track world like my dear half-brother! I've got Tir, and my work, and plenty of other interests.

"But just the same, I wish you *would* tell me. I'd

promise never to let my mother find out. Women who are chosen for eugenic maternity would always rather not know."

"Tell you what, Wia?"

"Who my father was, of course!"

McElroy's face was a study. Before he could find words, Wia forestalled him.

"Oh, Great Radiation! How stupid of me! Of course! I see it all now. If only that silly Gord had waited till you could make him understand!"

"I'm afraid I don't understand you myself, my dear."

"Certainly you do. You don't need to pretend. I'm not always as dense as I must have seemed just now. Naturally, for a momentous project like that, there was only one thing you *could* have done."

James McElroy's heart, which had ached for seven months, suddenly throbbed with joy. He smiled at his daughter, who, in this strange meeting, was of exactly his own age.

"Then you don't mind, Wia?"

"Mind? I should have known I could trust you. The idea of Gord's saying that you had made a freak of him! Did he think you picked out just anybody at random to become our father? It must have taken you months or years to decide on the man with the very finest mind and the best body alive in your time. Whom else *could* you have chosen, with the very lives of future beings at stake?

"That's all I need to know about my father. I'm not interested in his race or nationality or whatever you call it, or his age or what he looked like. That hot-headed Gord! He got himself so wrought up I honestly think he'd have believed any silly balderdash you told him." Wia laughed merrily. "Why," she went on, wiping her eyes, "he probably would have believed you if you'd told him the most ridiculous thing you could think of—even that you yourself were the man!"

Her eyes were mirrors of innocent candor.

"Then you wouldn't consider me a—a good eugenic specimen, Wia?" McElroy asked painfully.

Wia sobered contritely.

"Oh, dear," she apologized, "that wasn't very polite, was it? But really, James, don't you have mirrors in your era? You seem about the same age as Gord and I are, yet even with your smaller life-expectancy, I can see that you're going to be prematurely old. Why, look, there are grey hairs at your temples. And you seem unable to see without that glass thing across your eyes. Besides, I noticed right away how unstable you are emotionally.

"I'm sure," she added courteously, "that you have a fine mind. You must have, to have thought of this whole thing in your primitive era. And you must be forward-looking, or you wouldn't have believed in time-travel when other people didn't. I like you very much. But naturally, as a geneticist yourself, you would hardly select yourself as the best possible ancestor for anybody, would you?"

McElroy smiled with stiff lips.

"You're very perspicacious, my dear. I hope you won't ever regret the father I did pick out for you."

"I shan't. And don't worry about Gord, either; he'll get over his shock. Anyway, neither of us will ever have children of our own now. And that other little boy—Mark Iverson—died when he was five. So the line ends with us, and you can set your mind at rest."

She took McElroy's cold hand in her warm one.

"Paternity means a lot to people in your time, doesn't it?" she said sympathetically. "More than it does in ours—or maternity either—and much more, evidently, than it does in Gord's.

"Look, James, I know how you're feeling. You must feel responsible for our existence, Gord's and mine, almost as if you really *were* our father. Don't. We'll get along all right.

"Do you know what I think you ought to do? I think you ought to have a child of your own. I'm sure you're as good a potential ancestor as lots of people of your time, and any defects you transmitted would be diluted out in the generations after you. Have you any children already?"

"I had—I had a son—but he was killed."

"Like poor little Mark Iverson. Well, have another."

"His mother was killed with him. We—I loved her very much."

"Oh, I'm sorry. But even so—oh, I forgot; you people are sort of monogamists, aren't you?"

"Sort of." To his surprise, McElroy found himself smiling faintly.

"Then perhaps—don't you think you might find someone else you would want to have a child by? I'm afraid that's a clumsy way to put it; your customs are so unfamiliar to me. But I do feel you're the kind of man who ought to marry—isn't that the word?—and have sons and daughters of your own again."

"You may be right, Wia. I hadn't thought of it that way. Thank you for coming today. I feel my whole experiment was justified by its producing you."

"What a nice thing to say! I've liked meeting you too, James. I don't expect they'll want me to come to see you again, but I'll never forget you. Neither will Gord. And think about what I said, won't you? Why, just think, if you take my advice today, I may know some remote descendant of yours myself!"

He took her hand.

"Goodbye, Wia. I promise you I'll think about it."

He stood at the door and watched his daughter stride across the lawn to the bushes where her time-travel machine was hidden. There were tears in his eyes, but his heart was strangely light.

Throwback

Stop being so jittery," Kathrin admonished herself sternly. "The only way you're going to see this thing through is by keeping your head."

Nevertheless, her hands shook a little as she parked by one of the rows of meters on the roof, and her knees trembled as she stepped out of the copter.

If she had only let Jon into this first it wouldn't have been so bad. Together, somehow, they might have worked it out. She hadn't been sure enough of him: that was the inescapable fact. And now she had involved and imperiled him as well as herself. It was up to her. It had been so overwhelming an impulse that it had swept her away. She didn't see the glimmering of a solution, but one would have to be found, and quickly; and she was the one who was going to have to find it.

As she dropped down the shaft Kathrin tried to remember if she had ever known an unregistered child. There was Bill North—people used to say he must have been unregistered; but that was probably just slander, because he was so odd. Come to think of it, his forehead was unmarked, and once she had seen him vote, so it was just libel and he must have been a full citizen. The colonies, of course had plenty of them—they didn't need an optimum population law yet, and everybody there was as good as everybody else. They said the mayor of Venusberg was an unregistered.

Kathrin shivered. She didn't want to leave the earth forever, to be a permanent exile—though she would, if she had to. All her friends, her associations, were here on earth; in all her twenty-six years she had made only two vacation tours to the Moon and one to Mars, and she hadn't the least desire to become a permanent resident of either of them. Where, in the provincial life of the colonies, would there be a market for Kathrin Clayborn's sophisticated plasto-ceramics, which were earning banked credits and a solid reputation for her here?

And Jon. The colonies wanted hydroponic farmers and sub-atomic engineers and prefabrication builders; they had no need for a specialist in fourteen-tone music. But if Jon wouldn't go, there was no reason to live at all.

The carrier stopped at the 141st floor and Kathrin opened the door to the lobby of the suite of offices. Baby-faced Lane sat facing her at the visiboard. She smiled good morning. Lane was one of the fancier touches of Amalgamated Art Enterprises; an ordinary business office would have had a robot visicom operator.

"CCD's been calling you, Clayborn," Lane said brightly.

"Put them on for me."

This was it: she would have to think fast. She entered the studio that was more like a laboratory—fitted in light blue and silver, she always noted amusedly, because Amalgamated Art Enterprises never missed a bet and Kathrin Clayborn was a silver blonde—and almost immediately the visiscreen flashed.

"This is Central Contraception Department, Clayborn," said the robot voice. "Our records show that you missed your contraceptone injection which was due on February 28th."

Good old government procrastination! It was now April 28th by the new thirteen-month-plus-Year-Day calendar. Kathrin had been banking on that.

Alternative excuses flashed through her mind with the speed of neutrons. "I should have notified you," she apologized smoothly. "I'm applying to the Selection Board."

"You are not supposed to do that without giving us six months' notice," said the robot voice severely. "The matter will be investigated and we shall report back."

Now she *really* had to work fast. "Get me the Selection Board," she told Lane.

As she asked to have the application forms sent to her, she was calculating swiftly. They would have to be returned before CCD got around to verifying. But the Board would take at least three months, she was sure, before making its examination. Then she would be in trouble for fair. But at least she would have a breathing-space in which to plan what to do next.

Kathrin started work on the day's orders, but it was hard to keep her thoughts away from her problem. It was futile now to wish that she could have been telling the truth to CCD. Never in her life had she thought of applying to the Selection Board in all sincerity. She didn't want motherhood as a career, to spend all her fertile years incubating and bearing children at ordered, stated intervals. And she didn't want babies by artificial insemination, either, carefully chosen in somebody's laboratory and guaranteed to be the best eugenic combination. She wanted Jon's baby.

That was how it had started. Like everybody else, Kathrin had had plenty of temporary affairs. But this was permanent, the real thing, what they used to call marriage, a thousand years ago; Jon and she both felt that. The yearning, the excitement, perhaps even the vast tenderness, they could get and had got, both of them, from others; but not this feeling of belonging, of being necessary to each other, of being safe together against the world.

But now they weren't safe, and it was she herself who had jeopardized their safety. Musing, as her hands deftly shaped a plastic abstract, Kathrin reflected that she must be feeling as it had been normal for a woman to feel in—oh, say, the twentieth century. She wanted the old primitive unit, man and woman and child. And not a child to be taken away as soon as the pediatricians and psychologists ruled it ready for mass rearing, but a child to be reared with its parents, knowing them, loving them and being loved by them. In other words, what they used to call a family.

Kathrin blushed as if she had said an obscene word aloud, but she might as well be honest with herself. By some quirk of heredity, she was a throwback, an atavistic reversion, a freak.

And yet, in spite of everything—in the face of loss of citizenship, imprisonment, death itself—she had obeyed that atavistic impulse. And now she faced the probability of losing the child even if she contrived to bear it. Even worse, she might lose Jon as well.

As if she had called to him, the door opened and Jon stood there.

"Jon! What in the galaxy are you doing here?" Instinctively she darted a glance at the door, at the visiscreen.

He laughed and stretched out his arms.

"My shy girl! I have permission to call on you, my love. I'm running over to Capetown this afternoon, and I find I'll have to stay and look over Bloemer's stuff, so I can't get back till tomorrow."

As always, Kathrin felt a brief twinge of envy of Jon's mobility. In a sense he was a World Government employee, commissioned to find and evaluate the latest compositions in fourteen-tone scale music, and was likely at any moment to hop to Australia or Greenland. Kathrin, tied all her working life to office hours, and knowing few persons except Jon who weren't, often wondered what it would be like to be free to go here and there at will. Instead, she might find out soon what it would be like to be confined in a rehabilitation camp!

"Why didn't you just visicom to tell me you'd be gone for the night?"

"Because I couldn't kiss you goodby by visicom. Like this." He demonstrated thoroughly. "Great Sun, Kathrin don't be such a roboty little mouse! Anybody'd think you'd broken a law, the way you tremble at every tiny breach of government regulations."

"Jon—" she said suddenly. If he only knew. No, this wasn't the time or the place. She would have a night alone now, to think how she could tell him.

"What?"

"Nothing, darling. Did you check to see if your overnight things were in the plane?"

"I did. Good-by, dearest. I'll be there when you get home tomorrow."

"Good-by, Jon. I hope you find Bloemer's wonderful."

He waved and was gone. Kathrin was alone with her problem again.

What did one do when one had a problem too hard for one's own solution? Go to the Counselor, of course.

But would the Counselor help when a question of—almost of treason was involved? What was even more important, was the Counselor really safe? There was supposed to be only one copy made of the microfilm record, which the consultant took away with him. But suppose, unknown to ordinary citizens, a secret duplicate was made which went to the consultant's dossier in World Government files?

Kathrin had been to the Counselor twice before, once to have her talent evaluated, to see if it was worth while for her to take the intensive art training, once at the time she had first met Jon, when she had had a tempting offer of a position in Turkey to balance against the growing realization that Jon, whose work was based in America, was going to be one of the most important factors of her existence. Both times she had received sound advice and was glad to have followed it, and neither time had she heard any echo from the consultation. But this would be different.

Back in the suburban apartment, a hundred miles from the city, Kathrin set herself to serious meditation. For the first time in her life she really thought about unregistered children.

They were something people didn't talk about; something the poor creatures themselves couldn't hide, and that decent people pretended to ignore. How did they happen? Contraceptone never failed; either the mother must have let her injection date go by through pure stupid carelessness, or she had deliberately skipped it as Kathrin had done herself. But that meant that other women must be throwbacks too. She had a sudden vision of a vast, secret society of women whose atavistic emotions had impelled them into this dangerous adventure.

What about the fathers of the unregistered, she wondered. Men, of course, did not have to undergo contraceptone injections; any man might be chosen at any time by the Selection Board, and she had never heard of one who had refused his common civic duty. But had some of the fathers of unregistered children known and approved beforehand, hoping too for the impossible—were there male throwbacks as well as female? Or if they hadn't known, what a shock and grief when they learned about it, if they loved the women concerned! For inevitably as soon as the fact became unhidable, the woman was taken into custody, and as soon as the baby was old enough to be taken away from her and reared in a Pediatricum—with that dreadful red circle tattooed on its forehead, to make it recognizable for life—the mother was either sent to a rehabilitation camp or euthanized. The government could take no chances on upsetting the balance of nature by an epidemic of unregistered births.

Suddenly Kathrin remembered a tragedy of several years before—a couple she had known slightly, who were found dead in their apartment. The man had ray-gunned the woman and then himself, and nobody ever discovered why. Was that the reason? Had the woman confessed, and had this been his heartbroken way out? Kathrin thought of Jon, and shivered. What a fool she had been; what an impulsive fool! But she realized why she had not tired first to secure Jon's co-operation. The impulse had been too overwhelming. She could not risk his probable recoil and refusal.

Now it was too late.

No sleep-inducer vibrations did any good to Kathrin that night. But desperation brings its own calm.

Her voice was quite steady the next morning as she asked the Counseling Office for a special appointment. Fifty credit-units extra for not waiting her turn, but what did that matter?

The robot clerk in the waiting-room checked her number, then let her into the little room where the towering Counselor took up all of one wall. She shut the inward-locking door, peered through the one-way glass to watch the robot go back to its desk, and lay down on the long couch.

The Counselor lighted up immediately. The mechanical voice repeated her number, indicating that her dossier was before it for reference, and recited the opening formula: "This is a confidential consultation lasting one hour. What is your problem?" The microfilm began to pour out from the slot into the plastic container in which she would carry it away afterwards.

It was hard to begin. For a moment Kathrin had the embarrassing feeling that the Counselor was a human being, like the human psychoanalysts in ancient times she had read about. The voice had to reiterate: "What is your problem, please?"

Again, she felt with a sinking heart, she had been too percipitate. Most certainly she should have waited for Jon to come home; she should have told him everything, have made sure of his cooperation, before she made an appointment with the Counselor. But last night it had seemed such a wonderful inspiration. Now she must go on with it.

"As my dossier shows, Counselor," she began hesitantly, "I am by profession a maker of plasto-ceramics. Most of these have been designed for use as interior decoration or as house furnishings. But I have also made some advances in the use of plasto-ceramics as pure sculpture. I have twice won the World Prize for rhythmic three-dimensional art."

"All this is on record," said the Counselor, in what

would have been an impatient tone if a machine could display emotion.

"Just so. My dossier also shows that for two years now I have been in unitrelation with Jon Grover, who is conceded to be the foremost authority on fourteen-tone scale music. Naturally we have talked much together about our separate arts.

"And now—" Kathrin took a deep breath and prepared for the plunge—"we are on the verge of something altogether new in cultural history—a synthesis of the two aspects of rhythmic force."

"The Counselor is not competent to give technical advice."

"That is not my—not our problem. It is that such a project requires much time and complete attention. It has become apparent that we shall not be able to bring it to fruition while both of us are actively engaged in our usual work."

"How much time would be required?"

"That is difficult to say. No one could even promise success in such an experiment; we might find in the end that it could not be accomplished at all. All I can say is that we feel we are on the right track, and that if we could have—oh, say a year, under suitable conditions and with the opportunity to devote ourselves exclusively to the task, without demands or interruptions of any sort, we should at least be able to demonstrate whether or not such a synthesis could be brought about."

"One can see the magnitude of such a discovery. It would be as important as was the color-touch synthesis of Stjern and Harasuki. You would both be willing to undergo a year of unmitigated isolation and distasteful privacy to conduct your experiment?"

Kathrin's heart beat fast. She stifled the joyful relief that rose in her. Throwback she might be, but she had been reared in this era; she knew very well its compulsive gregariousness, its horror of being alone even in couples.

"If that were the only condition," she said carefully,

"our devotion to the progress of civilization is great enough to make us willing to endure even that."

"It might be possible," the Counselor said, "for you both to secure a year's leave of absence and for arrangements to be made for you to spend it in Patagonia."

"We would have to live in reasonable comfort, with facilities for our work," Kathrin interposed quickly.

"Your knowledge of geography is deficient," retorted the Counselor. Patagonia, it is true, has been for some four hundred years preserved as an example of natural uninhabited terrain. But its climate has been adjusted to human requirements, and buildings have been erected for the use of visiting scientists from the earth and the other planets. There is even a resident curator, who is a Martian, naturally, since Martians do not mind loneliness as human beings do. You could have one of those buildings, fully equipped for human habitation; your food and the materials and supplies you might need could be teleported to you on order; and of course you would be in visicom communication with all World Government areas.

"If you and Grover are willing to undertake this onerous task, and believe you could bear such isolation without physical or mental breakdown, application to the World Arts Department would probably be granted. The Counselor would add its own recommendation.

"But be very sure, before you apply, first that there is at least a good chance of your succeeding in this project, and secondly that you feel confident of your ability to endure the strain. Remember, not even the Martian curator nor the occasional visitors would be permitted to associate with you, and your visicom would be strictly censored so that you could use it only for utilitarian purposes, not for social communication."

"I understand."

"Make your application, then. The reputation you both possess in your respective fields of art will eliminate the need of any extensive inquiry or examination."

"There is one difficulty—"

"Oh, yes," replied the Counselor smoothly. "You mean

your recent application to the Selection Board. It is the latest item in your dossier. Why did you do that?"

"It is hard to explain, I know. It was the outcome of discouragement. Discouragement with the prospects of being able to devote myself to this synthesis experiment, I mean," she added hastily. "Naturally I realize that to be chosen by the Selection Board is the highest social honor that could be given any citizen. So I thought, if I couldn't serve the World Government by advancing cultural progress, perhaps it would let me serve it by producing worthy offspring."

"And then you changed your mind? That does not augur very well for your psychological stability."

"I did not change my mind. Actually, as you will notice, I have not even really applied to the Board. All I have done is to ask them to send me the blanks. That does not commit me unless I send them in. What I wanted was to be provided with an alternative, if you could give me no hope of an opportunity to accomplish this other project."

"Citizen, you are a little too free with your individualistic schemes and actions. The government is willing to make allowances for the aberrancies of people with artistic talents, but you are in danger of carrying it too far. However, in view of the real importance of the project you have in mind, the government will probably let this too be adjusted. Your application to the Selection Board might be withdrawn without prejudice.

"But in your dossier there appears another serious discrepancy. You are two months overdue for your contraceptone injection."

"Yes, I—I let it go when I first thought of applying to the Board."

"Now that, citizen, is what is meant by carrying your individualistic tendencies too far. You must know the danger you have run by failing to keep your injections up to date. Suppose in consequence you had become pregnant? Then, no matter what your potential value to the community, it would have been necessary to treat you like any other lawbreaking woman who conceives an unregistered child.

"In fact, irrespective of this other matter of the synthesis experiment, it is imperative that some penalty be inflicted on you for this criminal carelessness.

"The Counselor will strongly recommend that you and Grover be given a year's leave in Patagonia, with full pay and maintenance, to make your experiment. But it will also recommend that, as a penalty for your disobedience to a fundamental law, you be debarred from the protection of contraceptone until after your return to civilization. You need a lesson in self-control, citizen. You will either exercise it during your leave, or you will take your chances on having an unregistered child, with all that that implies. And since, if that should happen, it would also obviously implicate your companion, he would incur the same consequences.

"Do you still wish to go ahead?"

"I still wish to go ahead," Kathrin said quietly.

She glanced at the ceiling, on which, as on every ceiling on earth, moving hands on a lighted dial told the time. Her hour was up.

"Your consultation with the Counselor is at an end," the voice intoned as the lights flicked off. Kathrin rose from the couch, picked up the microfilm container, and opened the door. The robot clerk checked her number as she passed its desk.

Kathrin Clayborn and Jon Grover sat hand in hand at the view window of their twentieth-story suburban apartment, watching the peaceful countryside, with the moon making silver lace of the shadows of leaves on the river bank below them. Behind them, in the rosy glow to which they had switched the wall-tubes, music like a muted echo played a soft uninterrupting accompaniment to their voices. Kathrin had set the stage with infinite care. This was the final, crucial moment.

"Jon."

"Yes, darling?"

"You love me very much, don't you?"

"More than I have ever loved anyone in my life."

"I have something to tell you. I have done something—perhaps you'll think it was dreadful. You may never forgive me."

He kissed her and laughed.

Then she told him.

There was a long silence. Kathrin sat stiffly, trying to master the trembling that had seized her whole body.

Through the long day many versions of Jon's possible response had passed before her mind. Sometimes, in moments of optimism, he cried: "You too? I never dared to hope! Now we'll fight it out together, we two—we three—!"

But in the version that came most often, a voice she did not recognize said bitterly: "You must be out of your mind. Had you no concern for your own work, or for mine? You have ruined them both, and us with them. This is 2952, not 1952. I fell in love with a thirtieth-century woman, not with a freakish reversion to the days of our primitive barbarian ancestors!"

Never, in her most fantastic guesses, had she been prepared for what he really did say.

"I know already, dearest. I know all about it. I've just been waiting for you to tell me yourself."

"You know? How could you?"

But of course. How had she been stupid enough to trust them, to believe that anything touching even the fringes of government could be really secret or confidential? Everything that had happened, everything she had said and done, had been taken down and put on file; and after her interview with the Counselor they had communicated with Jon immediately, before she could see him, wherever he had been, in South Africa or on his way home.

She turned to him uncertainly.

"Then what—"

He took her in his arms.

"It's all right, darling," he soothed her, his voice tender. "It was touch and go for a while; they gave me a real scare. They insisted you must be insane. You know what that would have meant." He shuddered. "But I used every bit of influence I have. I got some pretty important psychologists on the job right away, and we convinced the authorities it was only a temporary collapse from overwork and overstrain, such as might affect any highstrung artist. It helped a bit that this plasto-music synthesis you dreamed up really is quite logical—though at present it is also quite impossible.

"You're going to be perfectly safe; I have their absolute guarantee. Just a short stay in a mental hospital, and it will all be as if nothing had ever happened."

"But Jon—" Kathrin could scarcely find her voice. "You don't understand. I'm pregnant now—I told you that! They couldn't have known that."

"They guessed it, my dear," he said dryly. "But don't worry. That can be taken care of very easily; we're in plenty of time."

She looked at him, incredulous horror in her eyes.

"Jon—Jon—no! Our child!"

"Don't you understand, darling? You needn't *have* the child. You *never* need have one."

She tried once more, desperately.

"But I want it, Jon. That was my whole idea in getting the Counselor to back my plan—so that we could go to Patagonia together and then maybe escape on a space ship somehow and be together always—all three of us."

"Now, now, Kathrin! Don't you realize, dear, that this is all part of your mental upset? Just stop worrying and leave things to me. I've taken care of everything. It will be all right."

He held her to him, gently and firmly, and signaled with his head. His face twisted with loving concern, he handed her over—dazed, no longer protesting—to the two men in white uniforms who had been waiting in concealment.

One-Way Journey

We had the driver let us off in the central district and took a copter-taxi back to Homefield. There's no disgrace about it, of course; we just didn't feel like having all the neighbors see the big skycar with LYDNA PROJECT painted on its side, and then having them drop in casually to express what they would call interest and we would know to be curiosity.

There are people who boast that their sons and daughters have been picked for Lydna. What is there to boast about? It's pure chance, within limits.

And Hal is our only child and we love him.

Lucy didn't say a word all the way back from saying good-by to him. Lucy and I have been married now for 27 years and I guess I know her about as well as anybody on Earth does. People who don't know her so well think she's cold. But I knew what feelings she was crushing down inside her.

Besides, I wasn't feeling much like talking myself. I was remembering too many things:

Hal at about two, looking up at me—when I would come home dead-tired from a hard day of being chewed at by half a dozen bosses right up to the editor-in-chief whenever anything went the least bit out of kilter—with a smile that made all my tiredness disappear. Hal, when

I'd pick him up at school, proudly displaying a Cybernetics Approval Slip (and ignoring the fact that half the other kids had one, too). Hal the day I took him to the Beard Removal Center, certain that he was a man, now that he was old enough for depilation. Hal that morning two weeks ago, setting out to get his Vocational Assignment Certificate . . .

That's when I stopped remembering.

It had been five years after our marriage before they let us start a child: some question about Lucy's uncle and my grandmother. Most parents aren't as old as we are when they get the news and usually have other children left, so it isn't so bad.

When we got home, Lucy still was silent. She took off her scarf and cloak and put them away, and then she pushed the button for dinner without even asking me what I wanted. I noticed, though, that she was ordering all the things I like. We both had the day off, of course, to go and say good-by to Hal—Lucy is a technician at Hydroponics Center.

I felt awkward and clumsy. Her ways are so different from mine; I explode and then it's over—just a sore place where it hurts if I touch it. Lucy never explodes, but I knew the sore place would be there forever, and getting worse instead of better.

We ate dinner in silence, though neither of us felt hungry, and had the table cleared. Then it was nearly 19 o'clock and I had to speak.

"The takeoff will be at 19:10," I said. "Want me to tune in now? Last year, when Mutro was Solar President, he gave a good speech before the kids left."

"Don't turn it on at all!" she said sharply. Then, in a softer voice, she added: "Of course, Frank, turn it on whenever you like. I'll just go to my room and open the soundproofing."

There were still no tears in her eyes.

I thought of a thousand things to say: Don't you want to catch a glimpse of Hal in the crowd going up the ramp? Mightn't they let the kids wave a last farewell to their folks listening and watching in? Mightn't something in the President's speech make us feel a little better?

But I heard myself saying, "Never mind, Lucy. Don't go. I'll leave the thing off."

I didn't want to be alone. I wanted Lucy there with me.

So we sat out the whole time of the visicast, side by side on the window-couch, holding hands. I'll say this for the neighbors—they must all have known, for Hal was the first to be selected from Homefield in nearly 40 years, and the newscast must have announced it over and over: but not a single person on the whole 62 floors of the house butted in on us. Not even that snoopy student from Venus in 47-14, who's always dropping in on other tenants and taking notes on "the mores of Earth Aboriginals." People can be very decent sometimes. We needn't have worried about coming home in the Lydna Project bus.

It was no good trying to keep my mind on anything else. Whether I wanted to or not, I had to relive the two last hours we'd ever have with Hal.

It couldn't mean to him what it meant to us. We were losing; he was both losing and gaining. We were losing our whole lives for 21 years past; he was, too, but he was entering a new life we would never know anything about. No word ever comes from Lydna; that's part of the project. Nobody even knows where it is for sure, though it's supposed to be one of the outer asteroids.

Both boys and girls are sent and there must be marriages and children—though probably the death-rate is pretty high, for every year they have to select 200 more from Earth to keep the population balanced. We would never know if our son married there, or whom, or when he died. We would never see our grandchildren, or even know if we had any.

Hal was a good son and I think we were fairly good parents and had made his childhood happy. But at 21, faced with a great, mysterious adventure and an unknown and exciting future, a boy can't be expected to be drowned in grief at saying good-by to his humdrum old father and mother. It might have been tougher for him 200 years ago, when they hadn't learned to decondition children early from parental fixations. But no youngster today would possess that kind of unwholesome dependency. If he did, he would never have been selected for Lydna in the first place.

That's one comfort we have—it's a sort of proof we had reared a child far above the average.

It was just weakness in me to half wish that Hal hadn't been so healthy, so handsome, so intelligent, so fine in character.

They were a wonderful lot. We said our good-bys in an enormous room of the spaceport, with this year's 200 selectees there from all over Earth, each with the relatives and whoever else had permission to make the last visit. I suppose it's a matter of accommodations and transportation, for nobody's allowed more than three. So it was mostly parents, with a few brothers, sisters and sweethearts or friends. The selectees themselves choose the names. After all, they've had two weeks after they were notified to say good-by to everyone else who matters to them.

Most of the time, all I could keep my mind on was Hal, trying to fix forever in my memory every last detail of him. We have dozens of sound stereos, of course, but this was the last time.

Still, it's my business at the News Office, and has been for 30 years, to observe people and form conclusions about them, so I couldn't help noticing with a professional eye some of the rest of the selectees. (This farewell visit is a private affair, and the press is barred, which is why I'd never been there before.)

There were two kinds of selectees that stood out, in my mind. One was those who had nobody at all to see them off. Completely alone, poor kids—orphans, doubtless, with no families and apparently not even friends near enough to matter. But, in a way, they would be the happiest; life on Earth couldn't have been very rewarding for them, and on Lydna they might find companionship. (If only companionship in misery, I thought—but I shied away from that. In our business, there are always leaks; we know—or guess—a few things about Lydna nobody else does outside the authorities themselves. But we keep our mouths shut.)

The ones that tore my hearts were the boys and girls in love. They never take married people for Lydna, but a machine can't tell what a boy or girl is feeling about another girl or boy, and it's a machine that does the selecting. There's no use putting up an argument, for, once made, the choice is inexorable and unchangeable. In my work as a newsgatherer, I've heard some terrible stories. There have been suicide pacts and murders.

You could tell the couples in love. Not that there were any scenes. If there had been any in the two weeks past, they were over. But anybody who has learned to read human reactions, as I have, could recognize the agony those youngsters were going through.

I felt a deep gratitude that Hal wasn't one of them. He'd had his share of adolescent affairs, of course, but I was sure he was still just playing around. He'd seen a lot of Bet Milen, a girl a class ahead of him in school and college, but I didn't think she meant more to him than any of the others. If she had, she'd have been along to say good-by, but he'd asked for only the two of us. She was now a laboratory assistant in our hospital and could easily have gotten the time off.

It was growing late, almost midnight, and Lucy and I had to be at work tomorrow, no matter how we felt. I forced myself to talk, with Lucy's silent pain smothering me like a force-blanket. I made an effort and cleared my throat.

"Lucy, go to bed and turn on the hypno and try to get some sleep."

Lucy stood up obediently, but she shook her head. "You go, dear," she said, her voice firm. "I can't. I—"

The roof buzzer sounded. Somebody had landed in a copter and wanted us.

"Don't answer," I said quickly. "There's nobody we want to see—"

But she had already pushed the button to open the door.

It was Bet Milen, the girl Hal used to go around with.

I braced myself. This might be bad. She might have cared more for Hal than we had guessed.

But she didn't look grief-stricken. She looked excited, and determined, and a little bit frightened.

She scarcely glanced at me. She went right up to Lucy and took both Lucy's hands in hers.

"Well," she said in a clipped, tense voice, "we made it."

Then Lucy broke for the first time. The tears ran down her face and she didn't even wipe them away. "Are you *certain?*"

"Positive. And I got word to him. We'd agreed on a code. That's why he didn't want me there today—we couldn't trust ourselves not to betray it, either way."

I stood there staring at them, bewildered.

"What's this all about—" I demanded. "Have you two cooked up some crazy scheme to rescue Hal? I hope to heaven not! It would ruin all of us, including him!"

The wild daydreams I'd had myself flashed through my mind—the drug that would seem to kill him and wouldn't, the anonymous false accusation of subversion, the previous secret marriage. All impossible, all fatal.

Lucy disengaged her hands from the girl's and slipped her arm through mine.

"You tell him, Bet," she said gently. "You're the one who should."

I'd never noticed how pretty the girl was till then, when she stood there with her face flushed and her eyes straight on mine. A pang went through me; if only she and Hal could have—

"No, Mr. Sturt," she said, "we haven't rescued Hal. He's gone. But we've rescued part of him. I'm going to have his baby."

"Bet's going to live with us and be our daughter,

Frank," Lucy explained. "Hal and she and I worked it out in these two weeks, after they came to me and told me how they felt about each other. We couldn't tell you till we were sure; I couldn't bear to have you hope and then be disappointed—it would be enough for me to have to suffer that."

"That is, I'll come if you want me here, Mr. Sturt," said Bet.

I had to sit down before I could speak. "Of course I want you. But what about your own family?"

"I haven't any. My mother's dead and my father's an engineer on Ganymede and gets home on leave about once in three years. I've been living in a youth hostel."

"But look here—" I turned to Lucy—"how on Earth can you know? Two weeks or less is no time—"

Lucy gave me a look I recognized, the patient one of the scientist for the layman.

"The Chow-Visalius test, dear. One day after the fertilized ovum starts dividing—"

"And I ran it myself every day for over a week. That's one of my jobs in the lab and it was easy to slip in another specimen. And it didn't, and it didn't and I went nearly out of my mind—"

"Every time Hal entered the apartment, I'd look at him and he'd shake his head," Lucy interrupted. "It meant everything to him. And it would just have broken my heart—"

"Mine, too," Bet said softly. "And his. And today was the last chance. I was scared to try it. This afternoon at 14:30, just before the farewell visits, was the deadline for viz messages to any of them. If I'd had to send mine without the word we'd agreed on that would tell him it was all right—But it was, at last! And now he knows, even if I never—even if we never—Excuse me, please, it's been a strain. I'm afraid I'm going to bawl."

We let her alone. Kids nowadays hate to be fussed over. Us, we'd lost our son, and that was going to stay with us forever. But now we would have his child to love and—

An appalling thought struck me suddenly. I can't imagine why I hadn't realized it sooner. All this emotion, I suppose.

"Good God!" I cried. "An illegal child! We can't keep it!"

"Nobody's going to know," Lucy replied calmly. "Bet's going to live with us, and when it starts to show, she's going to take her allowed leave. We'll take ours, too, and we'll all go on a trip—to Mars, maybe, or Venus—one of the settled colonies where we can rent a house. Babies don't *have* to be born in Hospitals, you know; our ancestors had them right at home. She's strong and healthy and I know what to do. Then we'll come back here and we'll have a baby with us that we adopted wherever we were. Nobody will ever know."

"Look," I said in a voice I tried to keep from rising. "There are four billion people on Earth and about 28 billion in the colonized Solar planets. Every one of those people is on record at Central Cybernetics. How do you suppose you're going to get away with the phony adoption of a non-existent child? The first time you have to take it to a baby clinic, they'll find it has no card."

"I thought of that," Lucy said, "and it can be done, because it must. Frank, for heaven's sake, use your wits! You're a newsgatherer. You know all sorts of people everywhere."

"I don't know any machines. And it's machines that handle the records."

"Machines under the supervision of humans."

"Sure," I said sarcastically. "I just go to my ex-newsgatherer pal who feeds the records to Io or Ceres and say, 'Look, old fellow, do me a favor, will you? My wife wants to adopt a baby from your colony, so just make up the names of two people and give them a life-check, invent their ancestors back to the time Central Cybernetics was established, and then slip in cards for their marriage, and the birth of their child—I'll let you know later whether to make it a boy or a girl—and then their deaths; and then my wife and I can adopt that made-up baby.'

"What kind of blackmailing hold do you think I have on any record official," I asked angrily, "to make him do a thing like that and keep his mouth shut about it? I could be eliminated for treason for even making such a suggestion."

"Frank, *think!* Surely there must be *some* way!"

And then it struck me. "Wait! I just got an idea. When I said 'treason,' just now— It might barely be possible—"

"Oh, what?"

"It would have to be Mars, the North Polar Cap colony. The K-Alph Conspiracy messed things up there badly."

"I remember, Mr. Sturt!" Bet said excitedly. "They wrecked everything in the three months before the rebellion was crushed, didn't they?"

"Everything, including their cybernetics equipment. Central doesn't want it known, but I have inside information that it's still not in going condition. That colony is full of children who have never been registered. And I doubt if it will be in 100 per cent shape for the best part of another year. Those hellions really did a job. Let's see—this is the end of Month Two. We'd have to get away around Month Eight at the latest and the baby would be born—when exactly, Bet?"

"Early in Month Twelve. We could all be back here again by the first of next year, or even by the end of Month Thirteen."

"Well, I have enough accumulated leave for that and I guess you have too, Lucy; neither of us has taken more than two or three weeks for years. But what about you, Bet? You've been working less than a year."

"I can borrow it. Our director is crazy about travel and she'll be all for it when I tell her I have a chance to go to Mars for a long visit. Besides, she knows about Hal and me—I mean the way we are about each other—and she'll understand that I'd want to get away for a while now."

Asher, my editor-in-chief, would feel the same way, I thought, and so would Lucy's boss.

"I knew you'd find a way," remarked my wife complacently.

I looked at the telechron.

"We've all got to be at work in seven hours," I said, "if we expect to get through before the end of the afternoon. What say we turn in?"

"You stay here with us, Bet," said Lucy. "You parked your copter in our port, didn't you? Frank, I think we need a drink."

I pushed the buttons. Nobody said anything, but somehow it was a toast to Hal. I know the liquor had to get past a lump in my throat and the women were both crying. It wasn't like my self-contained Lucy. I guess she thought so herself, for she braced herself. But her voice was still trembling when she turned to Bet.

"A year from now," she said, "we'll all be back here in this room and, this time, part of Hal will be here with us—his son, our little Hal."

"It might be our little Hallie." Bet smiled through her tears. "It will be ten weeks before I can run the Schuster test to find out."

"It won't make any difference. Hal will never know that, but he'll know, way out there on Lydna, that his baby has been born. He'll know, even though he can never see it—or us."

Lucy blinked, then went on bravely. "Every time he looks in a mirror there, he'll say to himself, 'Well, back on Earth, there's a little tyke with my blue eyes and my curly hair and my mouth and nose and chin, who's going to grow up to be tall and straight like me—or maybe like Bet, but also a lot like me.'

"And as he grows older, he can think back to the way he was as a child and a boy and a man, and know that his son, or his daughter, will be feeling and thinking and looking some day just about the way he himself is then, and it will be a link with Earth and with us—"

That was when I had to go to the window and look out for a long time to pull myself together before I could face them again.

Lydna is top-top secret, but as I've said before, we newsgatherers get inside information.

I have a pretty shrewd idea of what the mysterious Lydna Project is. It's to alter human beings so they can adapt to the colonization of outer space.

The medics do things to them to enable them and their descendants to resist every possible condition of temperature and radiation and gravity. They have to alter the genes—acquired characters would be of use only in a short-term project, and this is long-term. But you can't alter genes without affecting the individual.

We'd have Hal's normal child.

But when Hal got to Lydna, he and the rest of them would be shocked and sick for a while at sight of some of the inhabitants. And if he had any children on Lydna, we, back here, would scarcely recognize them as human. Some of them might have extra limbs. Some might have eyes and ears in odd places. Some might have lungs outside their bodies, or brains without a skull.

By that time, Hal himself would have got over being sick—unless, some time, he got hold of a mirror and remembered the boy he used to be.

The Season of the Babies

A baby whistled from the Nursery, and Ilswyth rose hastily and ran to turn it over, feed it, and clean it. When she got back she noted the scowl on Ragnar's face. He had ordered everything held up till she returned; he was a stickler for full Council meetings, most of all in this extraordinarily important one. Ilswyth slipped apologetically into her chair and the conference continued.

"It's bad luck," Ragnar said, "that the ambassadors from Sol should be arriving at just this moment, in the middle of the Season of the Babies. A few weeks more, and the Choosing would be over. Then we would be in the best possible position to create the favorable impression we must give if we are to be accepted. But right now—"

"Couldn't we have put them off?" Only Eghar ever dared to interrupt the president.

"Hardly," Ragnar snapped. "We've been asking for Federation membership for nearly 100 years. How would it look if, when they finally send a delegation empowered to make the final decision, we had to plead that this was a time when we weren't exactly at our best? They probably manage their own Season more efficiently."

Ilswyth, as Nursery Chief, had an idea.

"If we could—not advance the whole Choosing, of course; that would be impossible—but select some that will obviously not be Chosen but are otherwise well along? And just say that the others weren't ripe yet?"

"Pretty difficult. They know already that in one respect we aren't up to the standard of half a dozen at least of the present Federation members—they have interstellar flight and we haven't; they can come to us but we can't go to them, unless they take us. We don't want to rub it in by acknowledging that we're not up to them in other ways as well—it's a matter of planetary honor.

"No," Ragnar stood up to indicate that the Council was about to be adjourned. "If we can't put our best foot forward, as we'd hoped to do, we must just do the best we can. Ilswyth, I want you to stay over, and we'll discuss your idea. The rest of you may leave, but stand ready for a final briefing as soon as I know the exact time of arrival. We're in constant communication with them, and I should know definitely by tonight. Any questions before you go?"

"Are the ambassadors all from Earth?" Harkon asked.

"Yes, naturally; the other inhabited planets of Sol are all Earth colonies, and with the Outer Galactic Federation capital on Earth, the ambassadors would be most likely to be from there also. But don't worry—they all speak Standard Galactic besides their own languages, just as we do.

"Now, Ilswyth, about—"

There were three ambassadors—two men and a woman. The crowd around the newly remodeled spaceport was vaguely disappointed; these were ordinary-looking beings, very much like themselves, and not even grandly appareled, but dressed like travelers to their own colonized planets. Nevertheless, there was an air about them of dignity and consequence, such as the people were accustomed to in their own High Council, and most of all in their president. They were proud to realize that their own could meet these important strangers on an equal footing. There were banners and flowers and music, but the welcoming exercises were brief. Gorth, who was in charge of entertainment of the visitors, had decided that too much ostentation might be read as complacent self-assurance: time enough for real ceremony when they were accepted into membership in the Federation.

By the time the three had been greeted in the Council Chamber, and then taken to the dwellings alloted them, for a rest, it was nearly two-moon hour. Tonight the guests would meet their official hosts at a light repast, followed by a moonlight tour in ground-cars to show them the capital city and its environs; the first session would be held tomorrow morning. Ragnar and the Council members, watching the Earthians, were gratified; the ambassadors were most courteous and complimentary, apparently delighted with everything they saw and heard. It was an auspicious beginning, and the plenary sessions could not but improve on the initial good impression.

The two men were named Gonzalez and Richter, the woman was named Andree. They must all be people of prominence and standing on Earth, though their precise positions were a little puzzling because of natural differences in political economy between the two planets. However, they had credentials of the highest kind, empowering them to investigate and query at their discretion and to make final recommendations, after discussion with the similarly empowered president and Council, which would be binding on both parties.

Everything went swimmingly as the first session began. Ragnar laid bare the financial status of the planet, its governmental makeup, its technical achievements (acknowledging frankly that in some respects these last might be inferior to those of Sol and perhaps of some others of the Federation). The ambassadors drew up a statistical list of the matters about which the Federation had to be satisfied before a planet was admitted into membership. They started to get down to details.

A baby whistled.

At the sound Ilswyth, as usual, rose to her feet. The

woman ambassador, Andree, stopped her. "What is that signal?" she asked, startled.

"Signal?" Ilswyth glanced, perplexed, at Ragnar. He answered for her.

"It's only a baby. We equip them with whistles so they can let us know when they're hungry or wet. Ilswyth will just run in and attend to it—she's in charge of this Nursery. We're only a small planet, you know," he excused himself. "We have to double up in some of our official positions."

"A baby?"

All of the Council were red with embarrassment.

"I'm sorry," Ragnar apologized. "We had hoped you wouldn't notice. By pure bad luck your visit has happened to come in the middle of our Season of the Babies."

"I don't understand," interposed the ambassador Gonzalez. His Standard Galactic had a strong Spanish accent. "Do you mean that here you have children just at one particular season?"

It was Ragnar's turn to be astonished.

"Why, of course," he faltered. "Don't you—doesn't everybody?"

"Of course not," said Richter bluntly; his German accent was as strong as Gonzalez's Spanish. "On Earth babies are born any day of the year. Do you mean that you here have a rutting season, like our lower animals?"

"I don't know what that means. In the spring, naturally, there is the urge to reproduce, and so in the next winter our women of reproductive age have their babies."

"That is a rutting season," said Richter dryly. "Then are all your marriages celebrated in the spring?"

"Marriages? I don't understand that word."

"What are you," Andree demanded crisply, "promiscuous?"

"Nor that word either, your honor." Ragnar was uncomfortable. "Perhaps we can get back now to our serious discussion, and later I can satisfy your curiosity about these minor trifles."

"But this *is* important," said Gonzalez, frowning. "Your family system seems to be completely out of line with that of any humanoid planet in the Federation. We might be willing to make adjustments, but we should have to know all the details. For instance, it seems to me that if all your women have babies at the same time every year, it must put a serious strain on your economy. All the extra expense—and all these women withdrawn from their work to care for their infants— And besides, unless you have a high infant mortality, which would be another indication of lack of social development, it would appear that you must have a constantly mounting population, with all the consequent depressive effects on your living standards."

The other ambassadors nodded their heads in agreement. The Councilors gazed at one another, puzzled. Gorth looked to Ragnar for permission to speak.

"I believe, your honors," he said, smiling, "this is merely a little semantic misunderstanding. Naturally, the bad effects you mention would ensue if, like the lower animals, we preserved all our offspring. But of course we do not—on the contrary, the Season is the time when our economy gets its annual uplift. We are fully as civilized as you, I am sure, in that respect." He hesitated, seeing the lack of comprehension on the three alien faces. "You mean," he ended lamely, "you do *not* have our system? We had supposed that it was common to all civilized planets."

"Are you saying that you let your babies *die?*" cried Andree, outraged.

"Please, Gorth, let me explain," Ragnar interrupted.

"Yes, explain," said Richter grimly.

Ragnar picked his words carefully, at a loss to make clear what to all of his people was the normal and universal way of life.

"In the winter all the babies are born. For the first three months they are cared for in the Nurseries—there is one in each city, with a government official, like Ilswyth here, in charge. Then comes the Choosing, when trained observers make careful surveys and decide which babies are physically and mentally superior. These we keep and rear. We—all of our people you have met—were once, of course, among the Chosen of our year. It is a eugenic measure."

"And the others? The ones not 'Chosen'?" inquired Andree sternly.

"They are disposed of, naturally—under the best possible conditions, I assure you. They are very young still—they cannot realize. And there is no pain whatever."

There was a long silence around the conference table. Then Richter said: "It seems at the best a very wasteful system. Why don't you practice birth control instead?"

"That would be immoral," said Ragnar stiffly. "Every human being has a right to be born, to take its chances on being Chosen for survival. Remember, we preserve *all* the superior ones and rear them so as to develop all their potentialities. We could not do that if the others—the ones who did not make the grade—did not provide the financial means."

"Provide the financial means—how?" Gonzalez asked. Andree broke in on him.

"But the mothers!" she exclaimed. "The poor mothers! How can you take a woman's baby away from her and—and murder it? The worst totalitarian regimes in our evil past never did that. I should think the mothers whose hearts you've broken—yes, and the fathers too—would simply rise up and wipe out a government that was so brutally cruel!"

The whole Council was in a turmoil, with everybody trying to speak at once. Ragnar, bewildered and frantic, tried in vain to restore order. Desperately he signaled to Eghar—least subordinate but most persuasive of the Council—to be their spokesman. He cleared his throat and said slowly:

"Your honors, let us reassure you. Our government is not cruel. We break no hearts. Ilswyth, you are the only woman on the Council. I suppose a baby of yours is among those in the Nursery here. Will you tell our guests how you feel about the Choosing?"

Ragnar flushed with vexation. He should have thought himself of calling on Illswyth. Here was another feather in Eghar's cap. If he wasn't careful, Eghar would be the next president. But he managed to smile benignly.

"An excellent idea, Eghar. Tell them, Ilswyth."

The three pairs of alien eyes fixed themselves on her.

"B-but we're all one, aren't we?" she stammered, shy to be the focus of attention. "I mean, no m-mother *owns* her baby, does she? Ever since we are little girls, we look forward to the day when we shall be able to produce children every year for our people—the boys do too, though of course they can't be sure which special ones are theirs. We are all so proud if at the Choosing there are unusually many who are good enough to keep, even though that means an extra call on the education fund. And if one of our own is Chosen, we almost burst with pride. I have had eight babies so far, and three of them have been Chosen; that is one of the biggest reasons, I'm sure, why I was elected to the Council last year."

"But what about the five who *weren't* 'Chosen'?" cried Andree. "How did you feel when they were killed before your eyes?"

"But they weren't!" Ilswyth exclaimed, horrified. "How can you think that? It is all done decently and in order."

"But a mother surely becomes attached to her own baby—"

"How could she? It is taken away at once to the Nursery, and she never sees it again. I am in charge of a Nursery, so I am pretty sure which one is mine, but why should I feel differently toward it than toward any other? We are all one people, all children are our children. Suppose a woman is a teacher—should she care more because one of the children she teaches happened to come from her body?"

"And doesn't she care when she knows that her baby has been—disposed of?"

"Why should she? We made them all, we do with them what is best for all of them and all of us. It is wonderful to know that one's own baby has been Chosen, but if not—neither are most of the others, and better luck next year."

The three ambassadors sat speechless, doubt, anger, and astonishment on their too expressive faces. Gorth, always a peacemaker, jumped into the breach.

"I think," he said smoothly, under Ragnar's approving nod, "that we have talked enough without a break. Let us resume our discussion—or, better, go on with more important questions, in the afternoon. It is almost time for the official banquet which is scheduled for today. Our cooks have outdone themselves to please you, and you will want to go to your lodgings first to rest and refresh yourselves. The ground-car is waiting, and it will call for you again in half an hour."

"I'd still like to know about 'providing the financial means,'" said Gonzalez stubbornly.

"Later, later!" Ragnar replied. Gonzalez let himself be persuaded, and the three were handed over to the ground-car driver. The Council members did not follow them; at Ragnar's gesture they waited until they were alone, then huddled for a hasty conference.

"This is most annoying," the president said abruptly. "It never occurred to me that there could be such a difference in customs between two advanced cultures. Apparently they do their Choosing before conception instead of after birth. It seems most immoral to me, and distinctly uncivilized."

"*And* ridiculously wasteful," Harkon added. "They must have to pay for the training of what children they do have, out of the public funds; we pay for it out of our government monopoly and the patriotic devotion of our citizens."

"People are so attached to their own ways," worried Gorth. "It's little things like this that divide them. This contretemps might cause the collapse of all our negotiations."

"Oh, I can't imagine it will be as bad as all that," Ragnar soothed him. "They can't be so provincial. But it *has* made things more difficult, I confess. To tell the truth, I think we've shown our civilization to be more advanced than theirs, and they'll surely be reasonable enough to realize that when they've thought it over. Certainly they haven't attained our solidarity, the oneness of empathy we take for granted. I suppose it's because only a few centuries ago the inhabitants of Earth were slaughtering their own kind in wars. You notice they still evidently keep up their separate national languages."

"And then they make a fuss about our disposing of our own babies as we see fit!" said Ilswyth bitterly.

"I know. But I'm afraid, Ilswyth, in our endeavor to do them the highest honor we've made a little miscalculation. Is it too late to change it?"

"I'll try. I'll go over there right away. It's upsetting, after we nearly broke our necks to make a special effort for them."

"Well, that was against my better judgment anyway, you'll remember—though I never dreamed they wouldn't be impressed by the honor. Do the best you can, but if you're too late it won't really matter. I'll just say nothing, instead of calling it to their attention, in a nice, modest way, as I'd intended. We'll simply charge up the waste to profit and loss. After all, it doesn't matter how much we spend if we get their recommendation for acceptance into the Federation."

"If!" snorted Eghar. "What new outlandish quirk will they show next?"

"We must hope for the best," said Ragnar.

The banquet went well. The visitors ate the unaccustomed food with grace, and drank the unaccustomed wine with pleasure. Once or twice they asked, "Delicious—what is it?" but only of the salad and the fruits. Ilswyth hadn't been able to have any major change made in the menu, but she'd arranged to have the delicate meat sliced in the kitchen and smothered in a complicated sauce, which quite spoiled the taste of the highly luxurious food for the natives; but under the circumstances that didn't matter. She sat next to Gonzalez, and saw to it that his glass was refilled as soon as it was emptied.

But Gonzalez was used to stronger wine than theirs. As soon as the meeting adjourned to the Council Chamber again, he repeated his question: "How does your system provide a profit to your educational fund?"

By this time Ragnar was ready. "Isn't it obvious, my dear sir? The fewer children there are to educate, the more money is left for the benefit of those who are preserved."

The woman delegate, Andree, had eaten little and drunk still less. "I'm afraid you will think me rude," she had murmured to Harkon, seated next to her, "but I'm on a slimming diet." Harkon, from a world that liked its women statuesque, was hard put to it to find a polite rejoinder.

Now she followed Gonzalez right up. "But you said— it was Gorth who said it, I believe—that your Season of the Babies was the time when your economy gets its annual uplift. Surely you didn't mean merely that you saved money by it?"

"In other words," said Richter harshly, "what *do* you do with those superfluous babies? Sell their bodies to the medical schools or the tanners, and use the proceeds to educate the ones you save?"

"Oh, your honor!" Ragnar was shocked. "We would *never* do anything as gross as that—we, a people as highly cultured as yourselves! Of course not—we wouldn't dream of it. We—how shall I put it? When farmers have the remains of a crop left over, they plow it back into the ground to benefit the next crop. That is what we do—the Unchosen babies are the part of the crop we turn back to those who made them."

He looked at the three horrified faces before him.

"But only to the very best of our people, I assure you," he explained carefully. "It is a great privilege to be allowed to contribute to the education fund. They must have a good record in every way before they are even allowed to bid."

Suddenly Andree screamed loudly.

"That—that meat!" she shrieked. "That tender, delicate meat!"

She collapsed in hysterics. Richter sat as if frozen. Gonzalez turned green and abruptly vomited into his handkerchief; he had eaten more than either of them.

The Council members fixed amazed eyes on their president. His face was flushed with anger.

"We had assumed," he said coldly, "that you of the Federation were at least as civilized as we. We paid you the greatest honor we can offer a guest—we made a special effort to provide you, though you arrived before the Choosing, before they were really ripe. We had not expected such a peculiar reaction—such an insult."

"What is the matter with you?" Ilswyth burst out indignantly. "The babies are part of us; they will go to make up next year's babies, too. Aren't *you* all one people, as we are? Or are you so upset because we turn them back to our people for money—money which goes to educate the Chosen? Would you like it better if we just wasted our substance?"

"But their souls, their souls!" Gonzalez shouted. Ragnar shook his head uncomprehendingly. Andree was still weeping wildly. "Cannibals!" Richter hissed, "Savages!"

White to the lips, Ragnar held up his hand to silence them.

"Forgive us," he said with elaborate courtesy, "if we have perhaps not understood your social standards as well as we had imagined. May I inquire, since you are so offended by our customs, what are your own in this respect? Since it seems so dreadful to you that we consume our own, how do you on Earth secure the proteins necessary for your health—from vegetable sources alone?"

"Why," answered Gonzalez, startled, "from meat, of course!"

"Meat!" Ragnar was triumphant. "You see—you do eat meat, just as we thought! Is it perhaps some taboo that forbids you to eat your meat young and tender? That seems very strange."

"Not human meat!" yelled Richter, "meat from animals, of course, you cannibal!"

There was a ghastly silence. None of the Council members dared to meet the eyes of another.

"From—" Ragnar could harly speak. "You actually mean," he said painfully, "that you, human beings like ourselves, take into your bodies, to become part of your own and your children's substance, the flesh of vile, alien creatures? Our earliest ancestors, even before they became civilized, never fell so low as that!"

He glanced at his colleagues. Dismay and disgust were on every face. Ilswyth suddenly clapped a hand to her mouth and dashed from the room into the Nursery.

For a long time nobody on either side seemed able to speak. Ragnar finally rose to the need for action, but it was his own Council he addressed, ignoring the strangers.

"I am afraid," he said, "that for 100 years we have labored under a profound misapprehension. We have applied constantly for membership in the Outer Galactic Federation, not so much because we needed anything it could give us, as because we felt it a blot on our planetary honor to be excluded from what we had supposed to be an alliance of highly civilized worlds.

"And now we suddenly discover that the very planet which controls this Federation has a culture so disparate from ours that it seems impossible we could even work together in amity. True, Sol and some of the other systems have interstellar travel; true, we do not, as yet. But such technical advances are extraneous. The very heart, the inner meaning, of our society, it appears, is abhorrent to Sol. And I need only look at you, or search my own feelings, to realize how infinitely more abhorrent theirs is to us.

"I am sorry indeed that these ambassadors"—he glanced at the silent three—"should have had to undergo the trouble and expense of a useless journey. . . . Shall we take a formal vote? If so, will you, Gorth, ask Ilswyth to—oh, here she is again: good. What is your pleasure?"

"No vote needed," said Eghar gruffly. "We agree." There were assenting murmurs all down the table.

"Then—" Ragnar had recovered his suavity; he even managed to smile at the flabbergasted delegates. "I regret that our conference has failed. I trust this will not have unpleasant political repercussions for you. But it seems obvious that our social systems are too far apart in spirit for us to wish any longer to be affiliated with you.

"You will be wanting to leave at once, I am sure. We shall do everything possible for your comfort and convenience. When you return to Earth, tell your principals that we withdraw our application for membership in the Outer Galactic Federation, at least until such time as other planets have reached the same high state of culture we have attained."

The aghast ambassadors came to life.

"Why you—!" The veins stood out on Gonzalez's forehead: His voice was strangled. "If you think for a minute we would admit—"

"Dirty cannibals!" yelled Richter again.

Andree, outraged beyond speech, merely sat and stared.

"Unspeakable non-human-flesh-eaters," Eghar retorted, under his breath. Ragnar stopped him with an abrupt gesture.

"Let's not act any more like barbarians than is necessary," he said quietly. "You have heard our decision. This conference is at an end."

"Let's get out of here," Gonzalez growled.

The Council watched the three ambassadors file silently through the door. Then Ragnar turned to them briskly.

"Harkon, if you will prepare the formal statement to be given to our people—and make special note of the fact that *we* rejected membership: I don't think we need harrow anyone's feelings by explaining exactly why.

"Eghar, you and Gorth had better get busy now on the preliminary setup for this year's Choosing. Illswyth—"

In the Nursery, a baby whistled. Ilswyth ran to turn it over.

"A quick crop this year," said Ragnar happily. "I think we'll get a really good boost to the education fund. In spite of the sauce, those precocious specimens we had today were extraordinarily tasty."

Featherbed on Chlyntha

I had just settled down to sleep in my cage after the evening inquisition when I heard the back door open softly, and Iri came in. It's never really dark on Chlyntha at night because of their two moons, but I'd have known anyway who it was—no mistaking that crest of blue-black iridescent feathers or those flashing amber eyes.

"Are you awake, space creature?" she whispered.

They knew, of course, that I could speak their language, because I obeyed orders. They'd never bothered to learn mine, any more than a man bothers to learn a dog's. Theirs is rather a simple tongue and I'd picked it up in a few months from listening to the conversation in the crowds gathered in front of my cage in the zoo in the daytime. But I seldom spoke it to them—they did all the talking.

However, if Iri was paying me a private visit I figured she rated a reply. So I yawned and said: "Yes. What do you want?"

She sat down, but I noticed she kept one hand on the open door in case I got violent. Maybe she was smart at that; I hadn't seen another girl on Chlyntha with her looks, and it had been a year now since I'd seen a woman of my own kind. But I was too beaten down to be much of a menace.

Iri leaned forward until the feathers on her crest tickled my shoulder. I drew away and apparently that gave her more confidence.

"Why do you think you're here, space creature?" she asked. "What do you think we're trying to find out when we give you all those tests every evening?"

"As to the first," I answered stiffly, "I'm here because I was kidnaped. As to the second, how should a subhuman creature from outer space understand the purposes of the scientists of Chlyntha?"

She frowned—I could see the feathery eyebrows knit above the amber eyes.

"None of that," she said sharply. "We've tested your intelligence, you know, besides everything else. You are distinctly humanoid, even if you're not really human."

"Very well, then. I haven't the slightest idea why you're putting me through this performance, unless it's just plain scientific curiosity. . . .

"After all," I added in my own language, "I'm a scientist too, and I can understand an interest in pure science." I said that deliberately to find out if she understood any Terran at all. Apparently she didn't.

"Speak Chlynthan!" she commanded. "You speak it quite intelligibly, in spite of your accent. That's one of the main factors in our decision that you have a relatively high intelligence."

"Thanks," I said. Naturally I hated them all, but I hated Iri the least. You don't hate as pretty a girl as that, even if she has feathers instead of hair and twelve fingers and twelve toes. Those were the only differences I'd been able to discover—outwardly at least, which was all I saw—between us and them.

I had been minding my own business, that day a year—one of their years—before, tooling along in my little one-seater between one Mars colony and the next, when I was snatched. My special field is fourth-generation Martian colonists. There's mighty little social anthropology left to do on Earth; we've observed, checked, rechecked, researched, described, till there isn't an ethnic group left that hasn't been investigated down to the last myth and the last folk-art. But opening up the other planets gave us anthropologists a new lease of life—now we have not only the remains of the extinct Martians to study, and the primitive carbon-breathing Venerians (the latter under difficulties, I acknowledge), but also the changes brought about by even four generations of life in our colonies on Mars and the Moon. I had a pretty good position for a man of only 31—half a year studying in the Mars colonies, the other half back on Earth in a college teaching job with time enough besides to put my findings on microtape. Now, thanks to Iri's people and their damned starships, I was just an exhibit in a zoo on Chlyntha.

"What we've been testing most—" her voice snapped me back from my bitter reflections—"is the sexual equipment of your species."

"Oh, yes?" I said in Terran. "Well, how about a practical demonstration, baby?" But this might be important, and I started to listen more closely.

"I don't suppose you can see past the front bars of your cage," Iri went on, with only an impatient wave of the hand for what she must have suspected was a verbal pass. "But you're far from our only specimen at present, though you're the most humanoid one, and therefore the most valuable. We've been scouting for years, ever since the population problem became serious—sending out scout ships all over the Galaxy, and picking up likely-looking samples. Ideally, where there is apparently a bisexual system, we ought to collect one of each sex, but so far we haven't been so lucky. You do have females on your planet, where we collected you, don't you?"

"To begin with, that wasn't my planet; I come from another planet of that solar system. And yes, my dear Iri, we do have females; I wish I had one right now. Incidentally, I have a name, and I don't like being called 'space creature.'"

"Of course," she said blandly. "Prizing one's special individuality is a common primitive characteristic that you'd naturally have. But you've never told us your name; what is it?"

"You've never asked. It's Duncan Keith. And I've heard them call you Iri."

"Oh, that. It doesn't mean me, particularly; it's the designation of my work on the laboratory staff. We have official names, but we seldom use them. I'm perfectly willing to call you Duncankeith."

"Just Duncan will do."

"As I said, most of the other specimens we've gathered have been so far from human that they could teach us nothing that would be of use in solving our problem. In fact, except for you, the present lot isn't worth bothering with, and we've finished examining them and are ready to dispose of them."

"Dispose?"

"Get rid of them," she said coolly. "Just as soon as the next scout ships come back, if they have enough on board to build up the zoo as a public attraction, we'll kill off this lot and mount and stuff them for the Space Museum. You're fortunate that you're worth further study."

"I don't suppose it would occur to you to return us poor devils to where we came from when you're through with us, would it?" I inquired sarcastically.

She smiled—and damn it, when she smiled there were two cute little dimples—

"Hardly," she said crisply. "It's a very expensive project as it is; we're not going to waste more money sending the specimens back. Besides, there is always the possibility that some day some other race somewhere in the Galaxy might reach the starship stage, and we don't care to inspire traditions of a dreadful place called Chlyntha which steals the inhabitants of other planets. If one of the places we've fished should ultimately learn to conquer outer space, they might find us and do some quite unpleasant things to us. . . .

"That is," she added with a deep sigh, "if there are any of us left by then."

When Iri sighed, it was quite easy to see that the

Chlynthans were mammals. I wrenched my mind away.

"Well," I said, "it was very kind of you to give me all this useful information, but I doubt if you dropped in just to brief me. What's this leading up to? The date of my transformation into an exhibit at the Space Museum?"

There was no answer. Iri had got to her feet and was pacing up and down, deep in thought, between me and the open door. I don't like to sit while a lady is standing, so I got up too. To show I wasn't trying to escape—where to?—or intending to assault her, I went and leaned gracefully against the front bars.

I was a very disobliging zoo animal—I just wouldn't perform. They wanted to see me doing my strange antics—eating at a table, drinking out of a cup, sitting in a chair, even using the latrine in a side cubbyhole. The keepers had provided me with reasonable facsimiles of all these objects after I'd drawn sketches of them. That was a week or so after I'd been thrown in the bare cage, when the first shock was over and I'd realized I might be in for a long term. I wondered how they provided proper gravity and air conditioning and food for all those "specimens" from nobody knows where; so far as I was concerned, Chlyntha was enough of an Earth-type planet to make no difference.

So leaning against the bars wasn't my usual daytime position; I was much more likely to be sitting with my back to the crowds. Sometimes they'd bang sticks on the bars to make me turn around, but the keepers discouraged that. I'd trained myself to attend to my natural needs of intake and outgo before the zoo opened or after it closed. I was comfortable enough, but the one thing I didn't have was privacy, except in the hours between the end of the evening session I spent doubling in brass as a laboratory animal, and the opening of the gates the next day. I'd had to grow a beard, though—they didn't trust me with a razor when I drew one, though they gave me a mirror and a comb and brought in a tub of bathwater early every morning.

Iri must have guessed some of my thoughts. A look of compassion fleeted across that lovely face.

"There may be ways we could make it easier for you here," she said. "Tell me, and I'll try to get you anything you want."

"Why all the come-on? Are you trying to tell me that I'm valuable enough to be kept alive indefinitely? And if so, why?"

"I'm trying to find the words to explain so you'll understand. Have you noticed anything about my people that seems different from what you're used to in your own?"

"Well, of course you have what we call feathers—" I used the Terran word.

"You mean our plumage, instead of those bristles on you? I didn't mean that; I meant a difference in the— let's say in the differentiation of the sexes here."

"How would I know? You people have been all over me with a finetooth comb, but I've never seen any of you without those cloaks you all wear. Your men seem a bit taller and heavier than the women, and they have feathers on their chins—"

"That's not what I meant," she said sharply. "Our men are made just like you, and I suppose our women are made just like yours; it seems to be a common Galactic pattern for the dominant race."

"Then what?"

She paused again, and then went off on another tangent.

"I am the child of a High Person," she said abruptly. "It is an honor to mate with me."

I stared at her, my jaw dropping. So that was what she was driving at! The one thing I hadn't expected was a proposition. The reflexes worked and I started toward her. She held up her hand.

"Just calm down, Duncan," she said calmly. "Impetuosity is a primitive trait."

I waited. There was hardly anything else I could do.

Safe from my primitive impetuosity, Iri sat down. She changed the subject again.

"What do you remember of your capture, Duncan?" she asked.

"Not much," I answered sulkily. "One minute I was in my ship, then something shining caught the edge of my sight. I turned my head, and the next thing I knew I was smothered in a net with a hook at the end of it. That's the last I remember till I woke up lying in this cage. And there wasn't so much as a cushion to lie on, that day," I concluded savagely.

There was another silence. Then Iri said: "I'm empowered to offer you a choice of two proposals, Duncan.

"You can go with one of our crews back where we got you, and guide them to a male and female of your species, of suitable age and other characteristics. If you do that, we'll drop you on your home planet. We'll take a chance of your talking—getting a couple of your promising sort would be worth the risk."

"Or?" I said. "I'm not a traitor."

"Or you can stay here, and your life will be spared. You will continue to be used as experimental material—this time on a practical basis."

"Meaning?"

"Meaning that you will mate with—with one of our women. The object will be to find out if our two breeds are mutually fertile. It's our last desperate chance to step up our population by introducing new blood before our people become too few to carry on our civilization."

A thought struck me.

"Did you volunteer for this—service? Or are you under orders?"

Moonlight doesn't reflect colors. But her warm apricot skin distinctly darkened.

"I'm under orders," she said. "I—I like you personally too, Duncan—that would be necessary. But I'm the nearest to the change of the women on our staff, yet I'm far enough away from it for there to be time to see if the experiment would work."

I looked at her skeptically. Women on Chlyntha must reach the menopause a lot earlier than ours do, or I was being kidded.

"Give me time to think," I said. "This isn't something I can decide in a hurry; my whole future's at stake. I take it that if I refuse either offer, I'll be—processed like the other 'specimens?'"

Iri nodded. "I'll give you till tomorrow night," she said, turning toward the door. I was still standing where she'd frozen me. She lifted her hand again, palm up, and I unfroze. She went out, locking the door behind her.

I didn't sleep much that night. And the next day I had too much to think about to take the trouble to keep my back turned to my public or to make faces at them, as I had rather childishly been doing. I had only till evening to make up my mind, and I hadn't a useful idea. I stood apathetically at the bars, gazing out abstractedly at the crowd clustered before my cage. It must have been some kind of holiday—there were more of them than usual: the men with their feather beards, the women, the children.

All at once I got a flash. I thought I must be wrong, but when I made a point of it I found I was right. What Iri had been hinting at snapped into place, though I still couldn't see the whole picture.

All the women were young. And all the children were little girls.

I remembered another thing. Naturally the conversation around me at the evening research on Specimen Me was mostly confined to the subject a hand. But one night I heard the man I thought of as the Chief Doctor say to Iri, of some fascinating X-ray plate of some portion of my anatomy: "I wish your parent could have lived to see this!" And Iri had answered: "Yes, it always predicted we'd find a specimen with an arrangement like that."

"Your parent," and "it."

Were the Chlynthans hermaphrodites?

No, plainly the men were men and the women were women. Then what? And where were the little boys? Where were the old women? But I hadn't time right then to puzzle things out. I had to figure out what I was going to do.

One thing I *wasn't* going to do, and that was to agree in good fatth to help the Chlynthans kidnap either a Terran or Martian-colony couple the way I had been kidnaped.

But the alternative was to spend the remainder of my life on Chlyntha, to all effects a prisoner even if perhaps no longer a zoo exhibit, and an experimental stud for Iri and presumably for any other Chlynthan woman who wanted to try me out or could be coerced into taking me on. And I'd always liked to do my own picking.

What I needed was something to bargain from. Perhaps an offer, if the experiment should be successful, to go back as a missionary and recruit a batch of unattached Terrans, male and female, to help them bring their population back to par? But there was no way, that I could make foolproof, to pretend such a scheme and then double-cross them, and I had no intention of doing any such thing in earnest.

I was so absorbed that I even let the crowd watch me eat my evening meal. One little devil got a nice long stick and poked me through the bars while I was eating, to see what I would do, and her mother—her parent?—only laughed instead of smacking her—it? I just went on eating.

Iri had said she was near the change. She might possibly be 25, though she didn't look a day over 20 of our years. The period of fertility of mammals is conditioned by their life expectancy. These weren't short-lived people; I once heard a white-feathered man in the crowd say to a woman: "You wouldn't remember that, child; it was all of 50 years ago, when I was young."

The synthetic but adequate food I was eating tasted vaguely, I thought in a corner of my mind, like fried oysters.

Oysters. I suddenly remembered the life-history of some species of oysters. Then I knew.

And I knew the only thing I could do that had even a possibility of success. I had about one chance in a thousand of putting it over. But nothing else I could think of had any chance at all.

I had thought my little confab with Iri would take place after the usual evening session of being punched and pinched and X-rayed and injected. But when they came for me I found the whole staff assembled in the consultation room, with the one I called the Chief Doctor installed at the head of the table. There were ten of them all told, two women besides Iri, and seven men. With my new perspective I noticed how young the girls were, and how far from young the men.

Nur, they called the Chief Doctor—I suppose, like Iri, it was a title rather than a name. He started in on me right away.

"I hear from Iri that you have learned to speak human language rather well, space creature," he began. . . . , "Iri tells me also that our two proposals have been submitted to you. Have you decided which you will accept?"

I went right to it.

"Before deciding," I said, "I'd like first to get some things straight in my own mind.

"As I gather from what I've observed and from Iri's hints, your people are all born female. After a time, I don't know when, some kind of hormone change takes place and you are transformed into males. We have some creatures on my own planet which go through a similar cycle. We call them oysters."

"Are they the dominant race?" One of the men wanted to know.

"Not exactly. But am I right?"

"Naturally," said Nur, looking at me like a teacher confronting a willing but particularly stupid pupil. "That is the normal development of a human being."

"On my planet that isn't the way human beings develop. We are born either male or female, about an equal number of each. And we stay whichever we are as long as we live."

I could feel a distinct tremor of shock going around the table. "Incredible!" murmured a woman; her head-feathers were quivering. "Obscene!" "Disgusting!" That was two of the men.

"We don't find it so. In fact, my people would feel the same way about you."

"But *we* are the normal ones," remarked Nur complacently. "Go on."

"The way I work it out, your women bear children just as ours do. Then after the change, they become completely masculine and can function as fathers instead of mothers."

"Of course. All the men here have been mothers, and now most of us are fathers."

"Then what's to prevent families getting all mixed up? I mean, women would be having children by—say the men who used to be their older sisters, or even their—"

"I won't stay to listen to this!" a woman exclaimed, jumping to her feet. Even Iri looked horrified.

"Sit down, Raki," Nur said. "The space creature knows no better. It didn't mean to be offensive." He turned to me. "That," he stated, "is something that never has occurred and never could occur. People don't change their personalities because they change their sex; relatives keep up their old ties. I am the mother of two daughters and the father of one, and I can assure you that the fathers of my older children and the mother of my youngest child are all completely unrelated to me or to one another.

"In fact, the very mention of such a thing is an obscenity so dreadful that this it literally the first time those words have ever crossed my lips—and if you'll glance around you at the faces of my staff you'll realize they have never heard them openly expressed before."

"I see. I apologize if I have offended you; as you say, it is only my ignorance that is at fault. And here is another thing in which I shall doubtless display my ignorance again.

"Our two species being so fundamentally different, I doubt extremely whether they could be mutually fertile. You probably took it for granted that all mammals have your sexual history. But even supposing we could interbreed, what makes you think that I, one single man, could restore the population-deficit of your whole planet?"

"We don't," said Nur calmly. "We have chosen Iri to make the experiment—we too have no idea whether it will succeed or not. You are merely the most promising of the creatures from every portion of the Galaxy we have captured during more than ten years of scouting. If the experiment does succeed, then naturally we shall invade and conquer your planet, and use its inhabitants as breeding animals."

Swell.

"Tell me," I said, "at what age can your females become mothers?"

"At about 15. And the change comes on about ten years later."

"That is a very short period—in my world it is about 30 years. Still, in ten years a woman ought to be able to bear four or five children. Why isn't that sufficient to keep your world populated and your civilization going?"

"You don't understand, space creature. The change doesn't come overnight; it is very slow. It takes over 20 years to be completed, and during most of our lives we are neither male nor female, but neuter, unable to either bear or beget offspring. And the period of male fertility also lasts only another ten years or so. That is why every woman during her fertile period must have as many mates as possible; out of 30 or 40 men she may find only two or three who are able to give her a child. And if a man fails with one woman, logically it would be useless for him to try again with another. Our female phase seems to be definitely more fertile than our male phase."

Ah! That was what I had been devoutly hoping to hear. I had made a lucky guess. Here was my one chance in a thousand.

"Nur, ladies and gentlemen, including my charming proffered mate Iri," I said slowly and solemnly, "I can solve your problem. I can solve it without involving any more of my own kind. Among other things I have made a special investigation—" I hadn't, but let that pass—"of fertility and sterility. Our research on our planet—and there is no reason why it should not apply equally to yours—shows that 75 per cent of sterility is chargeable to the female partner.

"In other words, you have been managing the whole of your society the wrong way around. If you want more people here on Chlyntha, you must reverse the process. Each woman much have only one mate, but each man must become a father by many women. Why, we have examples in our history where one man has fathered 200 or more children by what we call his wives and concubines. There is your solution."

And what a Moslem Paradise *that* would be, I reflected privately—a wish-fulfilment dream of Don Juan! I could see looks of disagreement on the faces of the staff; of bewilderment, of antagonism—but also looks of dawning revelation. There was a long silence.

"You are proposing," said Nur finally, "you, a half-human being from an inferior culture, not even evolved enough to have developed Galactic travel, that we alter the whole social structure of Chlyntha, with its antiquity stretching back for untold thousands of years?"

"If you want to increase your population," I answered stubbornly.

Most of the faces were stony. Only Iri's had a light in it; I always knew Iri was the best of the bunch.

"Try it," I urged. "Try it for a year. Compare the births at the end of the year with those of the year before. If it doesn't work out the way I predict it will, then I'll agree to the experiment you wanted. And if that doesn't succeed, you'll kill me and stuff me and put me in your museum—and you'll have lost nothing.

"Under no circumstances, I may add, would I ever have agreed to your alternative proposal, to put the finger on others of my own kind. That's out."

I kept my eyes on Nur. He was the leader. Whatever conclusion he came to, the others would follow. And whatever conclusion they came to, their whole world would follow—it was clearly one monolithic totalitarian state.

At last Nur smoothed back the white feathers of his head and looked me coolly in the eye.

"And if by some lucky guess you are right, space creature," he said, "what do you expect in return?"

"Only to be taken home again and left there."

"But if we do that, what guarantee have we that you will not reveal our location and arouse your fellow-beings to take vengeance against us?"

"You know I couldn't do that—we have no starships. And further, you could keep me under sedation all the way and deliver me unconscious. That way I couldn't possibly find out your co-ordinates."

"We might still be discovered ultimately by trial and error."

"In my world," I said, "We have a profound taboo. It is, among decent people—of whom I hope you have decided I am one—never to break a promise made on one's sacred honor. I so pledge you that I will keep this whole story secret forever."

Nur looked at me meditatively.

"Very interesting," he said at last. "Take it back, Iri, and then return here. We must discuss this for a long time."

My heart began to beat again, but I felt pretty weak. They hadn't said no. And if they said yes, even if my theory proved wrong, at least I'd have had a year's reprieve to think out another plan.

For a week I was left alone in my cage. The evening sessions had ended. Instead of the regular keepers, it was Iri who brought me my meals and cleaned up after me. She was as pretty as ever, but she didn't need to freeze me to keep me off. I'd lost my appetite for Chlynthan girls now that I'd become aware of their future.

I knew I had put it over, the day Nur himself directed my removal from the cage. I was taken to a comfortable room, furnished according to the sketches I had made for them when they first settled me in my quarters in the zoo. I couldn't read their tapebooks, and they seemed to have nothing to correspond to our Tridimens shows, but I kept myself busy.

I began this account about six months ago. I didn't dare ask for writing materials, but I found the absorbent plastic they use for towels makes a pretty good paper; by using it sparingly for both purposes (it's flushed away after use), I never required more than a normal amount. They have no typewriters, but I learned as a hobby in boyhood how to write by hand, and as a writing medium I used a fallen feather from the crest of one of my own attendants, dipped in a coffee-like drink they give me every morning, and which I poured into my extra cup—I pretended one day that I'd broken mine and thrown it down the disposal chute—which I kept secreted. I am rather proud of my ingenuity; it reminds me of an ancient book I once saw televised, called "Robinson Crusoe."

There was a window in my room, and I could look down from it. I was still in the zoo grounds—I could see the crowds of visitors, but they could no longer see me. It seemed to me I could see more groups of one man and several women, and fewer of one woman and several men.

I have wondered what emotional upheavals, what psychological crisis, must be stirring those beings whose age-long way of life was being forcibly reversed. What an opportunity for an anthropologist, as well as for a sociologist or a psychologist!

Iri had apparently gone back to being the Iri, whatever that was, of the laboratory staff. I didn't see her again. I missed her; I wondered if she missed me: she had been the nearest approach to a personal friend I had known on Chlyntha. The people who fed me and housekept for me were strangers. The door of my room was always kept locked, of course; I was still a prisoner. But outside my window was a balcony, where I could exercise and get fresh air and sunshine. The time went faster than I had anticipated—too fast, if my informed guess should prove wrong.

It was their summer when I was taken from the cage,

and now it is summer again. Yesterday was the pay-off. I had a sudden visit from Nur. I barely had time to turn the written sheets over to look like towels, and to put my cup and feather under my pillow. The keepers came at regular times, so I'd grown a bit careless.

"Space creature," Nur said gravely, "you are very fortunate.

"I don't know by what lucky fluke you settled on the solution of a problem that had baffled our best minds for so long. You are very popular with our men," he commented, with the first smile I had ever seen on his face, "but not quite so popular with some of the women, including your friend Iri. However, they can console themselves with the prospect of getting their own back later."

"You mean—" I said breathlessly.

"The statistics have been compiled. The number of births on Chlyntha is almost twice as great in the past year as in the year before."

I was dizzy with relief.

"And now—" my voice was unsteady—"when will you take me home?"

"The helicopter will come for you tomorrow. It will take you to our laboratory, which I'm sure you remember, and we'll administer your sedation there, so you'll be unconscious when you're transferred. That is the best way to manage your journey, don't you think?"

"Whatever you say," I answered. I was too excited to care about details. . . .

That tomorrow is today. I woke up very early for my last day on Chlyntha. Soon through my window I shall see the helicopter that is to take me to the laboratory, and then to the starship. With counter-gravity, no matter how many parsecs away from Sol I am, it can only be a few months before they land me on Mars or Terra, it doesn't matter which.

All that remains is to get rid of this manuscript before they come for me. I hate to do it—it has been the comfort and companion of my imprisonment—but of course I couldn't take it with me: that or anything else except the clothes I came in, which I suppose they have kept.

I wonder how long I have been away, in terms of our own time. Will the babies I left on Earth be old people now? Will it be safe ever to tell my story? Will they believe it if I do? How far, actually, am I bound by my pledged word to alien beings who kidnaped me and kept me captive?

Well, all that I can make my mind up about when I'm back again. And even if I have to remake my whole life and rebuild all my associations, I shall have come home!

"And now," said the museum guide in an impersonal monotone, "in this glassed case you see, just as it was in life, the most nearly humanoid creature from outer space in the entire collection.

"It is almost as intelligent as a real human being. In fact, it was even able, by a lucky guess, to be of some service to us, its superiors. But, like all nonhuman creatures, it was also stupid.

"In return for its service, it asked for replanetation, and it actually seems to have believed it would receive it. The Nur of that time, a Chlythan noted for its single-minded devotion to our glorious world, has recorded that it itself felt some compunction at having to 'break faith' with so remarkably humanoid a space creature; but of course, as the Nur remarked, the first and highest virtue is loyalty to one's own planet.

"The sheets of plastic lying beneath the creature's hand, written on in an indecipherable language, were in its possession when the museum helicopter pilot, approaching the window to pick the space creature up, arrested it by the freezing gesture. By the Nur's order, this diary or apologia or whatever it may be was preserved when the creature was prepared for the museum after a painless death at the Disposery. . . ."

The Transit of Venus

Nobody really knows when the rite of the Buti-contest began. Some archeologists place it as far back as the 20th century, which seems improbable; but it is undoubtedly very old. We do know that in its origin it was far from the quasi-religious ceremony it is today. Myths and legends seem to indicate that in the beginning it was merely a sort of display of physical pulchritude, and that any tests for superiority in other fields were very superficial. Indeed, the name itself is an adaptation of the word "beauty."

Nowadays, as everybody knows, the Buticontest fills the same place that was filled in ancient Greece by the Olympic Games. (It is interesting to note that our remote ancestors appear to have made some attempt also to revive these same Olympic Games, back in the Terran Era, with men as well as women participating; but as they made a fetish of the purely athletic aspects of excellence, and neglected the intellectual ones, advancing civilization put an end to them.)

It is no secret to the sophisticated that interplanetary politics and diplomacy play their part both in selecting the Buticontest contestants and in awarding the prizes. If contestants from the Colonial Planets were not given some latitude, a Terran girl would always be crowned as

Queen. Terra has so many more human inhabitants than any other planet that the choice is infinitely greater, and short of emergence of a supermutant elsewhere, the laws of probability would practically insure a Terran victory. If girls from Mars, Venus, Luna, Ceres, Ganymede, and Titan had to compete on equal terms with those from Terra, they would soon become disheartened and in the end we should have no entries from the colonies at all—which would mean the gradual extinction of our most important symbol of interplanetary solidarity. Nevertheless, there are rigid rules which apply to all contestants, breaking of which means disqualification.

It is for this same reason of interplanetary unity that the Buticontest is held every five years, instead of annually as once was the case; distances are so vast that more time is required for local elections and for the far-flung visits of the reigning Queen.

Since every child knows all about the Buticontest, and every girl almost from infancy dreams of some day being able to compete in it, the scanner may wonder why anyone should devote even a few feet of tape to it. What every child does not know, however, and few adults have ever known (for this story has been hidden in the official archives for centuries and has only recently been released), is that once there was a Buticontest which went wrong. It happened in 2945.

The sponsoring Terran Region that year was the American, and of course AR's twin colony is Venus, just as the Eurasian Region's is Mars, and so on. So Miss Venus of that year was a matter of special interest— though naturally that was no guarantee that she would win.

But win she did. And then all thunderation broke loose. For only two days later it was revealed (a) that Miss Venus was actually a Terran by birth (worse, from the northern section of AR), who had lived for less than a year on Venus; (b) that her doctorate in nuclear physics was a fraud; and (c) that she had not really paraded entirely nude, as was the strict rule then as now, but had worn a close-fitting plastic sheath which revealed her measurements but concealed any possible defects of surface.

It was, of course, what is still archaically called a newspaperman who first trumpeted aloud this glaring scandal.

"Miss Venus a Phony, Exposed by Anonymous Letter," videoshouted the Interplanetary Network in its Latest News Report, by Our Special Correspondent Kitsayo Okamura. "Buticontest Invalidated."

He went on. "Sobbing, lovely Aletta Braun, Miss Venus, this quinquennium's Buticontest Queen, confessed to Contest Director Tubaj Mgambo that she was a ringer. 'I did it for love,' she said."

And so on and so on.

The archives do not go much farther. A lid was clamped down, discussion ceased, the next Buticontest took place as scheduled, and pretty soon the whole affair was forgotten. If anyone wondered what had happened to the discredited Queen, he was met with bland evasions. So far as public knowledge went, she had vanished, disappeared.

Here is the real story.

Aletta Braun was, as said, born in the northern section of the American Region of Terra, in 2927. Outside of the few gangling years of pre-adolescence, she was noted both for her beauty and her intelligence; she was a bright and lovely baby, child, and young girl.

But from the beginning it was evident to her worried parents that she also possessed a strange atavistic quirk which made her almost a mutation.

She never adjusted. Her pedianalyst said she had never dealt with a child so obstructive to social conformism. She never wanted to do any of the things she should want to do, and what she wanted to do was things that were unheard of, dangerous, insane, and almost subversive.

For example, from kindergarten on she flunked elementary physics, biophysics, chemistry, and biochemistry. Her parents caught her several times reading smuggled tapes of ancient verse and fiction.

When she became nubile, she refused to have her mate-computation made; instead, she announced openly, to her parents' horror, that "somewhere there must be a man she could love and who would love her"—irrespective of their genetic compatibility.

As she developed physically, she made herself ridiculous and became the butt of her schoolmates by refusing any longer to remove all her clothing when she came into the temperature-regulated building; even in summer she wore some kind of garment reaching from her neck to her knees. She was expelled from three schools for this obscenity. Her pubertanalyst recommended that she be sent to a school for special children, but these all declined to accept her; they did not take cases so far removed from normality.

Her parents' duty was clear; they should have reported her at once to the Deviate Department, just as if she had been born with some physical or mental abnormality. They did not do so because they were weak, ashamed, and frightened. (This argues that they themselves were reportable cases, and perhaps accounts for some of their daughter's difficulties.)

When she reached voting age, at 18, she could not be enrolled as a citizen of the Federation, for she was not able to present evidence of a degree, an occupation, and listing in the Reproduction Selection roster.

What was to be done with her? With criminal foolishness, her parents, fearing discovery and disgrace, took her with them on a holiday trip to Venus—and abandoned her there.

The colonies, as is well known, are even more conventional and rigidly conformist than the mother-planet. There was no possibility that so deviant a creature as Aletta could make a normal life for herself there. The older Brauns simply fled like the cravens they were, leaving their problem child on the doorstep of the Venerian government. It developed later that they had doped Aletta with Narcosin one night, and departed while she was sleeping. By her bed they deposited a farewell tape they had spoken secretly in her absence, together with a substantial sum in Venerian credits. They had booked return passage without her knowledge, and by the time she awoke they were already on their way home. Back on Terra, they changed their name and moved out of the American Region altogether. To their new acquaintances they said that they had never had a child; that Reproduction Selection had listed them as N-3—permitted to mate but not to reproduce. All this was discovered by detectives employed by the Buticontest Committee after the fiasco and noted in the recently released secret file.

Their whole action was reprehensible, but not so callous, so far as Aletta herself was concerned, as it may seem. From the beginning, she had been mostly a source of distress and anxiety to them; how could they love a child who was like a changeling? And naturally Aletta reciprocated. As a matter of fact, when she woke up that morning and found the tape and played it back, her reaction was one of relief and gratitude. She checked with the hotel and found her parents had paid for her room for a month in advance. She had a month in which to plan a life on her own.

Since she could not qualify for any work requiring a degree, she was reduced to reading proof in the Venerian Microfilm Office. (It was that which gave her the opportunity to steal the forms for her forged certificate of birth on Venus and her forged diploma as a Doctor of Nuclear Physics.) It wasn't much fun, she was lonely and bored and resentful, but even a person as misdirected and aberrant as Aletta Braun was obliged to acknowledge that she had brought all this on herself by her wilful contravention of all the mores of her era.

She was ripe for trouble. And trouble came in the shape of another variant—this time a native Venerian colonist. Jonny Velanco was three years older than Aletta, goodlooking by rather outmoded standards (he was not balding in youth as is normal nowadays), with a greenish tinge to his dark skin that suggested a misalliance with an indigenous Venerian somewhere in his family tree. (In the first days of the colony, it will be remembered, Solar Federation laws were pretty loosely enforced.)

Jonny's parents had both died in the Great Flood of 2925, when he was only a year old. He had accordingly been reared as a state ward, which perhaps accounts for his own aberrations. He did not share all Aletta's peculiarities, but though he was a registered plastic engineer with a good government job, and though he was listed as A-1 on the Reproduction Selection roster, he had found some way to evade every proposed mating, and was perhaps the only bachelor of 21 on all Venus.

How an engineer met a mere microfilm proofreader is not known; it is almost unthinkable, but, considering the persons concerned, within the realm of possibility, that Jonny and Aletta may have become acquainted by what in ancient times used to be known vulgarly as a pickup. What *was* discovered later was that both these near-criminals fell immediately into a relationship which in Aletta's confession she fatuously described as "being in love."

The recently released story from the archives gives the confession in detail. The following points are of interest: 1. Reluctantly the discredited contestant acknowledged that the first suggestion of her entering the Buticontest had come from Velanco. She herself, she shamelessly added, agreed enthusiastically and welcomed it as "a good joke and a chance to get even with the stuffy old officials," and she it was who had forged the birth certificate and the diploma. Jonny, as a plastics engineer, was able to provide the skintight film which she wore in contravention of the requirement of full nudity. 2. (in her own words) "I wouldn't tell you that much, except that Jonny is safely hidden where you can't find him and punish him, and you will never get me to tell you where he is." 3. Who sent the anonymous tape to the authorities which betrayed her, she professed not to know: "I didn't think I had an enemy on Venus. All I can guess is that it must have been some girl who wanted Jonny for herself. But how she or anybody could have found out, I can't imagine; nobody knew but us. We must have been overheard."

The committee must have heard all this with disquietude; they had enough on Velanco to accuse him as an accessory simply from his having furnished the plastic film. But it was true that they had lost him.

And it was true that their detectives had not yet found any clue to the author of the anonymous letter. They were inclined to agree with Aletta that it was the work of a jealous woman, and that worried them more than anything else; it argued that the younger generation, on Venus as on Terra and perhaps throughout the Solar System, was more dangerously infected with this "love" heresy than anybody had dreamed. They would much rather have believed that Aletta Braun and, to a lesser extent, Jonny Velanco were merely solitary freaks. (As all students of history know, they were correct; such cases of atavism may still occur, very occasionally, but there has never been any wave of youthful abnormality such as they feared.)

That is where matters rested at the end of the first report from the secret file. All that remained was to decide what to do with the disgraced delinquent. No sentence had ever been set for such an offense, since it had never entered anyone's head that so audacious a fraud would ever be perpetrated.

Their first move was to clamp down on any more publicity. In their first shock they had let the thing get almost out of hand. When the anonymous tape arrived, and then, immediately on its heels, Special Correspondent Kitsayo Okamura videocasted his scoop, they had been caught completely unprepared; all they did was to call Miss Venus in to explain. If they had hoped she would disprove the videoman's charges, they were sadly disappointed. Very soon she broke down—in fact, her first words were, "How did he find out?"

(How he found out was soon discovered. Descendant of a people who were pioneers in nudism, his sharp eye had detected an infinitesimal wrinkle in the plastic covering. He had communicated his suspicion to a colleague in the northern section of the American Region, who had relayed to him Aletta's abnormal career on Terra. A robot clerk he kept bribed with daily oiling had then informed him of the anonymous letter—and was disassembled for it at once.)

Hastily the authorities took steps to hush the thing up. The 2945 Buticontest, they announced, would be considered as never having occurred. The next contest would be held, not in 2950, but in 2946, with the same contestants—minus Aletta Braun. Henceforth, they added virtuously, every entrant would be subjected to intensive personal examination and investigation of her eligibility.

The next tape released from the archives includes the detective's report mentioned earlier. Aletta's parents had now been located, but they refused to take custody of her, and since she was of legal age they could not be compelled to do so. Naturally, she was no longer welcome as a resident of Venus, and would never again be able to find a job there. Terra wouldn't have her back, and all the other colonies, when approached, refused her as an emigrant. One member of the Buticontest Committee was indiscreet enough to let remain on the tape his exasperated remark: "I wish to Space we still had those ancient scavengers known as Gungangsters, so we could hire one of them to bump her off quietly!"

But something had to be done with her. And the only remaining answer was the Deviate Department. Aletta Braun was ordered to report to them the following morning for a brainbath, to transform her (as should have been done in childhood) into a normal citizen.

If, even as long ago as 2945, they had had the equivalent of what used to be known as prisons, there would have been no further difficulties. But the officials underestimated the extent of Aletta's abnormality; it did not even occur to them that after their unanimous ruling she would not report for treatment the next morning.

The next morning Aletta Braun had vanished—as completely as had Jonny Velanco.

And now it is my privilege to announce that I myself, as an archeologist of some standing, have made and authenticated a discovery that will excite all historians, and that amply justifies the retelling of this perhaps trivial incident. To archeology and history no episodes of the past are trivial, for they all help to build up the detailed record of our civilization. To fill the smallest gap in this narrative is an important achievement.

For the past two years an expedition under my direction has been excavating in the ruins of Venus Northwest, destroyed in the Second Flood of 3102. In the site known technically as S-X 74, which before the flood was a reservation for Venerrian indigenes, my robots dug up, among the primitive artifacts, a 30th century enduramic tape, still in good recording condition.

This was a sufficiently startling discovery, since the indigenes, though of course humanoid and even fairly advanced, had a completely non-mechanical culture, and those living on reservations (the last full-blood died, as every student knows, some 500 years ago) were kept as living museum exhibits, with no access to civilized mechanisms.

It can be imagined with what curiosity I had the tape played off. And I could hardly contain myself when I found that it was—and this is the revelation I am now making popularly known, after a confidential technical report to an executive session of the Interplanetary Association for the Advancement of Science—a complete solution of that long-ago mystery arising from the failed Buticontest of 2945.

For 90 years after they vanished, Jonny Velanco and Aletta Braun lived as Venerian natives in that reservation in Venus Northwest!

After Velanco died, Aletta—still the arrogant rebel she had been at 18—taped and hid this record, so that, as she said, "it would be discovered on some faroff day how well she and Jonny had fooled the authorities and managed to live their own free lives." The account will thus be of interest to criminologists and deviational psychologists as well as to archeologists and historians.

Jonny Velanco had been a plastic engineer. It is possible, as I have said, that he had a remote Venerian ancestor of his own; in any event, he had always been interested in the natives and was familiar with their appearance, customs, and language.

When Aletta had caught up his suggestion that she compete fraudulently in the Buticontest, he had warned her that there was always a possibility she might be betrayed. She flouted the idea, but since she was, as she said, "in love" with him she agreed, to please him, to take the precautions he urged on her.

He made for both of them a perfect plastic covering—how I wish either of these had survived the centuries; the man must have been a misdirected genius—which, with various postures, gestures, and speech which he taught her, transformed them into undetectable indigenes. Since there were always a few "tame" natives in the cities, they would be unobserved en route to the reservation. Frequently, Aletta said in her narrative, they had donned these disguises and spent what seemed to her delightful evenings together, completely unsuspected.

When Okamura made his videocast, they acted at once. Jonny wanted her to disappear with him, but Aletta could not resist the "fun" of a public showdown and a confession adorned with fake sobs. As soon as she was ordered to the Deviate Department, she went home, put on the disguise, and followed him to the Venus Northwest Reservation. They had visited it together, in disguise, several times previously, and had been accepted by the indigenes as fellow-aborigines. They had no difficulty in settling down there permanently—and no repugnance to living the uncivilized life of the native Venerian. In the privacy of their own hut, of course, they could always shed their masquerade. They must never have dared, however, to have a child.

It may be wondered what would have happened to their "love affair" if Aletta had not been unmasked. As Buticontest Queen she would have moved in a very different sphere from his.

Jonny Velanco saw to that. He had planned from the beginning to make possible their strange future alone together. He confessed it to her on his deathbed, and it was the climax of Aletta's taped bequest to posterity.

He, who had put the idea in her mind in the first place, was also the author of the anonymous letter which brought about her exposure.

All in Good Time

Good morning, ladies and gentlemen, and welcome to your first session in my course.

Before we get down to cases ... That was a pun, class, and you're supposed to laugh at my jokes—haven't you been told yet that old Dr. Hunnicott is the campus character, the faculty's prize eccentric?

Before we get down to cases, then, let's get some things straight. You are first-year students in this law school, which is a graduate school of the university. You will find things a bit different from your experience in undergraduate work, wherever in any of the Three Planets your colleges were located.

Hitherto you have been instructed by tridimens and tapings, and your reports and papers have been graded by cybercom. They will still be so graded, but now for the first time you will be face to face with your instructors. You're going to be asked questions and will have to give immediate answers; I know that's going to be hard for some of you to take, unaccustomed as we all are nowadays to direct communication. But it isn't just an archaic holdover; when a few of you—just a few, I must remind you sadly—have completed your courses and taken your bar examinations and been admitted to practice in the Interplanetary Courts, you'll find that law in some respects lags behind the other learned professions.

For example, I see some of you having difficulty already in understanding everything I am saying to you. For those who have always spoken vulgar and colloquial Intervox, and know no other language, learning to understand and speak classical Intervox, with its outdated words and strict attention to grammar, is going to be almost like acquiring a new tongue. But that is the language of the courts, and you're going to have to reconcile yourselves to it. If you find it too hard or too distasteful, it's not yet too late to transfer to medicine or education or engineering.

But if our language indicates a cultural lag, I can assure you that our procedure does not. Law has kept abreast or ahead of all the other disciplines. To demonstrate this, it is my custom, at the beginning of every term, to plunge you eager embryo attorneys headfirst into consideration of some quite modern case. That will not only convince you of the contemporaneous nature of our jurisprudence—that's right, make a note of the words you don't understand, and look them up afterwards, instead of wasting our time now—but it will also give me a chance to find out how you respond to the give-and-take of a live lecture. Your other instructors will cover their particular specialties; old Dr. Hunnicott's function is to give you a broad orientation.

Yes?—you with the red hair—I don't know your names yet. Oh, I thought you were asking a question. No apologies needed—I often make people yawn.

The case I'm using this time as a preliminary example of the legal approach dates from 2160, only 23 years ago. It was quite celebrated in its day, and may even be known to some of you—though I should say your average age is about 25, so you couldn't have been very much interested at the time.

What's the matter, young lady? Didn't you get enough sleep last night, either? I promise you the dry part of my discourse is about over.

In fact, I hope it will wake you all up when I tell you that this is a criminal case in the realm of sex-relationships—to be precise, a trial for bigamy. It is the case of Government vs. Summers, Interplan 78,-239-60NY.

To give you the necessary background, Halton Summers, the accused, was at that time 38 years old, a historian by profession—in fact, I believe some of his historical tapings are still used in colleges, and some of you may have scanned them.

He was married, and in 2160 had been for 12 years married, to one Marion Garth, an architect—though her occupation does not enter into the case. They had no children, and apparently on the husband's side, at least, the marriage had ceased to be a happy one, though neither had any grounds for divorce. The wife seems to have been not so much jealous as possessive; she demanded a good deal more of her husband's attention than is customary in our modern unions. As a matter of fact, they were both bored with each other, but expressed it in different ways. With Summers, it took the form of spending as much time as possible away from home—home being a servo-unit on the edge of the metropolis, only 20 minutes, even by slow copter, from the old city of Manhattan: I mention this to note that they were not suburbanites or exurbanities, and therefore were not afflicted with any of the well-known emotional disturbances common among people suffering from agrarian neurosis. (You will find, ladies and gentlemen, that frequently legal problems are entangled with medical ones, as Dr. Singh, your professor of psychosomatic jurisprudence, will soon make clear to you.)

Summer's special interest in history was the mid-20th century—as those of you who may have scanned any of his tapes will be aware. As a registered member of the Interplanetary Historical Association, he had, of course, a license to use his regional time-traveler, in order to verify or elaborate points in his researches.

Yes?—the gentleman with the Martian haircut, in the third row.

Oh, perhaps I should explain that; neither Mars nor Venus has time-travelers yet, since the history of both colonies is so recent. On Earth we have government-owned instruments—I'm not mechanically-minded, and I've never seen one, but I understand they are collapsible capsules dialed for place and time and for duration of stay—in each of the five federated regions. Their use is limited to qualified persons—government officials, law enforcement officers and privateyes, historians and archaeologists, and some other scholars. Licensed users have to apply in advance for a booking, just as you would make a reservation for a space-berth. Does that answer your question?

Well, Halton Summers naturally had occasion to use the time-traveler a good deal. His usual system, when he was working on a book, was to go as far as he could with recorded secondary material—discs, microtapes, and the preserved old print-on-paper books which were still in use 200 years ago, and then reserve passage on the time-traveler, to consult first-hand sources—to talk to the persons concerned, read contemporary newspapers and magazines, see their newsreels and television interviews, all that sort of thing. According to his wife's testimony in the court trial, he usually taped a book every two years or so, and during that period was absent in the 20th century for four to six visits on each book, each visit lasting from three to ten days.

What? I don't think that's exactly relevant, but if it will make it easier for you to understand the case—

Yes, I believe all qualified persons must not only show complete familiarity with the exact language of the time and place they visit, back to 3000 years ago, as far as the time-travelers can reach in their present stage of development, but they must also know the customs, beliefs, manners, and technical development of the time and place they visit, so that they are able to pass without question as contemporaries. Government specialists provide them with the proper clothing and equipment. And all license-holders are conditioned psychologically, so that it is impossible for them to reveal to any person in the past that they have come from the future.

Well, as I was saying— Did somebody else have a question? Oh, yes, the lady from the African Region.

No, I don't think any of the visitors could—how did you put it?—influence history by any action of his in the past. Whatever he did would only change history as it has come down to us. And please don't raise the issue of his killing his grandfather—that old fallacy has long since been exploded. If he'd killed his grandfather in the past he would never have been born and so he couldn't be going back now for that purpose.

To return to Marion Garth's testimony during her husband's trial, she said that during the preparation of his last book, which he began late in 2157, his whole procedure had suddenly changed. Instead of going back for a few days, two or three times a year, he began reserving the time-traveler whenever it was not in use by anyone else, and finally it came to the place where he was spending at least three quarters of his time in the mid-20th century. The exact year he was visiting she did not know, since she herself had no access to the time-traveler reservation records, but since his book before that had brought the cultural history of the Newyorko-polis area (that was his particular field of inquiry) up to 1960, that was the most likely date.

Her always latent suspicions having been aroused, she determined to find out why her husband went away so often and stayed away so long every time. Another woman would have queried or challenged him—as perhaps she would have done in the earlier, happier days of their marriage; but by this time, though still living together, they were barely on speaking terms.

What she did was to hire a privateye, a well-known practitioner named Stanley Wiggins, to (as she put it) "go back there and see what Hal was up to."

Since Wiggins could scarcely have found out "what Hal was up to" unless Summers was on the spot to be observed, he had to use a time-traveler belonging to another region, at a time when Summers was using their local one. It must have cost her a lot of money, but that didn't seem to bother her. It was almost a year before the privateye could get the use of a free machine at the right moment.

Well, since I told you in the beginning that this was a prosecution for bigamy, you can guess what Wiggins discovered. Summers had married a mid-20th century woman—her name was Enid Harkness—and was cohabiting with her. Moreover, he was about to become a father by her.

Okay, I expected you to be horrified at the idea of a contemporary of ours mating with, and even having a child by, a virtual barbarian—as, from our standpoint, the people of 200 years ago undoubtedly were. Just take it in your stride; you'll learn many still more shocking things when you begin to practice law. And it ill behooves any of our young men who came back from occupation duty on Titan with aboriginal brides—

Sit down, sir, and calm yourself. I know nothing about the private lives of any of you, and there was nothing personal in my remark. If you are so quick to take offense, you don't belong in the law. Wait till some prosecuting attorney really lets go on you some time and you have to keep your temper or the bailifrobot will throw you out of the courtroom!

Very well, then. We now have the background of the Summers case. On information from his wife—his 2160 wife, I mean—backed by the testimony of Privateye Stanley Wiggins, Halton Summers was indicted on a charge of bigamy and tried in the Regional Court.

Now, of course you have no acquaintance as yet with either regional or interplanetary law. That is why, in this introductory lecture, I am taking as illustration, not a case depending on colonial relations or space-scope limitations, but one dealing with a situation as old as human marriage itself.

What I'm trying to get over to you is that law is not merely a set of arbitrary rules, but that common sense is a ruling factor in it. That is especially true of criminal law. Most of you—the ones that get through law school, pass their examinations, and are admitted to the bar— will find yourselves practising as defense attorneys; vacancies in the various Boards of Prosecutors, like vacancies in government service, are few and far between, and the civil service examinations to fill them are ferocious. Unless—which I hope every year, but I seldom find my hope fulfilled—I have a legal genius or two in this class, most of you, as I have said, will wind up in the lower courts, where plain horse sense is just as important as is knowledge of the minute points of recorded decisions. One of my objects in this whole preliminary lecture is to test your ability—since you are still completely laymen—simply to put two and two together and make four.

So I'll tell you right now that Halton Summers was acquitted. One statement by his attorney ended the whole case.

And I'll tell you that the reason for this was not the citing of some obscure decision, but an obvious statement of fact that even a jury—that body of lay citizens which in the old days used to decide whether the defendant was innocent or guilty—would have realized must end in his discharge.

I'm going to give you three minutes to consider the situation and discuss it among yourselves, and then I'm going to ask for suggestions from the class as to *why* Summers was set free. . . .

. . . The three minutes are up, ladies and gentlemen. Who will be the first to brave old Dr. Hunnicott's derision of an inept response?

Ah, there's a courageous young man. Stand up, sir, where we can all see you. What is your conclusion?

Now, that really is a lallapaloosa and a humdinger—which, if you want to know, is ancient slang for what you call a glub.

No, citizen, it was *not* because his 1960 marriage to Enid Harkness was not legal in our eyes. It was entirely legal by the laws of the place and time in which it occurred. And so—to forestall another foolish suggestion—was his marriage to Marion Garth in 2148.

Yes?—the gentleman who got so angry because he

imagined I was insulting his Titanian wife. I'm glad you've cooled down, sir. What is *your* idea?

No, I'm sorry to say you're wrong too. Summers had instituted no secret divorce proceedings against either wife. He was legally married to both of them at the time the alleged offense took place.

Anybody else? Come, come, class, surely you can do better than that.

Ah, our red-haired friend has waked up! Yes, sir, what do you suggest?

Oh, no, quite impossible—remember that the 20th century wife had no idea whatever that her husband came from the future. I suppose Summers gave her some excuse about a job that required traveling, to account for his absences from her. If he disappeared permanently, she could only think that he had deserted her—or that he was dead. Presumably she would make efforts to have him traced, but naturally they would be futile. So it is utterly impossible that she should have appeared suddenly in his defense or even given him any kind of affidavit offering to give him up if the suit against him were quashed. I doubt if people in the 20th century were civilized enough even to make such a gesture—aside from the fact that she had no inkling of his true status.

Dear, dear, this is discouraging. Why, ladies and gentlemen, it's as plain as—as the dome on a space-platform. Can't one of you guess it? Do I have to tell you myself?

All right, the reason Halton Summers was acquitted was—

Good! Let's hope that is a last-minute inspiration. You—the young lady from the African Region.

Ah, at last! Congratulations! At least one member of this class has some aptitude for the commonsense give-and-take of the legal profession as it is actually practised in the lower courts.

That, of course, is the correct answer.

All you had to do—as this young lady finally did—was to ask yourselves just what constitutes bigamy.

Bigamy, ladies and gentlemen, at all periods and in all places, is marriage to two women or two men—*at the same time*.

Simple, wasn't it? Let it be a lesson to you, the next time I call on you to use such brains as you were born with.

Now, before dismissing the class until Thursday morning— Yes, sir, did you have a further question?

How should I know what happened to Halton Summers after his acquittal? I never knew him—for our purposes he is only an interesting criminal case. I haven't the remotest idea whether he remained with Marion Garth or not.

One thing we can be sure of, however—he couldn't leave here permanently and go back to Enid Harkness in 1960, no matter how much he might have wished he could. For one thing, the Interplanetary Historical Association must have expelled him—they're very sensitive to scandal. That would mean he would no longer have access to the time-traveler.

Oh, come, my friend—I'm afraid your métier is to be a crime-fiction writer for the pulptapes, not a lawyer! Granted, he might by some lucky chance have been able to wrangle one last trip back before the IHA expulsion cost him his license—just happened to find the machine free. But he could never have ditched the time-traveler in 1960 and stayed there for good.

Why? Why, because as soon as he had overstayed the period he had reserved the time-traveler for, an officer would be dispatched in another to find him and it and bring them both back here—and that time he certainly wouldn't be acquitted; he'd still be serving a good long sentence in the penal camp on Ceres. And if all that had happened, it would have made a No. 1 story for the sensational tridimens newsreels, and I would certainly have known about it.

Oh, my own guess—I'm not much interested, but I should guess that Marion, who doesn't seem to have been a very pleasant character, would refuse, out of pure spite, to divorce him, and he had no grounds to

divorce her. Probably he's still alive—he'd be only 61—
and still tied to her, still eating his heart out for the little
barbarian of 1960, whom he seems, strangely enough, to
have loved very deeply. And of course he could no
longer earn a living as a historian, without membership
in the IHA, so if he's still living he must be doing some
kind of low-grade work just a cut above the robot occupations—epigraphy or translation or ghost-taping—the
kind of thing that brings in scarcely any money because
most of it could be done better by machines.

So if any of you in your future careers should have
occasion to visit the past, let Halton Summers's fate be a
warning to you never to go native! I'll see you again on
Thursday.

. . . Well, I have only a minute. What is it?

No, no, my boy, let's not go on with the Summers
case. You'll be late for your next class. Eh, *what?*

Oh, good space! Oh, how dreadful! If I'd had the
slightest idea—Do please believe me, I chose the case
just at random, because it made such a nice illustration.

I can understand you wouldn't take your mother's hobby of genealogy very seriously. But if your great-great-
great-great-great grandfather was Halton Summers, and
your great-great-great-great-great grandmother was Enid
Harkness—

Oh, no, I beg of you, *don't* try to look him up, even to
help him! The shock might well drive the poor devil
mad!

The Absolutely Perfect Murder

It was a quiet, domestic evening in the spring of 2146. Mervin Alspaugh and his wife Doreen, snugly ensconced in the viewing room of their living-yacht moored to the roof of a building in lower Manhattan, were separately occupied in private entertainment. Both, with hearing-plugs in their ears, directional conversion-glasses before their eyes, and Sensapills percolating through their blood-streams, were watching, listening to, smelling, tasting, and feeling their favorite telecasts. Doreen as usual was absorbed in advertisements of jewels, furs, new synthetics, and cosmetics; Mervin had switched on a science-ad program. (All telecasts, of course, consisted exclusively of advertisements, aimed at the individual interests of the viewers.) But he was *not* absorbed: under his surface perception his constant preoccupation, which was becoming an obsession, dug into him as always.

How could he murder Doreen and get away with it?

This project, which had begun as a faint wistful dream a year or two ago, had now become the substratum of all his thinking. It was threatening to interfere with his work as a cybernattendant, and that would never do: it must be either fulfilled or repressed.

Now that his situation was clearly and sharply in his

mind, he wondered often why he had ever married her. A combination of propinquity, lack of assertiveness, and loneliness, he supposed. The propinquity had become nerve-wracking, the lack of assertiveness had made him the victim of a nagging, bullying woman, and he no longer looked upon loneliness as an evil, but longed for it as a thirsty man for water. The truth was that he was not the marrying type, and he should have realized it and stayed out.

Divorce? Not a chance. He had no grounds whatever, no matter how lenient the divorce laws had become—not even incompatability, since Doreen had long ago substituted her interests for his and seen to it that he was properly involved in them; these blessed evening hours of separate telecast programs were her only concession. And nothing would have persuaded her to divorce him; she was completely, blandly satisfied with what to him was a persistent torture. The only time he had timidly and indirectly proposed the idea, she had laughed in his face. And if he merely left her without divorce, the police would find him and drag him back.

So there was nothing left, to avoid the wreckage of his own life, except to murder her.

But here again he was up against a seemingly impenetrable barrier. Never in his life had he physically attacked another human being; his knowledge of weapons was non-existent; and he shrank in distaste from the slyness of poison—even if he had known how to obtain any. More frustrating still, even if somehow he could find the means and the courage, there would be a body—a body bigger and heavier than his own—to dispose of. He had not the remotest idea how that could be accomplished. And if it weren't—if he were apprehended, accused, and convicted, as he most certainly would be—what kind of future would that leave him? There was no longer danger of his being executed, as in the old barbarous days, and the Rehabilitation Institutes would probably have seemed like heaven to inmates of even the most advanced prisons of a century or two earlier. But the essence of any imprisonment is the negation of liberty, the enforced absence of privacy, the prohibition of self-direction, and Mervin Alspaugh could see no profit in exchanging one kind of imprisonment for another, for years or for the rest of his existence.

No, there was no way out that he dared risk. And yet he could not endure much longer being tied to a woman he had come to hate.

A groan escaped him: fortunately Dorren, ear-plugged, failed to hear it. He forced his attention back to the program.

A white-coated man, wearing the full synthetic wig of the research scientist, was doing a come-on for the newest of scientific triumphs.

"Aren't we all honestly becoming bored," he was saying, "with what we might call horizontal travel—of 40-minute trips to the uttermost reaches of our little planet, or week-end tours around the solar system and vacation cruises in outer space? Well, a new thrill is possible for those of adventurous spirit—and, I must add, of financial means." (He laughed ingratiatingly, and millions of viewers receiving his message transliterated into their own tongues smiled dutifully at his little joke.) "You can be among the first to experience what might be termed vertical travel.

"Now at last you can not only visit the moon or Mars or Alpha Centauri, but you can travel back into the past. Yes, folks, public time travel has finally come true.

"You can witness the burial of Tutankhamen, the assassination of Julius Caesar, the coronation of Napoleon, the inauguration of the first World President in 2065—and not just see and hear and feel them on a screen, but actually *be* there at the real event. You can visit your native city as you remember it, even if years ago it was razed to provide room for a Redevelopment Complex. You can hunt extinct wild animals in a natural forest, fish in a long ago diverted river. You can relive your own youth.

"You can see the world as it was in any period of the past, behold once more those dear to you who have died before you, make history a living thing."

Mervin Alspaugh sat transfixed. Theoretically, he knew, time travel to the past had been possible for at least five years, ever since the startling discoveries of Haffen and Ngumbo. Carefully trained temperonauts— Okimatu Figlietti was the first—had made journeys up to ten years back and returned safely. But the project had been incredibly complicated, and inexorably secret. The computers in his own department had played a small part, very hush-hush, in the earliest developments, or he would not even have known of them.

But that the range of the Time Transporter had been so far extended, that the general public could participate, that time-travel could now be offered on the same basis as space-travel—that indeed was something new, and the white-coated scientist on the screen was making the first announcement.

A sudden warmth crept through Mervin's chest. Oh, he knew it wouldn't be as easy as the come-on indicated: it would be ferociously expensive, hedged about with all sorts of restrictions, all sorts of rules about secrecy, non-interference, non-liability of the dispatching agency—

But if his life's savings were enough—if he agreed to any and all conditions—if somehow, when he got to a selected time and place, he could escape, lose himself forever and never, never come back to a time with Doreen in it—

He sighed deeply, deflated by common sense. How could he earn his living in a time that did not yet know the only profession for which he was equipped? How could he hope not to be dragged back by the authorities of his own time as soon as he did not return at the scheduled moment? How could he endure the primitive conditions of any century before his own?

The little warmth died. He wrenched his attention back to the tele-ad.

"Now," said the speaker genially, "I know there are all kinds of questions and objections that will immediately occur to you. We are not in a position yet to offer luxury cruises in time as you know them in space. By the very nature of the mechanism of the Time Transporter, there will be strict limitations on where you can go and what you can do when you get there." Mrvin felt himself nodding in sad agreement. "At first this is going to be a project barred to the very old, the disabled physically, and those of modest means.

"But just one week from today, the first Time Transportation offices will open in every city on earth. Your local visinews will give you the details. You will be able to get full information there. And some of those whom I am addressing now will soon discover for themselves the marvels of the most wonderful journey Man has ever made. Some day it will be as common to spend holidays in the past as it is now to visit a friend in Lunapolis. And some other day, not too far away, we shall be able to visit the future, just as, within another week, we shall be able to visit the past.

"Now let me save the energies of our Information Clerks by answering at once some of the questions that will most probably arise."

Mervin listened apathetically while most of the objections that he had already considered were outlined and disposed of. It was no use. There was no way out for him. He was still confronted by the urgent need to eliminate Doreen.

The scientist smiled, his perfect permateeth gleaming.

"And in conclusion," he said, "let me disabuse your minds of a notion that may sound amusing to some of you, but that has been brought up seriously over and over again in the course of our studies.

"No, you *can't* go back into the past and kill your grandfather, as people used to fancy, for the very good reason that if he *had* been killed, you wouldn't be alive now to make the trip. You would never have been born. So—"

Mervin lost track. He turned off the set. For a long time he sat, his eyes closed, thinking. . . .

This was 2146. Doreen, in a weak moment at the beginning of their marriage, had confessed that she was seven years older than he. That made her 52. So she had been born in 2094.

For the first time he was grateful for her garrulous, egocentric recitals about her undistinguished family. "I was an only child," she had droned so many times. "I was born the year after my parents were married, and my father died suddenly when I was only four."

At first he toyed with the idea of going back to a time when her father had been a child. It would be so much easier to overpower a child. But he knew he couldn't bring himself to harm a little boy. It was hard enough, driven as he was to utter despair, to confront another grown man.

But at whatever cost, he must nerve himself somehow to that. He began to calculate. Doreen's father and mother were married in 2093. Give it another year to be safe—he would aim for 2092, nine years before he himself had been born.

Even he was taken aback by what the journey cost. But by almost wiping out his bank account—the secret one he had managed to keep hidden from Doreen—he could just make it. He agreed to all the conditions, signed all the papers. He acquired clothing of the proper fashion, studied intensively the booklet on a half century's differences, to avoid suspicion.

He got his vacation changed to June, instead of the usual time in September: he couldn't stand waiting that long. He steeled himself to tell Doreen—at the last possible minute—that the department had ordered him to take his holiday earlier this year, and that therefore (since her own would still come in September) he must go away without her. It was a nasty scene, but he was desperate enough to go through it without giving in. Of course he lied about his destination: by the time her letter-tapes were returned from the false address he gave, there would be no need for him to worry any more.

On a day in June, 2092, Mervin Alspaugh found himself in New York, then still a separate city from both Philadelphia and Boston.

He knew where to go—he had listened to enough long-winded reminiscences. He found the apartment house without difficulty, only a bit confused until he remembered that there had still been surface transportation in cities in those days.

It was an ordinary 40-story formaglass apartment building of those years before most people had been crowded out of Manhattan except for the dwellers in moored living-yachts. It looked about as he had expected. What did surprise him was a concourse of small children—five or six of them—gathered on the stoop and in the doorway, playing. Mervin Alspaugh viewed them with disfavor; in his day the neighborhood robonurse would have put them to bed an hour before. Presumably their parents lived in the building and let them play outside till dark. He glanced at them sourly as he mounted the steps. A little girl, surely not more than four—a pudgy, unattractive child with sallow skin and a mean mouth—made a face at him and gave vent to a loud razzberry. Apparently she was the leader of the mob; the others immediately stopped their game and followed suit.

He ignored them; he had other things on his mind. He pressed the button for 1410.

He was face to face with the moment of truth.

Thanks to Doreen and her fond memories, he knew that Roger Tatum in his bachelor days had lived alone in the same flat to which he had taken his bride, and in which Doreen had spent her childhood until her father died. His life before and after his marriage, she had often remarked admiringly, had been "just like clockwork." He had got to the office by nine, was home again by half-past 18, after an early dinner at a nearby restaurant, then was home all evening listening to video lectures at the University of the Air, preparing himself for promotion in his job, and was in bed every night by half-past 22. "Why, even when he was going with my mother, he never went out with her except at week-ends."

And then she would invariably add: "He was a *serious*

man, my father, always trying to improve himself. Not like you, with your head forever in the clouds."

An excellent regimen—for Mervin's present purpose. And when he rang the bell downstairs, it was just 19.53.

The buzzer sounded promptly. If the paragon of perfectin was to be interrupted in his studies, then apparently he wanted the interruption disposed of quickly.

As Mervin mounted the escalator to the 14th floor he fingered nervously through his pocket what he thought of always, in capitals, as The Weapon.

He had pondered longest of all about this. Often, even as he made his preparations for the journey, it had seemed an insoluble problem—just as it had been when he had dreamed of eliminating Doreen directly. A blaster? He had never fired one in his life, and wouldn't know how. A knife? A blackjack? His blood turned cold. From Doreen's sarcastic comparisons—what a memory she must have had at four—he knew only too well how inferior he was in size and strength to Roger Tatum. So strangling or a blow was out of the question.

Only one thing that he knew of could kill a man instantly and painlessly, and that had not yet been invented in 2092. At first it had seemed impossible that he could get hold of one even in 2146. Mervin shuddered as he remembered the depths to which he, a man of hitherto blameless life, had descended to get The Weapon. It had cost him all that was left of his secret bank account, and he had risked his own life by venturing after dark into the notorious inner reaches of Central Park. (Overtime work, he had told Doreen, and she had been too indifferent to question him.)

He had succeeded, though he had had nightmares ever since. In his pocket, as the escalator carried him to his waiting prey, was a charged freeze hypo. Heaven knew from whom it had been stolen by the drug-ridden derelict who had furtively thrust it, wrapped in a dirty plastic rag, into his hand in exchange for the thick wad of credit notes.

Part of the Time Transport agreement he had signed was a prohibition against carrying arms into the past.

But no one could have imagined that in this case the little Sleepwel pillbox everybody carried held instead that tiny, deadly needle, which once it penetrated the skin immediately froze its victim, reduced his temperature to an incredible degree, turned his blood to ice, and held its grip until no recovery was possible.

He took the box gingerly out of his pocket, opened it with care, and extracted the freeze hypo by its safe end.

He rang the doorbell of Apartment 1410, and in a minute the door opened.

He would have known anywhere that it was Doreen's father. The same cold grey eyes, the same tight mouth, the same scowl, and the same grating voice as the man snapped: "Yes?"

"Mr. Tatum—Mr. Roger Tatum?"

"Yes. What do you want?"

"I have a package for you." The package—plastic and Sealfast containing nothing—was under his arm.

Tatum glared suspiciously.

"I'm expecting no package. I haven't ordered anything."

Doreen's meanness again—somebody must be trying to put something over, extort money somehow.

"There's no charge."

Expertly Mervin Alspaugh proffered the dummy parcel. Over and over, while Doreen snored, he had practiced holding the freeze hypo unseen under it.

Tatum stretched forth his hand grudgingly to take it. The needle went through his palm.

Without even a gasp, he turned rigid and then fell.

Mervin wheeled to leave. There was no need to touch the icy body—death was always instantaneous. He paused only to recover the hypo, harmless now that it had spent its charge. For a moment he thought he heard footsteps inside the apartment, hurrying to the door at the sound of Tatum's fall. (Perhaps father's studious bachelor evenings had not been so solitary as his doting daughter had fancied.) But he was on the escalator and out of sight before anyone could have glimpsed him.

The children were still gathered on the stoop. The pudgy little girl grimaced at him and yelled "Yah!" But a voice called from a downstairs window, and when Mervin reached the corner and looked back he saw the children, summoned, entering the building one by one for their belated bedtime.

Weak with a horrid churning mixture of terror, relief, and ecstasy, Mervin dared not linger longer in 2092. He hurried to the center where the Time Transporter, invisible to others because it did not yet exist in that era, waited for its passenger. If they wondered at the other end why he had returned so soon, he would say that life 54 years earlier had proved too uncomfortable, and probably they would be only too glad to get the Transporter back early for the next traveler.

Everything went smoothly. As he taxicoptered from the Time Transportation office to the living-yacht—now all his again, haven of peace as it had been in his happy days before Doreen—the horror of having killed another human being, the fear of being caught before he escaped, were swallowed up in the rapture of his triumph. He savored his new freedom with delight.

Roger Tatum had died two years before his daughter could have been born. There had never been a Doreen.

Delirious with happiness, he matched the doorpattern and stepped into his home—*his* home only, forevermore.

And then he saw a light in the viewing room.

Shaking, he burst into it.

Doreen sat there, watching her telecast. Ears plugged, eyes encased, she did not even notice him.

And in that awful moment, Mervin Alspaugh suddenly realized the truth.

Never in the world, as long as he lived, would he be able to get hold of enough money again to buy another freeze hypo, or to take another trip, to an earlier date, on the Time Transporter. Nor had he been wrong in thinking he had heard footsteps running to Tatum's door: he *had*—they were the footsteps of Mrs. Tatum.

And as for that pudgy, greedy-faced little girl on the stoop—now he knew why he had taken so instant a dislike to her—not seven years his senior, but eleven—at least eleven—

Doreen, that insatiable, incorrigible woman, had lied about her age!

Operation Cassandra

I woke up slowly, as if from an ordinary sleep. For a moment I couldn't orient myself, then I remembered everything. We had been carefully briefed—how long ago was that? We were to kept alive automatically, though the staff would be on constant watch—so much Somnotone injected to keep us asleep, so much (or so little, for hardly any was needed) of intravenous feeding and elimination of waste, our temperature kept at 85° F. The idea was that when or if the catastrophe came, and when it was safe afterwards, they would discontinue hibernation, and then we would wake of our own accord. Then, they told us, we would be given at once the anti-radiation serum that would surely be isolated and ready by that time.

What they hadn't told us—hadn't dared to imagine, themselves, was what really happened—that most of the staff would be killed; that the few left would be too near death to do anything about awakening us; that no serum would have been discovered; and that we would lie there in the Hibernatorium until the automatic machines ran out of supplies and gave up. Neither had they told us that most of us would die when the nourishment and nursing gradually ceased before the Somnotone gave out.

I got the picture little by little. First when at last I sat up shakily, shivering and hungry, and found no one near except the other silent forms ranged row by row in the big room, men on one side, women on the other. Then when I called and no one came. Then when I stumbled from bed to bed and, terrified and horror-stricken, gazed on rows of skeletons, a few corpses long gone in decomposition, a few more still lying as if asleep, but dead. And three who began to stir, as I had stirred a few moments before.

There were two men and a woman left alive besides me. They were just beginning to sit up, as I had done. I knew them all.

Ole Arnesen had been born in Denmark and brought to America as a child of three. His father was a dairyman in California, and Ole had gone to the Agricultural College of the State University. But both his parents and his only sister had been killed in the great earthquake of 1976, and he had sold the farm and drifted east. He was a few years older than I, and had served two years in the Air Corps. Arnesen was somebody you could depend on. I was glad that if so few of us had to survive, he was one of them.

About Jim Forbes I knew less and was more doubtful—and embarrassed by my doubt. Just as they say radiation sickness carries on in the genes for generations to come, I suppose any Southerner born carries somewhere in the remote recesses of his subconscious mind the prejudices of his ancestors. It had been a quarter of a century since the last vestiges of racial discrimination had been wiped out in America, and yet I still couldn't feel comfortable with a Negro. Yet probably Forbes was the only one of us who had joined the project out of pure patriotism, with no personal reasons. (Like me, he had been too young for the draft after they started it at 25). He was a New Yorker, a Harvard graduate who had majored in philosophy, and the author of two published book-tapes of poetry. He had enlisted in Operation Cassandra as he might have enlisted in the Defense Forces in time of war.

The woman was Amy Sackett. I remembered her from the briefing weeks—small, finely made, with flyaway light brown hair and big, intent blue eyes. She hailed from a small town in the Middle West, which before this she had left only for the four years she attended one of the big colleges for women in the East.

As for me, Roger Campbell, all I need say is that I come from Virginia, that I'm tall and bigboned, that I've been an orphan from birth—all of us had to be without parents or siblings, unmarried and unattached, besides being between 21 and 30, physically and mentally sound, and American citizens able to pass security tests—and that I've been on my own since I was 16. I've worked as a seaman, a longshoreman, a farm laborer, a construction worker. I've had darned little formal education, but I've read a lot in public libraries all over the country.

We came to Washington in answer to newspaper ads for "an important government research project." "Maximum pay and bonuses. Permanent," the ads said. Permanent was right.

I can imagine some of the screwballs that answered—I saw some of them before they were screened. There were ex-convicts trying to go straight under difficulties, youngsters turned down by the armed forces (very few of those got by the physical and psychological tests), kids who had flunked out in college, budding scientists attracted by the word "research," people fired from their jobs or just fed up with them. And, I suspect, an awful lot of recent widows and divorcees, and people of both sexes who had been jilted or were suffering from the pangs of unrequited love and wanted a change of scene.

Also, since the year was 1984, we got some of the disillusioned ex-Orwell Cultists.

Ever since Orwell wrote that book, way back in 1949, 1984 had come to stand for calamity and terror. Around in the early '70s a cult actually arose, something like the Millerites of the 19th Century, only political instead of religious, which devoutly believed that Eric Blair (which was Orwell's real name) had been, not a novelist, but a prophet—and that his prophecy referred to America instead of, or as well as, England. They didn't propose to fight against his prophesied totalitarian victory; that, they thought, would be futile, since the point of true prophecy is that it cannot be resisted or evaded. Instead, the cult members were pledged to commit suicide on December 31, 1983. A lot of them did—and a lot of them killed their immediate families as well. The courts and mental hospitals were full of the poor fanatics who tried it and failed. Nothing of particular moment happened in 1984, after all. (And I might add, for the benefit of those who, not really knowing anything about it, had some muddled inkling of the existence of our super-hush-hush project, that it was pure accident that it was 1984 when Operation Cassandra started functioning: it had nothing whatever to do with Orwell's book.)

Once we four survivors realized what we had awakened to, we could no longer bear to stay in the charnel-house which the Hibernatorium had become. By one impulse we left the big room behind us.

But we did not dare yet to leave the building. It had been elaborately equipped against radioactive contagion; some said there were inner walls of solid lead, but that may have been a myth. Outside, the very air might be lethal, for all we knew. We weren't scientists; we were only guinea-pigs, and all we knew about radioactivity was what they'd allowed us to read.

We found the door open to the Administration Office, on the first floor, with nothing worse in it than thick dust everywhere. (Have I mentioned the dust?) We had to talk, to realize, to plan—if there was anything we *could* plan. We didn't even know where we were, except that it was somewhere in the Southwest; we'd been flown here blindfolded.

"First of all," Arneson said, "we've got to find something to eat, whether it's safe or not. I'd rather take my chances of poisoning than die of starvation."

"It's safe enough, I imagine," I told him. "The food supplies were canned and packed with every contingency in view. Let's adjourn to the kitchen wing, see what we can find right away, and then inventory the supplies."

Forbes was standing at the sealed window, looking out. I'd been keeping my eyes away from there. Forbes had talked very little. Now he said:

"Even the out-buildings seem to be intact, so if it was a nuclear blast, it couldn't have been very near here. But the trees are dead, and there's not a blade of grass in their Garden in the Desert they worked so hard over. What I've been watching for is some kind of animal—anything, even a rat or a snake—that would show us we could live out there."

"Nothing?" asked Amy Sackett.

"Nothing."

"Let's eat first, as Arnesen said," I urged. "Then we can begin to draw up a program. I'm parched as well as starving, and I wouldn't dare drink tap-water even if any is running. There ought to be some fruit juices in the kitchen."

"Best thing for us anyway," Ole agreed. "My father used to go on a fast once in a while—he was a good deal of a food faddist. And he always told us a fast must be broken on liquids, or it might be fatal. We don't know how long we've been without food. I know by looking at you three that you're down to skin and bones, and I guess I am too."

He was. We didn't need any mirrors to show us—the synthetic Everclean pajamas we'd been put to sleep in were hanging on us all like tents.

We adjourned for breakfast. In the big shelter-safe built against the kitchen we found cans of orange juice, and after we'd tested them with a Geiger counter—each of us wore a portable, naturally—we drank them and felt better. Amy scouted around and took a rough inventory. When we had the strength for solid food, there was going to be enough to last the four of us indefinitely—there had been supplies for 200 plus the staff. But the electricity was off, and how we were going to cook, none of us could think. It didn't matter; there was plenty we could eat cold until we figured that one out.

Without saying anything, we all avoided the Hiberna-torium. But we men got into the outfitting room on the men's side, and Amy on the women's, and we managed to rig ourselves out with clothes to fit our new waist-lines; the things we'd worn when we arrived were much too large for us at present. Then we trooped down again to the Administration Office to talk things over.

I know there were two things uppermost in my own mind, and I suppose in everybody's. First, of course, just what was the situation outside? Was the air breathable? Was there any non-poisonous means of subsistence? Above all, were we the only living human beings around? Perhaps this had been the worst-hit of all sec-tions of the country, perhaps the least; we had no way of finding out. We didn't kid ourselves about there being any more tridimens or news-tapes, but there might be planes or surface cars still usable. A subsidiary worry that might determine a lot of other things was the date, but how we'd ever discover that I couldn't imagine.

And the other thing we had to think about was the bare fact that we might very well find out that we were the last survivors in the whole country, perhaps in the whole world; that it might be up to us to re-form civili-zation, and to repopulate the world, or our portion of it.

And that we were three men and a woman.

We kept getting off the track in making plans and guesses, until finally we had to face it. On the surface we were all very calm and matter-of-fact. But I know how I was feeling underneath, and I guess the others felt the same way.

It was Amy herself who brought it to a head.

"Look," she said, "we might as well settle this. Either we're going to stay right here and keep going as best we can, until somebody rescues us or we die, or we're going to make ourselves the nucleus of a new community—maybe the only one in existence, unless there are other little pockets of survivors somewhere else who have escaped radiation sickness or got over it. We're all ma-ture, intelligent human beings—we were carefully se-lected, and we might as well acknowledge that we're a kind of elite. So how about discussing that phase of it, before we go on to other things? What we do will depend a lot on the solution of that problem, anyway."

None of us was looking at the others, I noticed; everybody was staring at the floor or out of the windows.

Ole cleared his throat.

"Well," he said, "one thing is obvious, Amy. Let's be objective about this. If there's going to be a new population, it's going to have an ancestress, and as things are at present you're the only one qualified."

I found myself saying foolishly: "That not a very polite way to approach the subject!"

"This isn't the time or place for compliments, Rog," Amy said. "I'm not picturing myself as a *femme fatale*— I'm just, as Ole says, the only *femme* of any variety in sight."

Ole, gazing over our heads, spoke in his slow Scandinavian way.

"If Amy prefers any one of us, that's that. The other two, I think, in that case ought to clear out as soon as possible. Or if she has no preference, we could have some kind of lottery. We're all fit and we're all willing—"

"Not me," Jim Forbes cut in. "Count me out. This is a white man's country and you're the majority left in it, around here, anyhow. I agree with Ole—let the loser join me in trying to find a way out of here, and perhaps locate some more survivors. I'd rather have a woman of my own kind, just as you would."

I didn't say anything, though I had the grace to feel ashamed. Ole shook his head and started to speak. Amy interrupted him.

"Wait," she said. "There's another consideration."

We waited. She flushed, gulped, and went on, her voice carefully controlled.

"We're in an unprecedented situation. We don't know what shape the country's in, or the world, or ourselves, for that matter. Has it occurred to you that some or all of us may be sterile right now? We don't know for how many years we've been subjected to radiation from fallout, right up there in the Hibernatorium, no matter how tight the building is. We've agreed that no nuclear bombs could have fallen very near here. But that still leaves fall-out—to say nothing of germs."

"What are you driving at, Amy?" Ole asked. "If we're all sterile anyway, that's the end."

"You know perfectly well what I'm driving at. Maybe we all are, maybe none, maybe one or two or three of us. There's only one way we'll ever find out. Perhaps I'm the one; in that case, as Ole says, that's that—there won't *be* any future population—not if I'm all that's left to provide one. If I'm not, it may be one or more of you. If I pick one, and the others go away, perhaps the only one who could father a child will be one of those who leave. You see?"

We saw. And none of us liked it. We'd been picked, among other things, because we were free and unattached sexually. But that didn't mean we hadn't had pasts, and it didn't mean we'd shed all the preconceptions and attitudes of our culture. We weren't brutes or throwbacks, any of us. We were normally sexed, healthy young men, but we'd been bred in the tradition of romantic love, and this cold-blooded approach was distasteful to us.

Yet the alternative was worse, and I don't mean the alternative of turning ourselves into a celibate community and letting mankind, so far as we could know, come to its end with our deaths. If we couldn't consider this problem objectively, and act on it in a civilized manner, then sooner or later one, or more, of us men would develop the fixation we call falling in love. So, probably, would Amy herself. Outside of the unlikely contingency that Amy and some particular man, and only he, would be the ones affected, that would mean the end of any communal co-operation—it would mean jealousy, and strife, and disaster.

Besides, what Amy had said about possible sterility among us made sense. We had reached an impasse.

I might have known it. It was Ole, the ex-dairy farmer, who came up with an idea.

"It's not necessary—we needn't—" he stuttered. "Oh,

hell, I've inseminated hundreds of cows. That way, we'd never know who the father was."

"We might," said Jim Forbes dryly.

It was up to me—I was the Southerner here.

"It might be lucky for the future of humanity, Jim," I said, "if the paternal blood-line came through somebody with more intellect than a roughneck who never finished grammar school."

It cost me a lot to say it, but I felt better when I had.

Yet when Amy threw me a look of gratitude, a thrill of alarm shot through me: did that mean she actually was attracted by that—? At least, I kept that to myself; I wasn't proud of it.

Ole's common sense rescued us again.

"This doesn't mean we have to start raising a family today or tomorrow," he said gruffly. "We've got more immediate jobs to think of first. If nothing else, I'd have to scout around and see if there's a syringe somewhere— they must have had some kind of laboratory or at least an infirmary.

"In fact, I think it would be a good idea—if the rest of you agree, that is: we want to do things democratically—"

"Go ahead, Ole," Jim said, and we other two nodded.

"Well, let's find out first of all just what there is in this building. Amy's inventoried the food supply, but let's get after the clothing and equipment. For one thing, let's find something we can make lights with after dark. Our big problem's going to be water, but for the immediate present we can go unwashed and drink fruit juice. In this climate we're not going to need much in the way of heating, but we do have to discover some way to cook.

"Let's divide these tasks up and each of us make lists so we know what we've got. Then tomorrow we can see about the possibility of getting out of doors and inspecting that. And next, if that is O.K., we must hunt for means of transportation elsewhere, if only for exploration."

"The very first thing to do," I said firmly, "is to lock and bolt the doors of the Hibernatorium, and seal if off from the rest of the building." They all nodded. "And since I made the first inspection, before the rest of you were awake, there's no need of subjecting anybody else to the ordeal; I'll take care of that myself."

There were no candles, but we found some flashlights with perpetual batteries. We turned in soon after it grew dark. The staff had done themselves well; there was a comfortable bedroom for each of us upstairs, with others to spare. There were bathrooms, too, but they were of no use without water. We would have to contrive something in the way of a latrine; meanwhile we could use a disposal can in the storeroom.

My last thought as I fell into an exhausted sleep was about Amy.

We were all up with the first light. We ate, and then Jim volunteered to try the out-of-doors. We found an entrance with a small vestibule he could close behind him. He was back in a few minutes.

"The Geiger counter kept clicking," he reported. "I think we could breathe without danger if we had somewhere safe to get to quick, but not otherwise."

"That settles it," said Ole. "This building is tight, and the air in it has kept fresh so far. We'll have to postpone that part of the program. For the present, this is where we stay."

"A fort against the enemy," Amy murmured ... An enemy we couldn't see, and didn't know how to fight. There was a long pause.

Then Jim said, "I've been thinking. This will have to be a very short postponement, whether the air outside is entirely safe or not."

"What do you mean, Jim?" asked Amy.

"I mean that we're acting like a bunch of blind idiots. This place is a prison, not a fortress; and it's a prison where we ourselves have thrown away the key. We can't go on long without lights and cooked food and stay civilized; and we can't go on without water and stay alive at all. Even the air we breathe will give out eventually, huge as this building is—to say nothing of the fact that we're living in a charnelhouse, with that Hibernatorium upstairs."

"We have every intention of leaving when it's safe," Ole objected.

"And when will that be? We don't know how long it's been already; we don't even know how much older we are than when we were put to sleep. We look the same to one another—our hair hasn't turned grey, we're still young—but how young?

"As for our becoming the nucleus of a new population, no matter what scheme we devise, it's an utter impossibility while we stay here. Could we raise children under these conditions? Could Amy or any other woman *have* a baby here that would be born alive?"

"I've said all along," Amy interposed, her cheeks pink, "that I was willing to do anything we all agreed on soberly and conscientiously."

"Exactly, and how much sobriety and conscientiousness are we displaying? Let's cut out the romantic nonsense. Let's face the fact that what we have here is just four human beings shut up in a concrete box.

"Whom do you expect to rescue us—explorers from some other planet? Either we're the world's only survivors, or we're not. The only way we can find out, and make reasonable plans for the future if we are to have a future, is to protect ourselves as best we can and go on out, whatever the Geiger counters say, take our chances, and try to discover what the situation really is.

"Then if we do find we're all there are, we can either come back here and die slowly, or stay out there and die fast. In either case, we might as well give up any idea of reconstructing a civilization on a base as narrow as this. When it comes down to it, what are we without other human beings to co-operate with?—just one woman and three men. If the two others of you want to fight to the death over the one woman, you're welcome: no offense to you, Amy, but I'm just not interested. I have other concerns, more important to me, to think about—such as keeping alive as long as possible."

We three others sat in somber silence. We knew Jim Forbes was right; we just didn't want to believe it, or to give up our grandiose dream of becoming the founders of a new (and of course better) humanity. To go out into that perilous, problematic world was like leaving the womb for the second time.

"We're safe here for another day or two anyway," Ole said slowly at last. "Let's sleep on it tonight and decide tomorrow."

That night it rained—a rare event always in this desert country. We had no idea what season, even, it might be—calendars were out as well as clocks, and in the Southwest there is little change in temperature between summer and winter, except that summer is hotter, if possible. It's always cool at night, the year round, on the open desert.

I was awakened by the rain. I got up—our windows were all sealed, of course, but I could see the drops streaking the one-way glass. I had some crazy idea of going outside and collecting rainwater, till I woke sufficiently to realize that it would probably be pure poison. It was while I was standing at the window that I heard a faint, furtive sound.

At once I thought of Amy's room—had she locked her door? Then I listened intently; and I knew.

The sound came from outside.

I peered out into the darkness, and at first I could see nothing whatever. Then my eyes caught a shadowy movement.

One by one they separated themselves from the solid dark behind them. Were they animals? Had wolves come to the desert? No—they were crawling, but they were men.

They could not see me, but gradually I could see them plainly. There were ten of them. I could even see the rags and tatters in which they were clad. Their heads were down, and inch by inch, foot by foot, they were encircling the building.

Very quietly I dressed and left my room, and opened the unlocked doors of Jim's and Ole's rooms. I shook them awake, and whispered my news. Luckily, they understood at once, jumped up, and threw on some clothes. But we had no weapons of any kind.

"What about Amy?" Ole whispered.

"Let her sleep," I replied.

"Nonsense,'" Jim retorted. "We're going to need everyone we've got."

He was right; this was no time for medieval chivalry. I scratched at her door until she woke and came to it. I explained hastily, and she said calmly, "I'll be with you in a minute." Amy, I reflected with relief, wasn't the fainting or hysterical kind.

My eyes were most accustomed to the darkness, so I ran again to the nearest window. They were posted all around—I could see them to either side. They were standing now, and they were big, burly men who looked like savages. How many years, I thought in a sudden panic, had it been? Long enough for our countrymen to turn into those frightening creatures outside? I fought the panic down, and hurried back to the others; Amy had joined them.

"Perhaps they only want refuge," she suggested.

"In that case they'd have come openly by day, not waited for the first dark night since there have been signs of life in this building. No, they're enemies: I know it."

"Here's the best plan," said Ole. "We'll wait downstairs in the hall until we hear where they're trying to break in, then we'll concentrate on that point and meet them with everything we've got. They outnumber us more than two to one, but they've lost the element of surprise they must be counting on. At least, the building is securely locked, and they're not likely to break in easily."

Jim Forbes started violently.

"Oh, my God!" he exclaimed. "I didn't lock the door behind me when I came back from testing the air!"

"You fool—" Ole began, but I stopped him.

"Shut up!" I snapped. "How was Jim to guess anything like this? It just means that that's where we'll wait for them. Now, how about something to fight them with?

Amy, can you get about in the dark and hustle up anything you can find that can be used as a weapon? Get some knives from the kitchen, and anything heavy that can be used as a club or a blackjack."

That kept her away from danger for the moment, anyway, and we men could meet them with bare fists if she hadn't got back by the time they broke in. They might not discover the unlocked door—they might have reconnoitered before and found then that all the entrances were barred.

I had a nasty second when I wondered if they were waiting for reinforcements. But I kept quiet; they didn't look like an organized group that would know anything about strategy. A minute later I knew I was right; somebody tried the door behind us, then there was a muffled call from the one we were guarding, and the sound of running feet.

The door burst open.

We were waiting and they didn't expect us. That was our only advantage. If they had been watching the building, they must have seen our lights, and known that some of us had revived, but in the middle of the night they must have thought we were all asleep. Probably their real object was not to attack us, but to steal whatever they could find. They must have tried many times before without success, and hoped, now that people were up and about in the building, it would be easier to find a way into the hitherto impregnable fortress. Unfortunately, they were right.

It was as dark within as without, and none of us could see one another. But that didn't matter. We three men had hurriedly discussed our tactics. Not only were we badly outnumbered, but we were all still emaciated and weak from our long coma. In our normal shape, we were quite capable of tackling the invaders one by one as they entered and knocking them out, but we couldn't count on doing that, in this battle with tough, half-wild enemies. They must be tough, or they could not have survived unknown years of struggle in a world such as their must have been since the big blow-up.

We ranged ourselves against the wall near the door, Jim and I on one side, Ole, the biggest of us, on the other. Back in the kitchen wing, I could hear Amy rummaging for weapons, and hoped she would come soon. As the first figure sneaked through the door, Jim tripped him neatly, and I brought the heel of my shoe hard against what I hoped was the back of his head.

He yelled, so I hadn't put him out. I kicked again, and this time I made it—he grunted and lay still. But he had alerted the rest of them. I'd had a faint hope that when they discovered they were going to meet opposition, the others would run; but no such luck. They burst in now in a pack, and the brawl became a free-for-all. I had no time to see what Ole and Jim were doing; I had somebody on my back trying to pull me down, and somebody else holding my throat in a death-grip.

I felt my lungs collapsing; then I managed to pry one of the fingers loose and bend it backwards until my attacker bellowed with pain and let go for an instant. I heaved and kicked sideways, and my shod foot hit a naked shin. I'd learned some judo in my day, but there wasn't room to practice it. I kept wishing desperately that Amy would arrive with those knives—but if she did, how could she get into that melee and deliver them to the right people?

She'd had the same thought. And—I found it afterwards on the floor, where one of the invaders had grabbed it and then let it slip—she'd acquired a heavy iron frying-pan. Standing back at arm's length she swung it, and fortunately the heads she hit weren't ours. "Rog! Jim! Ole!" she called. "Catch!" Ole and I did, and they were good hefty meat knives. Jim wasn't so lucky; at the time, he was down under three husky brutes; but the knife she threw him went point first into the back of one of them, and he screamed and jumped off Jim. It was only a flesh wound, but it bled plenty, and he ran howling toward the open door.

That started a stampede. They had no weapons, and they'd had enough. Probably they thought there were more of us than there were, and they couldn't know how weak and shaky we all were. Three minutes later the hall was empty except for two silent huddled figures lying on the floor, and we were trying to get our breath back.

We listened till the running footsteps died in the distance; then we bolted the door by which they had entered and started to assess the damage. Somebody found two of the flashlights and we turned them on.

We were all bruised and battered; my neck ached from the fingers that had tried to choke me. Jim's nose and lip were bleeding and he'd lost a tooth. Ole groaned with every breath and kept holding his side; my guess was that some ribs were broken.

Jim and I bent over the prostrate figures. They weren't dead, just unconscious. Jim was for throwing them out in the rain, but we weren't up to it; they were both big burly guys.

"There's some rope around somewhere," I said. "Let's tie them up to keep them safe and when they've come to we can deal with them. We can use them; if we can get them to talk we may find out a lot we don't know."

"If they *can* talk," said Ole sourly between groans.

"Good Lord, they're just people—they're just like us," Jim objected. "There can't have been enough time gone by for another generation to have grown up, or we'd all be old and grey, and we aren't. They're not mutations—just tough babies who've survived conditions that have killed off the ones who couldn't take it. They prove the air is breathable, anyway. And they'll talk, once we can talk to them."

"Amy!" I called. "Find that coil of rope we saw and bring it here, will you? It's O.K. now—everything's quiet again."

There was no answer. I waited a minute, and then left Jim and Ole to guard our prisoners and went back in the kitchen wing to find her. She wasn't there.

I brought the rope and we trussed the two up. We had no water to revive them with, but we stretched them out and put blankets over them and pillows under their heads. One of them had a lump on his head the size of a walnut, though the skin wasn't broken. I hoped that was the one I'd kicked. He'd been the first one in and might be their leader.

Jim and Ole went off to the infirmary to try to find something to clean up Jim's cuts and to tape Ole's sore side, and I started through the building looking for Amy. It wasn't like her to hide from a fight, especially after she'd already been in it wielding her frying-pan, but she was no Amazon and she might have blacked out from the excitement and be lying somewhere in a faint.

She wasn't in her bedroom, or in any of ours. I went systematically, more and more puzzled and then scared, through the entire big building. The Hibernatorium was still securely locked on the outside. I went in every closet, and in rooms we hadn't entered since we awoke. I even looked under the beds. The other two came out of the infirmary to see what I was about, and joined me in the search.

We scoured the whole building thoroughly. There was only one answer.

Amy wasn't there.

We looked at one another in shocked silence. Ole broke it.

"Good God," he said huskily. "They were all men!"

"Let's go!" I cried. "We can catch up with them yet!"

"Take it easy, Rog," Jim said quietly. "Let's use our brains. They must have a hideout, and by now they may have reached it. We couldn't find it in the dark and the rain. We've got to plan.

"And what could we do, in our condition, against heaven knows how many of them?"

"It's easy enough for you to talk—"

I choked up. "I'm sorry."

"Forget it. And don't think I'm not with you. Amy's one of us—aside from being a girl. We'll get her, and we'll bring her back, and we'll get even with anybody who's done her harm. We can't help her unless we do it sensibly. Look at Ole—he can scarcely walk."

"I can navigate," Ole growled. "But Jim's talking sense —we haven't a chance if we just rush off helter-skelter after her now."

Horrible visions flashed across my mind—Amy dead, Amy helpless in the grasp of those ravening beasts. I groaned aloud. It had taken something like this to make me realize how I felt about her.

"Besides," said Jim, "are we sure that's what happened? We saw those fellows leave—maybe we were too confused to be sure, but we'd have known if they'd been carrying her with them. And she has a voice— she'd have cried out, wouldn't she? We, none of us, have any idea of her whereabouts since she called to us to catch those knives."

"What else *could* have happened?" Ole demanded.

"She could have left while we were busy with that bunch here."

"Left? For where? Why?" I wanted to know.

"I don't know any more than you do. I just want us to consider everything. The important thing is to get her back. It can't be long now till daylight. Let's make our plans."

We'd drifted into the Administration Office again by now. As if by agreement, Ole and I yielded the floor to Jim. I was the fittest of us physically, but he was the boy with the brains and education. He paced up and down while we huddled in chairs; Ole looked as if he'd never be able to get out of his again, and I wasn't feeling any too hot. Jim's cut mouth and nose made it difficult for him to talk, but he managed a sort of muffled monotone.

"Let's discuss this objectively," he said. "There are only two possibilities. Either she was kidnapped, or she left under her own steam, with some purpose we don't understand. If she'd simply run away because she was frightened, and hidden somewhere, she'd be back by now yelling to us to let her in; besides, that's not like Amy, even the little I know her.

"Ole's in the worst shape of us three. He ought to stay here to guard our prisoners and to let us in and out— shut up, Ole; you got wounded in a good cause, but you're not up to heavy exercise right now. Besides, someone's got to be here in case Amy does turn up of her own accord.

"That leaves only two of us—one to try to find that hideout and somehow get Amy out of it if she's there, and one to try to figure out where else she could be and hunt for her. One man can't fight a battalion, so if she's been captured she's got to be rescued by strategy, not force. The same is true of any bad situation she might have got into if she left here under her own power."

"I want to be the one for the hideout," I put in. "When I think of those brutes—" I shuddered.

"O.K., that's your job, then, if you can promise not to burst in like a one-man rescue army. Now, how are we going to trace her?"

There was a moan from the hall; one of our captives was beginning to show signs of life.

"Let him lie," said Ole. "I'll attend to them when you're gone."

"Footsteps?" I suggested. "The rain has softened the ground."

"It stopped raining long ago—hadn't you noticed? I doubt if footsteps will show much by dawn. But of course that would be our first clue—both Amy's and the men's, if we can track them. You'll have a better chance than I will on that—there were eight of them pounding out of here in a hurry. On the other hand, wherever they've gone to is likely to be a lot farther than where Amy is if she left here by herself.

"My guess is, the hideout is in caves in the foothills, and that's five miles or more away. That will be your objective; all I can do is scan the desert in the other direction and keep circling till I find something—if I do."

I felt myself getting the shakes again. Suddenly I remembered bitterly that earnest, unemotional colloquy right here in the Administration Office, only two days before. "Mother of a new humanity!" If Amy was going to be the mother, I knew damned well I wanted to be the father. And now—

I tried to keep my mind off it; I needed all my wits if

I was going to be of any help in this crisis. I glanced at the window. The sky was graying. It was almost dawn.

"Wait a minute!" Ole cried suddenly. "I just had an idea. Why should we go out hunting blindly for what these fellows out in the hall can tell us? They both ought to be out of it by now. And we can make them talk," he added grimly.

"How stupid can we get?" Jim assented disgustedly. "Come on!"

We trooped out to inspect our captives. One of them was awake, all right—he stared at us malevolently. The other was still out, but he was stirring and muttering.

Jim prodded the conscious one with his toe.

"Talk:" he ordered gruffly. "Who are you and where did you come from? What did you want here?"

The man grimaced. It was light enough now inside the building to see it, and to see them. They were big and well muscled, both of them, but skinny, with unkempt beards, long, tangled hair, and weatherbeaten skin. They were dressed in torn rags of shirts and trousers that looked as if they were made of sacking, and their dirty feet were bare.

"Go on, you," I chimed in. "You heard what the man said. Talk, if you want to get out of this place alive."

The man's dry lips opened.

"Water!" he croaked.

We had no water. But Ole gave me the nod and I went back in the kitchen and fished out a can of orange juice and opened it. I handed it to Ole and he knelt painfully and let the man drink. Jim held his head up so he wouldn't choke. He swallowed some of it and cleared his throat.

And then, to our utter amazement, this tough guy, who a few hours before had been trying to kill us, whined in a baby tone: "Why you fellers treat us like this? We never done you no harm!"

"No, you merely broke into our house and—" Ole began contemptuously.

"It *ain't* your house," the man objected. "It belongs to everybody. We don't know what it's for, but we know it's guvvimint propity. We're Americans just as much as you are. And you jumped us—all we did was defend ourselves."

"Swell story!" Jim retorted. "If you thought you had a right here, why didn't you come in the daylight, like honest men, instead of waiting for a dark, rainy night?"

"We was afraid. Our scouts seen the lights last night and we didn't know who was there. It's always been empty and we always thought the guvvimint people cleared out after the big crash. We tried lots of times to get in, but the doors and windows was all tight. We figgered maybe if somebody's opened it up again we could sneak in while they was asleep and pick up some things our folks could use. It's ours just as much as it's yours."

"To hell with that!" I shouted. "What did you do with the girl?"

"What girl?" He sounded astonished. "I never seen no girl. We got—"

A voice interrupted. The other man was awake again too. He must have been lying there listening.

"There *was* a girl screamed something, Bill," he whispered huskily. "She musta had a knife—I seen Garth bleedin' like a stuck pig."

"Gimme a drink," he pleaded. "I'm dyin' of thirst."

I turned automatically to fetch another can of orange juice. My eyes caught a glimpse through one of the front windows. The sun was coming up by now and it was almost full daylight.

"Jim! Ole! Look!" I screeched.

Walking up the roadway, calmly and serenely, was Amy Sackett!

We all three dashed for the front door, but I got it open first and ran.

"For God's sake!" I sputtered. "Where have you been! What happened? We've been nearly crazy!"

She gazed at me with mild surprise.

"Why Rog," she said. "I should think you'd have guessed. I couldn't be any more use in that fight, and when they started to run out, the only sensible thing was for one of us to follow them and try to find out who they were and where they came from. I was the only one who could, so I did. I knew I could breathe the air if they could."

"You damned fool!" I cried: I was almost weeping. "We had you kidnapped and raped and murdered and I don't know what! If anything had happened to you—"

"Why, Rog!" she repeated softly, and the loveliest smile lit up her face. At which second, of course, Jim and Ole caught up with us.

We hustled Amy back into the building, all of us explaining at once about the two captives and about our plans to go searching for her. The first thing we did was to unbind them and help them to their feet. They were stiff and sore but neither was badly hurt. We pushed them into chairs in the Administration Office and they both sat there staring dumbly at Amy.

"What I started to say," said Bill slowly, "was that we got plenty of girls of our own. But she's sure a pretty one—ain't she, Joe?"

Amy yawned widely.

"She's sure a tired one," she countered. "I must have walked all of ten miles in the dark after about two hours' sleep. Did they tell you about their colony? I got a good look at it."

"Not yet, but they will," Jim answered. "They understand now that the whole fracas was a misconception on both sides. You tell us what you've found out, Amy, and then get yourself some sleep, while we check with our friends here."

"Well, it's in the caves in the foothills—"

"Just what I thought," Jim interrupted.

"And there's about 40 of them—is that right?"

"Fourteen men, 18 woman, and ten kids, the last count," said Bill. "That's funny, ain't it, when you come to think of it?—the women turned out to be tougher than the men."

"Biological superiority," said Ole Arnesen from his agricultural learning.

"Huh?"

"Never mind. What we want to know is—are the kids all right?"

"All right? Sure—why not?" said Joe in a surprised tone. "Oh, I see what you mean. No, none of them ain't got two heads or 20 fingers, if that's what's on your mind. We're the ones that *wasn't* affected. Most of us was miners and was below ground when it come. Not the women, of course, but like I say, they was tougher. The ones that wasn't, men and women alike, died off—or we got rid of 'em," he added harshly.

"How long has it been?" asked Amy abruptly.

"Since the crash? Well, we ain't got no calendars, but going by the seasons, I'd say it was about 11 years."

"Oh, my goodness!" Amy squealed. "I'm 34 years old!"

We all laughed, and I swear it was the first time I'd heard anybody laugh since they put me to sleep in the Hibernatorium. Not that it made me any too happy myself to learn I was 36.

"And another thing," Bill remarked. "We're all kinds, and we aim to stay that way. We've got Mex, and Navaho, and a Chinaman, and even some—Oh!" He seemed really to notice Jim for the first time, and his jaw dropped. "I guess that's all right with you," he ended weakly.

We laughed again.

"What we was aiming at," said Joe, "what we'd kinda planned on when we thought this place was empty, only we couldn't get into it, was to move in here and make it a kind of headquarters till we could build ourselves homes again. We don't want our kids to grow up savages."

"Truly, don't you know what this place is?" Jim asked him.

"No, just some sort of top secret guvvimint thing. What is it?"

We told them.

Joe scrambled to his feet.

"Come on, Bill," he gasped. "I'm gettin' out of here! How do we know they ain't all contaminated? And I ain't stayin' nowheres with a room full of dead stiffs upstairs!"

"I can assure you it's safe and so are we," I declared. "We've been protected here—we were afraid to leave. Now we can open up and stay.

"As for the Hibernatorium, all of us working together can carry out the bodies and bury them and disinfect everything. It won't be a nice job, but we can do it."

"I don't like it, Bill," said Joe uneasily. "I'm gonna go back and vote to go hunt for the Center, like we said we might if we couldn't make do here."

"Well, I dunno," Bill pondered. "We can't stand the caves much longer, specially with more kids on the way, but we don't know how far off a Center is, and if we could fix this place up and move in with these folks—"

"What's a Center?" Amy interrupted.

"They're places, different parts of the country, where they've got survivors collected in underground shelters. There was a man scouting around a year ago, in a jet plane, found us and wanted to fly us in to one. But it didn't sound much better than the caves, and we wouldn't. Now maybe we ought to, but we let the man go and I don't know how we'd find out where the nearest one is. He said they was going to gradually—how did he put it, Joe?"

"Redeem the blasted areas, he said. He called the Centers—what was that egghead word?—something like 'atoms' or—no 'nuclei,' that was it."

"Yeah, I remember now," Bill agreed. " 'Nuclei of reconstruction.' But how we'd ever—"

He stopped dead. We all did, startled speechless by a sound.

A familiar, commonplace sound.

The visiphone was ringing.

For a second we all stood paralyzed, then there was a mad dash.

It was Jim who reached it first. His hand shook so that he could scarcely lift the receiver.

A face showed on the screen, dim and distorted, but still recognizably a human face. A voice spoke, and it was speaking English.

"Come closer," the voice said. "This thing isn't working right yet, and I can't see well. How many of you are there left?"

Jim opened his mouth, but no sound came out. "F-four from Operation Cassandra," I managed to answer.

"Is that all?" The voice sounded disappointed. I felt like apologizing.

"And we've got two men here from a cave colony in the foothills," I added hastily.

"Oh, yes, I know about them. We'll get in touch with them later. But it's you people I'm concerned about now. We were afraid you might all be dead."

"The rest are," I said. "Locked in the Hibernatorium. And the staff's all gone. They were gone when we four woke up, three days ago."

"I know about them. Dead of the sickness, all but one. Brock's left—he was the chief medico: remember him? He's with us in the Center. He insisted we try to reach you when we finally got the visiphone working.

"Only three days ago—it's lucky we didn't get through earlier. When our man was out last year, scouting, the cave people told him there was nobody in the building. Do you know about the Centers?"

"We just learned about them."

"We've got room for you here."

Ole stepped to the speaker.

"We thought we'd stay here and take the cave people in with us—" he began.

"Nonsense!" said the voice brusquely. "You're still under government orders, remember. We're going to burn the whole place down, with the dead in it, once we get you out and remove the furnishing and supplies.

"We'll pick you up in a jet tomorrow. Get yourselves ready. As I recall, there's plenty of flat desert around you for a landing-field. Tell the colonists we'll come for them next, if they've changed their minds—you can let us know, when we come for you."

"O.K., will do," I said. "Who's this speaking, anyway?"

"Enderby Houghton," said the voice dryly.

I did a doubletake. The six-star general, the chief of staff of the Army of the United States!

"I—I beg your pardon, sir," I gulped. "I should have recognized you."

He chuckled sadly.

"We're all changed a lot, son," he said. "And there's no Army left, and no enemy, either—we're all one world now, what's left of us.

"Well, we can tell you when we see you. No time to talk longer now—this power's getting weaker."

He rang off.

As you'll have guessed, this is written from Center 50, near where Salt Lake City used to be. The Center will be closed soon; we've got a lot of territory around here cleaned up, and in ten years more we'll have farming country and towns again.

Amy's and my marriage was the first one celebrated here, though Jim's wasn't long after; Althea was one of the girl from the cave colony whom he met after they all joined us here. Ole married Helga, who was at the Center when we came. It's been a good life, these last five years, full of useful work. We were scared after Amy became pregnant, but our Billy (he's named for our friend Bill, our captive that night) is a perfectly normal boy, and he's nearly three years old now. We aren't worried about the child who is coming.

One day recently I finally got up my nerve to say to Amy:

"Look, honey, tell me something. Why did you really go off by yourself in the desert that night? It was such a foolhardy thing to do."

Her face dimpled, that cute way it does.

"Haven't you ever guessed, darling?" she asked sweetly. "As soon as I saw there were other men alive, I wanted to get away from you, of course!"

"Have it your own way, my love," I responded loftily. "If you're too modest to let us make a famous heroine of you, we'll have to submit, I suppose.

"But I notice when you'd taken a· look at the other men, you came chasing right back to me!"

I had the last word that time—unless you count a kiss as a reply.

The Last Generation?

No attempt was made to conceal the accident that occurred in the desert of New Mexico on May 11, 1975. It would have been impossible to keep it secret, since two internationally-known physicists, a high-ranking Army officer, and a prominent Senator from the Deep South lost their lives in the disaster.

The explosion itself was singularly small. The seventeen men killed—the rest were workmen and minor scientists—died from concussion and asphyxiation. There was no fire. A lake of green glass suddenly appeared in the sand waste, but the atomic waves were dissipated quickly. There was no delayed bodily erosion as in Hiroshima and Nagasaki.

Something had slipped. But the fact that the world still existed was proof that no chain reaction had been started. The organizers of the experiment counted their dead and breathed freely again.

The first significant date after that was May 31st, the next one June 2d. These passed unnoticed. Rats and mice still infested fields and houses and peopled laboratories. Perhaps some laboratory workers observed that no litters of white mice appeared after the beginning of June.

A Dr. Wardour, of Melbourne, seems to have been the

first to make public a suspicion of the horrible truth. Doubtless other physicians had already confirmed it so far as they themselves were concerned, but kept it quiet on the supposition that it applied to them alone, and was a reflection on their professional standing. But Dr. Wardour was so popular an obstetrician that he felt morally sure it was not some sudden boycott that caused him to have no new patients after early in June. By discreet inquiry, he discovered that no physician in Melbourne had been visited after that date by any woman newly pregnant. None of them had any deliveries scheduled for after the following March.

The alarmed investigation spread throughout Australia, then to the entire civilized world. Reluctantly at first, and then in panic, medical associations queried their members. Maternity hospitals followed suit. By the end of 1975, the answer was given with appalling finality.

So far as could be ascertained, every mammal on earth, male and female, from the lowliest platypus to man himself, was sterile.

The unmanageable and unpredictable rays from New Mexico had done their work.

Initial endeavors to keep the terrible news quiet were, as might have been foreseen, entirely futile. An enterprising reporter on a New York paper nosed it out almost at once. For months the front page of every newspaper in every city dealt with no other subject. Second-rate scientists erupted in predictions and pronouncements: the damage was temporary; it would last a year, ten years, a few more months; it would affect only this generation; a way to reverse the action was in course of discovery, had already been discovered.

The first-rate scientists kept their mouths shut, or said frankly that not enough was known about what had happened to make any predictions at all.

Quacks with sure-fire cures ran riot, until in most countries they were rounded up and jailed. Among the masses of the ignorant, in the depths of undeveloped countries, witch doctors became the dominant rulers of the frightened people. There was the usual rise in the suicide rate which occurs whenever people balanced delicately on the edge receive a sudden unbalancing shock.

A Mrs. Jenkins of Lancashire, England, for a while became world-famous by her insistence, with supporting evidence, that she was going to have a baby. When, against her protests, she was examined by a London surgeon, she was shown to be suffering from a tumor. Mental hospitals and psychiatric clinics were crowded by women convinced that they were pregnant; so common did this psychosis become that it received a name as a special form of mental disorder.

Meanwhile, time went on and there was no change. Observation of other domestic animals—such as sheep and swine—was limited because of their set seasons for breeding. Experiments with cows and horses showed that they were affected just as were human beings.

The last child known to have been born on earth was the youngest daughter of peasants in southern Sweden. Her birthday was April 16, 1976. Her mother had carried her four other children a correspondingly long time. The child's name was Ingrid Anderson.

As it became definitely certain that, for an unforeseeable period at least, the human race, together with all other species of the mammalia, had come to an end, large mass-effects began to be felt.

If the variation in the genes caused by the atomic rays were permanent, then humanity's day was over. When the youngest children now alive were dead—say by 2095 at the very latest—mankind would have ceased to be. Indeed, except for a few surviving elephants and whales, the world would by then be left to the birds, the fish, the reptiles, the insects, and other submammalian orders.

Even if this suddenly induced sterility were not inherited, and the next generation were able to continue the race, a severe dislocation of life was inevitable. And even by the end of 1976, three major results of the disaster had become solidified.

In the first place, children became the only hope of

humanity. For the first time in the world's sad history, children became so valuable that nowhere on earth was a child hungry, or cold, or abused. The death of a child was the supreme calamity, the killing of a child the most atrocious and severely-punished crime.

Next, with universal death staring it in the face, mankind at last turned in horror from the thought of war. The struggling and weak United Nations unanimously transformed itself into a true World Federation, with plenipotentiary powers. Humanity, bent only on survival, at long last became one.

And in the third place—though many branches of science were neglected in despair—the physicists, biophysicists, chemists, and biologists became the most important and powerful people on earth. Education in these fields was widespread and intensive. Anything research workers desired was theirs—except experimental animals, for after two or three years, there were no more rats or guinea pigs to be had, and jealously cherished dogs and cats were guarded by their owners.

There was no lack, however, of men and woman who eagerly offered themselves for experimental purposes. Most of these were young people frustrated of parenthood; others offered themselves solely for the good of humanity. There were not lacking also those possessed by an itch for publicity; and as the years went on, many persons sought their livelihood by this means, since gradually one trade and industry after another ceased to exist. Makers of baby foods and clothing for infants went first, together with obstetricians and midwives; then, in order, followed all the occupations devoted to children and the young—kindergarten teachers, nursery school managers, writers of juvenile books, toymakers, and all the rest.

Long before the first child of the latest generation became nubile, it was dishearteningly obvious that the transformation caused by the 1975 accident was hereditary; for the last kittens and puppies grew up, came into heat, mated—but no offspring appeared. Young people were allowed and urged to marry as young as possible, and by 1995 millions of them had done so, all over the world. But no child was conceived.

By 1996, nobody on earth was less than twenty years old.

There were hardly any dogs and cats left on earth, and only a few old cows and horses. Rats, mice and squirrels had long been gone, and with them some diseases, such as plague, typhus, and tularemia, had practically ceased to exist; the effects of the accident were not all maleficient. There were no schools of lower than college grade, and soon there would be no need for any except those for advanced study. Zoos were almost depopulated, most of their live exhibits having been replaced by cleverly stuffed and mounted animals. Hundreds of professions and occupations had ceased to exist; either because they had catered to children or adolescents, or because they depended on animal industry. In many—though far from all—cases those trained in these fields were able to make adaptations; pediatricians, for example, became specialists in geriatrics; plastics took the place of leather or furs, though surviving specimens of these vanishing commodities became far more valuable than pearls or diamonds. Dairy farmers and their subsidiaries were hard hit, since there was no more milk, butter, or cheese. Butchers and cattle ranchers were out of a job; there was no more beef, pork, or lamb, and people lived entirely on chickens and other fowl, fish, vegetables, and fruit.

Even the most overpopulated portions of the globe were beginning to look empty, as the older inhabitants died off. This was least apparent in such places as India, partly because of the removal of tigers and other predatory animals. However, the huge increase in cobras now that there were no mongooses almost balanced that slight advantage. In Europe and America, and in the Antipodes, the lowering of the population was easily observable. Ironically enough, the human race in dying became also healthier than it had ever been. There was enough food for everybody now, even the poorest; moreover, the imminence of universal extinction gave sharp impetus to medical research. If a man could no longer hope to survive in his descendants, then at least he wanted to stay alive as long as possible. (The earlier suicide wave had dropped to almost nothing.) On the other hand, the impossibility of handing on property beyond the next generation killed the urge toward accumulation of great wealth, and rich men quite willingly allowed themselves to be taxed of nearly all their fortunes for the benefit of the general public.

On April 16, 1996, Ingrid Anderson, the youngest human being on earth, celebrated her twentieth birthday.

By pure chance, this girl had become a symbol. It was on this date that the World Government formally established four research commissions, with quarters in Shanghai, Chicago, Paris, and Moscow, for a final intensive effort to discover a way to reverse the disaster of May 11, 1975. They became known as the Ingrid Anderson Research Commissions—popularly known as IARC.

IARC had a specified life-span of twenty years. When the youngest woman on earth was forty, she might still, in the old days, be quite capable of child-bearing for several years to come; but it was unlikely that if the scientists discovered a means of reinducing human fertility, enough women in their forties would conceive for the first time to repopulate the earth and preserve our intricate industrial civilization.

Nearly all the most eminent scientists alive were workers in IARC. Their salaries were munificent, their facilities unlimited. At first they were all members of the generation alive in 1975; gradually young people from what was (rather hopelessly) universally known as the Last Generation joined the staffs. After 2005 most of the men and women who had been active scientific workers thirty years before had grown old, resigned, or died. At that date the average age of IARC was 42.5.

The four sections of IARC communicated daily with one another by television-phone and teletype, besides which the chiefs of staff held frequent conferences in one or another of the headquarters cities, since by this time every part of the earth was within five hours of every other part by rocket plane. The language they employed was Esperanto. When the World Government, now permanently located in San Francisco, celebrated the sixtieth anniversary of the first United Nations Conference for International Organization, in 2005, the directors of IARC were the principal guests of honor.

But in spite of great genius, terrific industry, and limitless facilities, none of their lines of investigation and experiment had proved successful.

It was understood, of course, that no announcement would ever be made unless it was the one great announcement for which a sick and terrified humanity waited. IARC was heavily guarded; no leaks ever seeped out to cause panic or frantic hope. And the years went on, and still IARC was silent.

In 2013, the youngest people in the world were thirty-seven years old. There was no youth left on earth, and very little laughter. A realization even more dreadful than humanity's extinction itself had seized the Last Generation: for the first time its members were brought face to face with the horrifying probabilities of their future. Unless IARC could work a seeming miracle, inevitably the time would come when all living men and women would be at least seventy years old, then eighty, then ninety, then a hundred or more. How could civilization be maintained by a handful of feeble old people? What of the day when in all the world, with its machines still and its great cities falling to ruins, there would be only half a dozen centenarians?

As the dreadful possibilities grew more clear, two parallel waves struck the Last Generation, affecting particularly those in the most advanced centers of culture—a wave of religious mysticism, drowning fear and horror in a dream; and a colossal wave of suicides, far greater than that at the beginning of the era.

Mankind as a whole began to divide roughly into three categories: those who had given way to despair and terror, who lived only to escape from reality, either by the feverish pursuit of pleasure, the ecstasy of mysticism, or the desperate gate of suicide; those too bovine and inert, too unimaginative, to face the future; and those who still had faith in IARC.

On August 21, 2013, a special meeting of the chiefs of staff of IARC was called in the Paris headquarters.

IARC was strictly international; its staffs were of all peoples, and it was seldom that anyone was attached to a headquarters situated in his own country. The chief of the Shanghai IARC was an American Negro, Arthur Ramsdell. The Chicago chief was Joseph Callahan, whose father had been Irish, his mother descended from a German Jewish refugee settled in Mexico. These represented the older generation—both had been boys in 1976. The other two were younger. The Moscow chief was a woman, Renée Loisy, who despite her French name had also English and Russian blood. The Paris chief was Chinese; his name was Liu Chen-ping.

All of those attending the conference, and indeed all the more responsible members of their staffs as well, knew why the meeting had been called. It was a crucial conference—the most crucial IARC had ever held.

"Loisy is read to make her report," said Callahan.

"Fellow-workers," said Renée Loisy, without preliminaries, "I have to announce that I am pregnant. The father of my child is my husband, Karel Batak, who as you know is also a member of our Moscow staff.

"I need not remind you that as this new line of investigation began to look more hopeful, I volunteered to be its subject, since by its very nature it might be fatally dangerous if unsuccessful, and we did not consider it right to allow anyone outside our ranks to undergo that peril. You will also remember that a year ago this council voted to permit Karel Batak to join me in the experiment.

"What seventeen years of research by means of radioactive waves, glandular therapy, serology, infra-red light treatment, and every other conceivable method has uniformly failed to accomplish, has at last been brought about by the simple but revolutionary means you all know—the means so brilliantly suggested in 2011 by our colleague, Arthur Ramsdell."

She paused. Modestly Ramsdell waved away a respectful murmur.

"What has succeeded with Batak and me will undoubtedly succeed with every healthy man and woman of proper age," Loisy went on. "There remains now only to plan making our announcement to the world in such a way as to avoid undue excitement and confusion, and then to make our final report to the World Government and to dissolve IARC.

"The human race has been saved from extinction!"

For a minute there was an awed silence. It was interrupted by Liu Chen-ping.

"One moment," he said in his soft voice. "I think there is more than that for us to determine."

"What, then?" asked Joseph Callahan.

"I ask you to hear me out before you comment on what I am going to say," Liu continued. "To some—perhaps to all—of you it will seem monstrous. But I should be lacking in my duty to my conscience if I did not speak.

"What I want you to consider, straightforwardly and solemnly, is whether it is after all desirable to preserve the species to which we belong.

"I can see your horror at my words. But increasingly, for fourteen years, I have had before my mind's eye a contrast—a contrast between the world as it was in 1975, and the world as it is today.

"I was not born in 1975. But I have read—read not only the literature of before that date, but also the innumerable works on history, economics, and politics published since. I have, I think, as keen a grasp on the realization of the past as has the oldest man or woman alive.

"In the half-century preceding 1975, the whole globe had twice been ravaged by a devastating total war, and a third such war was imminent. Today there is no war.

"In 1975 the world was divided among more than a hundred sovereign nationalities, each jealous of its borders and its prerogatives. Today we have a universal World Government, democratically elected and conducted, and with full and beneficient authority over every human being on earth.

"In 1975 mass starvation and famine, and disastrous economic depressions were endemic. Today everyone in the world is well fed, well clothed, well housed, well educated.

"I need not mention other aspects of the situation—the prevalence of crime in 1975, its virtual absence today; the treatment of alien races and nationalities by people numerically superior to them; the relative position of the sexes then and now.

"Re-people the world, and how can we guarantee that we are not thereby bringing back all the evils which in 1975 made life hardly worth the living to at least a large minority of its inhabitants?

"You will say, I know, that even this is better than extinction of the human race. All I ask you to consider now, deeply and soberly, is: is it?"

His voice dropped. Callahan was the first to speak.

"I am sure," he said, "that all of us have known these doubts. Nevertheless I am not in agreement with Liu.

"The contrast he has drawn is true and painful. But the worst he foresees is still only a possibility. There is the other possibility that this hard experience has taught humanity a lesson—that the human race may never, especially since his first new members will be guided by us of this generation, go back to the bad old days.

"And there is another and vitally important matter which I think we have forgotten. Loisy is to have a child—"

"If Liu's voice carries," said Renée Loisy in a low murmur, "I agree that that child can never be born. The first child to be conceived since 1975 will also be the last child to be conceived, forever."

"That too, Loisy," Callahan continued. "But I was thinking of something else. We must face facts. A complete and radical variation in evolution such as overtook all mammals thirty-eight years ago is a revolutionary thing. It is not simple and unconnected; it must have infinite ramifications and repercussions.

"How do we know that a re-reversal such as we have brought about by Ramsdell's method will not be equally complex? To put it baldly, how do we know that the children born henceforth will be physically and mentally normal? The answer is that we do not know. We have no way, short of waiting to see, to find out how far heredity itself has been altered by this twofold wrench at its foundations. We should have to proceed blindly with our experiment.

"As I said, I am, in spite of everything, opposed to Liu's opinion. But if we override his proposal, then I am in favor of keeping our secret not only until after Loisy's child has been born, but until enough other children have been born (probably, for the sake of secrecy, to other members of our staffs) to be sure that they are healthy, sound creatures. In other words, I recommend that we reserve our announcement for the date when, in any case, we must disband—April 16, 2016.

"Ramsdell, what is your feeling on this matter?"

Arthur Ramsdell's deep voice spoke hesitantly.

"It may be because I come from a race with a deep biological instinct," he said slowly, "but I cannot agree with Liu. I hope you will believe that it is not because by chance I hit on the method which finally solved our problem. I feel merely that life itself is sacred and desirable, at all costs and at all risks. For myself, I would rather be a Negro child born in America in 1960, as I was—with all that that implies—than never to have been born at all.

"I want to say, though, that if the majority opinion is against me, you can count on me loyally and faithfully to obey; and I know we can all say that of ourselves and of those members of our staffs who have even a glimpse of precisely what our recent work has been. In that case, we shall have to suppress permanently our latest researches, and announce on April 16, 2016, that we have failed. I suggest that if we decide to do this, we devote the remaining two years and eight months of our existence to the solving of another problem—a date and a means for euthanasia of the last remnants of our species. The fate of a few old people, waiting only to die of hunger and neglect, is too horrible for any civilized person to contemplate.

"However, I think the person most concerned in this decision is the one who has not yet spoken—Loisy. I believe hers should be the deciding voice."

"I do not concur in that," said Renée Loisy promptly. "Ours is a democratic body; the majority must decide. Indeed, I do not think we as chiefs of staff have the right to determine our stand without consultation of our colleagues. My recommendation is that we place the entire question before a general meeting of IARC—probably to be held in Chicago, since our largest hall is in that city. We need not, if you think it undesirable, give them the exact details of our successful experiment. But IARC has for seventeen years been the most important body on earth. Every person connected with it is an eminent scientist in some field. Only a vote of the entire membership, together with a pledge of secrecy, which I am certain every one of them will keep, should determine whether humanity is to live or to die. I do not suggest that the matter should be put to a vote of all the people on earth; I do not, and I know you do not, think that a valid opinion could be obtained except from people fully informed and, because of their lifelong scientific preoccupations, emotionally aloof—or at least relatively so. But my unchangable belief is that only IARC as a whole should decide."

Renée Loisy's proposal was adopted, and the meeting was held as arranged. Liu, Ramsdell, and Karel Batak were the principal speakers, Batak siding with Ramsdell. Many other of the world's most famous biophysicists and biologists also spoke, together with several noted historians and economists whom the chiefs of staff had invited under special pledges of necessity and secrecy. World Government guards insured the complete privacy of the meeting, which lasted for an entire

veek. Groups of IARC members discussed and debated
lay and night.

Finally, on September 3, 2013, the vote was cast. The
allots bore only two words, with a square after each for
registry by the voting-machines. The words were "Life"
nd "Death."

On the morning of September 4, 2013, which was a
'unday, the members of IARC gathered, in silent sol-
mnity, to hear the results of their vote. Over the sound-
roof hall a religious hush prevailed as Joseph Callahan,
hief of staff of their host city, stood before the micro-
hone.

"Comrades of IARC," he said, "yesterday you cast 820
allots. Previously you—or rather, I should say we—had
ll agreed that whatever the vote, the minority would
bey it, and that if it were for the action recommended
y Liu, each of us would forever keep the secret of the
ctual success of our researches, however strongly he or
he might feel opposed to the decision.

"Fellow-scientists, fellow men and women, the fate of
he human race has been decided. By your ballots you
letermined whether mankind was to live or to die. I
hall now read the vote."

What was the decision?
I cannot tell you. As I write, it is not yet 2013.

In Science Fiction
Ballantine Books Brings You
the Best of the Established Authors
and the Most Exciting New Writers